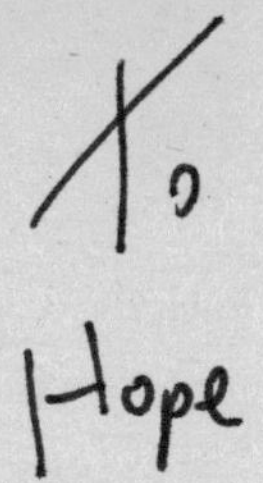

DROP DEAD GORGEOUS

WAYNE SIMMONS

snowbooks

I'd like to thank everyone who has supported my writing career thus far. In particular, I would like to thank Patty Smith, Ryan Fitzsimmons and everyone at Snowbooks.

This book is dedicated to my very own drop dead gorgeous Rebecca.

Proudly Published by Snowbooks in 2011

Snowbooks Ltd.
120 Pentonville Road
London
N1 9JN
Tel: 0207 837 6482
Fax: 0207 837 6348
email: info@snowbooks.com

www.snowbooks.com

British Library Cataloguing in Publication Data

A catalogue record for this book is available from the British Library.

ISBN 978-1-906727-98-7

Printed and bound in the UK by J F Print Ltd., Sparkford

BELFAST CITY
SUNDAY, JUNE

He'd been at it all day.

They'd been in town since half nine in the morning, and Jimmy had gawked at every single girl they happened to walk by. Siobhan was getting sick of it. She didn't consider herself the jealous type by any stretch of the imagination, but this was taking the piss.

The last one he looked at hadn't even been a girl. Siobhan was sure of it. Looked more like one of those emos you would see hanging around the city hall every Saturday and Sunday. Place was crawling with them these days, their skinny-jeaned legs spilling out of the Europa bus station like ants, shuffling downtown to pick up whatever release-of-the-minute MTV was whoring. And she could understand why Jimmy was staring: they looked like girls, what with their pale faces, floppy hair and all that make-up they wore. Jimmy no doubt clocked the make-up on the lad, automatically giving his tits—or lack of them—the once over, and decided he was a looker. Easy mistake. But she wasn't going to let him away with it.

"That wasn't a girl..." she said to him, her lips twisted like she was chewing a wasp.

"What are you on about?"

It had got to the stage where he didn't even realise what he was doing. Sometimes he forgot himself and nudged Siobhan, as if to let her in on the secret, as some half decent piece of skirt wandered by. It made her heart sink. She didn't feel sexual anymore. It was like their relationship had deteriorated to that of a mother and child: all Jimmy seemed to need these days was someone to wash his clothes, cook his dinner, and clean the house once in a while. She looked down at all the new clothes she'd bought, packed tightly into swollen plastic bags like parachutes. And they looked like parachutes, too. As she got older, and Jimmy's eye wandered further and further from her to find younger and slimmer girls, Siobhan saw her taste in clothes change. Out went the short skirts, the high heeled shoes and fancy tops. In came the oversized (and overpriced) t-shirts and functional, flat sandals. She wanted to just drop all her bags and walk away. They were suddenly useless to her.

Sighing, she slipped her credit card back in her purse, remembering all the bills coming out of their joint account this month. Swiping plastic about town wasn't going to pay the electric.

"Is it not time to go home?" Jimmy said, sniffing. Siobhan could see him look at her shopping bags, wondering, no doubt, just how much she'd spent this time on the card. "There's footie on tonight, and I told Frankie to call round at about seven. You need to get dinner ready and all."

Yeah, I need to get dinner ready. That'll be right.

He'd hardly lifted a hand around the house in all the time they'd been together. Siobhan often wondered why she even bothered with him. But life with Jimmy was just kind of the norm. She couldn't imagine him not being around every day, not sniffing and spluttering in bed every night, not belching loudly after a good feed of dinner.

Yet, were she to be completely honest, and were this a day that was going a little better for her, Siobhan would admit to seeing another side to Jimmy. She still remembered their first night out, all those years ago, when he was a skinny bundle of nerves, palms sweating, voice stuttering, trying so hard to be some version of romantic. He'd taken her out to Burger King. It was the first time she'd been there, what with it only having opened in Belfast in the nineties. She remembered him choking on his Coke. She had laughed at him, at the time, but she'd felt just as nervous.

And were she to think really hard, Siobhan might also be able to recall that big teddy bear he'd sent into her work on their first St. Valentine's Day together, and how all the girls in the factory told her how much he must love her. She still liked to believe that. *Deep down*, she thought. *It's still the truth.*

And it *was* still the truth. When it mattered, anyway...

Her mind travelled back to that dark day around Halloween last year, when Jimmy came home from work to find her in hysterics, standing in the rain outside the house, hands gripped tightly around her mobile phone, bawling her eyes out. He didn't even ask Siobhan what was wrong. He just took her in his arms and held her for days, rocking her to and fro. He fixed it so her mother's funeral seemed to just happen all around her. That was her Jimmy, and he wasn't all bad, Siobhan decided, as they marched towards the car.

...

Caz sat cross-legged on the 11.20 to Belfast. She was daydreaming, a collage of all-things-bright-and-beautiful dancing to the humdrum rhythm of the train.

She was sixteen years old, and as something of a romantic, Caz savoured these moments, when her quasi-adult mind would dip back into its inner child. Her token trashy magazine was lying face down on her lap, as if dead. Her eyes glazed over. The mishmash view of her own reflection, some grassy banks and rail track, did little to bring Caz back to reality—that was the way she liked it. The world blew by like smoke in the wind, fields and roads blending together as the train moved along its track.

Caz suddenly remembered that famous quote about a writer staring out the window of his room.

"What are you doing?" someone had asked him.

"Writing," came the reply.

—Or maybe it was painting?

It didn't matter. The story had always struck her as extremely bland. Not just because it didn't make sense to her, but because it shouldn't make sense to *anyone*. For Caz, there was nothing more natural in the world than unleashing the imagination, than uncorking the creative juices and letting them flood over. It wasn't something only for writers (or painters). It didn't need to be for *any* purpose. It should be something you do just for the hell of it—just because you could.

Somewhere close by, a random noise made her look up. One glance at the train's sliding, automatic door and Caz's hormones were bouncing, shaking her out of her self-induced trance. Her heart skipped with instant and sudden euphoria as the tall, gangly frame of Tim Adamson, the cutest lad in her GCSE History class—and possibly the whole school—slouched into the car she was in. His eyes peeked out from under his hoody, searching for somewhere to sit. His MP3 player was blaring loudly enough for her, and everyone else, to hear. *Don't sit here*, she thought to herself. Her face grew suddenly and powerfully red. His eyes were drawn to her, as if the heat radiating from her was a huge beacon. She watched him clock the empty seat opposite and slide himself into it. .

Crossing her legs, she picked up her magazine like it was a weapon of some sort. She stole a glance from under her fringe, and then pretended not to care.

...

Even though it was barely noon, the car park was a lot more packed than it had been when they'd first arrived. The afternoon was always the busiest time. That's why Siobhan had dragged a hungover Jimmy out of bed early to drive her into town. She hated crowds almost as much as he did. It was one thing they shared in common.

When they'd first opened the city centre on Sundays, it was fairly quiet all day. The place was like a ghost town. Siobhan had once told Jimmy that she felt like one of those celebrities who could get shops to stay open just for them. Meant fuck all to Jimmy. He just did what he was told. He was good at that.

Like clockwork, Jimmy unloaded the bags off her arms and packed them into the car. It was a well-practiced routine, carried out methodically without any need for communication between the couple. All the usual suspects were present and accounted for: Topshop, TK Maxx, and Siobhan's personal favourite for that cheap and cheerful bargain: Primark. Jimmy had absolutely no interest in the contents of those bags. He just needed to get them into the car in order to get home quickly. Fashion, to a man like Jimmy, was a dark art. Usually he just wore whatever Siobhan or his ma bought him. Day-to-day wear consisted of joggers and trainers. A night out usually called for one of the stripy shirts his ma had got him for Christmas and a pair of jeans. A trip downtown also merited the latter; Siobhan insisted on it.

You needn't think you're going out like that.

Yeah, whatever. He just did what he was told. Made life a lot easier.

Siobhan and Jimmy lived about ten or fifteen minutes drive out of town, in a place called Finaghy. It was just south of the city centre, an area wavering between the middle class suburbia of the Upper Malone Road (or "Mauuulone Rowd" as Jimmy called it, affecting his usual broad Belfast sneer) and the red, white and blue of Taughmonagh. Where Jimmy and Siobhan lived sported a more autumnal green, white and gold. Colour set the boundaries in Belfast. Like piss against lampposts, paint marked walls and pavements, flags and buntings riding high above them. Jimmy had once entertained the thought that the same person could be doing murals for both sides of the community (*Tenner an hour, mate. Cash in hand. Not bad work if you can get it.*) But it wouldn't have mattered to him, even if it were true. Jimmy thought it best just to ignore all that shite and get on with life. Politics was as dark an art as shopping was. Sometimes he pretended he cared, just to go with the flow, indulging his friends who, like most people in Belfast, had sectarianism inherent in their blood, but underneath it all, he couldn't give a rat's arse.

Siobhan changed the radio station as Jimmy was driving. A sudden tut showed it wasn't a move he liked.

"Fuckin' gay music's what that is," he muttered.

"No gayer than that hip hop shite you listen to," Siobhan replied, putting on her usual indignant face as she turned the volume up on whatever country rock Real FM was churning out.

"Aye, whatever you say."

"Just you keep driving and never mind what music's playing."

And there it was. Their third conversation of the day wrapped up in seconds.

Had it gone on, Jimmy would have said he was too tired to bicker. He might have pointed out the fact that he'd been tripping around town for the better part of two hours, and it hadn't helped either his hangover or his mood. Siobhan then would have brought up the fact that he had spent most of this time perving on other girls and might even have mentioned how one of them was a wee lad—and a wee lad that wore make-up, for that matter. But they hardly even argued anymore, such was their predicament. Their relationship was stale, like out-of-date milk. It looked okay but smelled funny.

Jimmy's belly growled a little, reminding him that he'd missed breakfast, his beer-soaked gut not having felt up to it earlier. His mind began to think of food as he turned onto the Lisburn Road, finally getting a bit of speed up.

"We stopping for a fry-up on the way home?" he asked Siobhan, hoping to win her back out of her huff with an offer to pay for it.

Then he dropped dead at the steering wheel.

...

Tim Adamson was sitting right across from Caz. His band played the Christmas party in school, although word had it that Tim had quit them. He was without a doubt the most talented one in the band. Everyone said it. Even Kelly Cullen, who had once also told Caz that she thought Tim was a dick. Of course, Caz knew she really fancied him. Kelly Cullen was a stupid cow like that.

As all of this rushed though her head, Caz sat with a defiant expression of nonchalance painted on her face. She was pretty sure that Tim wouldn't even recognise her, and despite herself, that realisation was starting to annoy her.

Fixing her glasses, she peeked up from her magazine and ventured another look at him. He lay back in the seat opposite, arms crossed over his belly, gum bouncing around his mouth. His legs stretched far and wide, one nudging into the old lady sat beside him, the other hanging out the end of the seat.

He was probably going down to the City Hall, no doubt to hang out with Kelly and all those other silly bints. Caz hated that crowd, hated how affected they all were, with their heavy make-up, kitsch backpacks and stripy tights. God, they were getting younger and younger, too. Even her little brother, Jan, was starting to hang around there with his teeny-goth mates, and Jan was barely fourteen.

It pissed Caz off to no end that she found a guy like Tim Adamson so attractive. He was like a nemesis to her, so image-conscious with his baggy jeans, sneakers and the constant drone of MP3s being the only thing resembling vocabulary to come out of his head. He was so beneath her.

The train jerked suddenly, causing Caz to fall forward into the personal space of an unsuspecting Tim. She had barely time to recover herself, hardly even the time to go red with the absolute humiliation of it all, before another much more violent jerk sent her sprawling back into her own seat. As if having some sort of seizure, the train jerked a few more times, finally throwing Caz onto the floor before coming to an abrupt halt somewhere close to Balmoral Station.

She was just about to pick herself up, confused and absolutely mortified, when the limp body of the old lady fell on top of her.

...

“Jimmy!” Siobhan screeched, leaning across and grabbing the wheel, steadying it to keep the car from mounting the pavement. . His heavy-set, hungover eyes peeked out of his bouncing, lopsided head, staring at her the way dead people did in movies. It was almost funny, were it not so grim; her boyfriend of nine years and two months simply having expired before her, without even as much as a whisper.

Jimmy!

Ironically, even now, he was pissing her off, his lifeless (useless, big, stupid) foot still keeping the car going over 40mph. She battled with him, trying to shake him off the wheel, to no avail. A car in front swerved right, dramatically crashing through a shop window. One of the new minis could be seen in her rear mirror, jittering and then slowing down, the limp body of a cyclist somehow strewn across its bonnet. Another car, this one bigger, jerked violently, as it crashed into a lamppost, uprooting an attached waste paper bin. As the contents of the bin spilled into the light wind, crisp bags, sweets wrappers and cigarette butts flailing about merrily, a small car in front of Siobhan crumpled into another vehicle. Siobhan stretched further across her boyfriend’s body, jerking the wheel again in time to narrowly avoid collision. But Jimmy (good ol’ Jimmy) kept the pride of his life (afforded more affection than Siobhan, lately) revving like a bastard, tearing up the Lisburn Road, a road going to hell right before Siobhan’s panicked eyes.

Birdhouse In Your Soul by They Might Be Giants played on the radio, its quirky innocence taking on a whole new sinister undertone as its famous drum beat bounced in time with Jimmy’s bobbing head. Siobhan didn’t even hear the song. It was lost in the riot of her brain, the spinning of her own engine as it tried to work out how to deal with this new and sudden insanity.

Another car swerved in front of her, mounting the pavement. A dog stood barking, its owner nowhere to be seen. Siobhan turned her head as the swerving car made a beeline for the dog. It stopped barking.

Siobhan wasn't a driver. Truth be told, she knew damn all about cars—how they moved, why they needed water as well as petrol (*does it get... thirsty?*). She couldn't tell a brake pedal from a carrot. As if mocking her, Jimmy's body remained rigid, his ever-increasing beer belly providing much of the weight that was currently pressing one foot on the accelerator. The speed of the small car held, maybe even increased, as Siobhan struggled with the steering wheel.

"Come on, Jimmy..." she whimpered, tears messing up her mascara. "Wake up, for God's sake!"

But it was no good. Jimmy's sleep was the eternal type. His eyes remained fixed at some indeterminable spot, his head bouncing on the steering wheel, twisting eerily as Siobhan fought for control.

The long road stretched out ahead, deadly straight. Carnage was building as the light traffic ground to a halt, cars smashing against each other like some fucked-up demolition derby. The sound of metal against metal and breaking glass seemed to echo, in stereo, somewhere beyond the noise of the radio. The body of a motorcyclist lay on the road dead ahead. It was ironed out, like something from a sick cartoon. His corpse was contorted, having already suffered some injuries from the fucked up road rage. The leather of his jacket succeeded only to keep his arm in its sleeve as Jimmy's much-loved Suzuki Swift drove over him like a rolling pin. The poor bastard didn't feel his lifeless body shake, nor hear it squelch against the hard tarmac road as two wheels cut a perfect line through his neck, the second wheel separating his head from his body like the popping of a cork. Siobhan's eyes shut only momentarily, only whilst she felt their blue Suzuki —recently polished by a doting Jimmy—bumping over the hard bone and soft flesh. Only long enough to avoid a glimpse of the scarlet spray against her rear window. But it was enough time for her to lose what control she had left of the car.

...

The old lady tumbled over Caz, her arms flapping around the sixteen year old's petite frame like a broken puppet. Caz screamed, struggling frantically to brush the body away.

"Holy s-shit..." Caz stammered.

She fixed her glasses, staring at the woman's vacant face. There was something about the eyes. They were peaceful, content, as if the old dear didn't know she was dead yet, as if some part of her still sat on the 11.20 train, reading The Times.

So quiet... so doll-like...

Is this what death is like?

Caz looked for Tim Adamson. He wasn't in his seat.

She stood up, slowly. She was worried the train might jerk again. But nothing stirred. The train remained still, as if waiting for someone important to get on, someone otherworldly. It was as if they had suddenly jumped into another dimension, like an episode of Dr Who or one of those comics her brother would read. Everything felt *that* different, suddenly, and Caz was scared.

She looked out into the aisle. She found Tim, face down on the floor, his MP3 headphones now silent. She drew closer to him, her heart racing....

...

As the car soared onto the pavement, seeming to actually gather speed as it revved angrily towards the railings of the Balmoral railway bridge, Siobhan gave up the fight. *This is it*, she thought to herself. Unlike Jimmy, she was very much aware of her impending death. Time seemed to slow down for her, offering a clichéd attempt to grab every last second and pull each breath close to her chest in a final embrace, her previously flailing hands no longer struggled with the wheel, instead reaching to tossle Jimmy's curls one last time. She was satisfied that she had done all she could. *A good effort*, as Jimmy might have said...

...

All her embarrassment was gone, all her teenage immaturity suspended as Caz stared at what looked to her like the second lifeless body she had witnessed within two minutes.

A sudden noise turned her attention to a window somewhere behind. As Caz gazed wide-eyed towards its source, she caught the incredible sight of something large and metal soaring through the air from the bridge above the train. She watched as the blue Suzuki Swift containing Siobhan Laney and Jimmy Ferris crumpled brutally against the driver car of the 11.20 to Belfast. The whole train shook again, throwing Caz on top of Tim Adamson for the second time that morning. There was no explosion, even though Caz thought that there should be (*That's how it happens in the movies, isn't it?)* but she could definitely smell smoke. She could also feel a sudden heat looming up from the train car in front, and a dull throbbing pain in her head.

She struggled back to her feet, Tim's body beneath her spread legs. She felt for the small silver crucifix around her neck. Her mother had given it to her a few years ago, telling her to grip it tight it when she needed extra strength (God knows it hadn't helped her through her French exams last summer). But as Caz's hands felt the naked torso of her little silver Jesus, everything changed.

There was movement at her feet.

Tim Adamson suddenly lifted his head and stared vacantly at the flames lapping against the door straight ahead.

"*Fuck me*," he muttered.

PART ONE

"Here's to the crazy ones. The misfits. The rebels. The troublemakers..."

Jack Kerouac

ONE

Mere moments after ninety-nine percent of Belfast's population stopped dead, like wound-down clocks, The Silence descended. Nothing moved. Small, isolated pockets of carnage gave a sombre accompaniment to an otherwise dead city. Flames flickered here; a soft (almost mourning) wind whistled there...

But nothing moved.

Behind Queens University, in the usually vibrant Botanic Gardens, a single dog could be heard barking. A warm breeze whispered through the trees, their leaves flourishing with late Spring, whilst branches danced quietly in the morning sun's smile.

Then there was nothing again.

Nothing was the new something.

A thin layer of clouds hung in the blue sky like lazy ghosts, haunting the dead city below.

Outer city generators remained active, faintly buzzing on their own, whilst employees slept on the job. Lights of shops shone seductively, their sveltely pale mannequins perhaps more life-like now than the fallen shoppers slumped quietly around them. Factory production lines kept moving, transporting fallen workers amongst incomplete products, up the line to nowhere. Well, nowhere useful, anyway.

Nothing.

Was.

The.

New.

Something.

A sudden fuzz from various radios throughout Belfast snapped back at The Silence, briefly off the air. The fuzz evolved quickly, soon forming a unified sound.

Like a vicious rumour, the noise spread with haste and defiance. Before long, it took definite shape, blaring obnoxiously from radios in cars, houses, offices, and shops across the city, finally dissolving into the all too familiar form of the Thin Lizzy classic, *Whiskey in the Jar*.

Utterly clueless to events outside, Sean Magee reclined back into his chair. The disc spun in the player, his mic turned away from him as he whistled along with the record. Swivelling his chair around (this one was comfy, not like the last one the station had left him sitting in for the better part of a decade), Sean stretched across his vinyl-cluttered desk for the small mug of coffee he'd left cooling for the last ten minutes. He hated things being too hot, always had. Swigging on his drink, secretly livened up with a sizable nip of vodka from his hip flask, Sean picked up the sleeve of the single currently rolling.

Man, oh man… how he loved this tune. Over the course of his twenty-odd years as a DJ, Sean had played this particular wee gem an incredible two thousand, one hundred and twenty-one times. Not that he (or anyone else, for that matter) was counting.

Sean was an old-school DJ. A veteran, with the receding ponytail to prove it. His style was minimalist. No fancy quizzes, no phone-in competitions, less talking bullshit and more good tunes. He liked to think he enjoyed his job. Hell, he lived for it.

Real FM weren't that difficult to work for. Sure, there had been a few changes over the years, most of them for the worst, and the musical output on the whole was questionable, to say the least, but Sean had always felt that his years of experience earned him the respect of his fellow DJs, grudging though that may be. More importantly, Sean knew he had the respect of the listeners. No matter how often his time slot had been changed, Sean's listening figures remained fairly consistent, proving his show was one of the station's most popular. The suits weren't fans. They wanted a more contemporary sound, a lively programme including promotional interviews with local celebrities plugging their wares, and political satire. Listeners weren't enough. They wanted *active* listeners, an audience not shy of phoning in with their questions, their praise, their fifty-pence-per-call opinions on whatever bullshit news-of-the-day negativity the local politicians were dragging out. The suits wanted revenue and lots of it, because that's what their bosses wanted. Sean couldn't give a high-flying fuck. He'd watched one suit change to another suit over the years, one grand plan getting shot out of the water by another. He'd slept through enough staff meetings where the direction and vision of the station had been hammered out ad nauseum, only to return to his swivel chair, fix himself a coffee (not too hot, with a nip of vodka) and wire on some solid tunes.

He largely ignored the play list that was encouraged by management, sticking to what he knew best himself, what he had learned to be the music that Belfast wanted to hear, over his twenty years as a DJ.

He'd defiantly ignored the station's no-alcohol policy since its inception. Sean had always drunk, always would drink—so fuck anyone royal who told him that he couldn't enjoy a tipple whilst spinning his favourite vinyl.

Whiskey in the Jar? How could you not drink along to a tune like that?!

As Thin Lizzy faded out, Sean expertly faded in *Free Falling* by Tom Petty. *Perfect*, he thought to himself, taking a heavy swig of his drink and looking up at the window facing him. It surprised him to find no one looking back in through the glass. Round about this time, of a Sunday morning, the most recent time slot for his unashamedly folk rock show, the room opposite would always be occupied by his producer and whatever news reader was working. Noon would be coming up soon, yet there wasn't a news, sports or weather reader anywhere to be seen.

So, where the hell were they?

...

Star wore something akin to a bemused scowl as she sat uselessly poised for action, leaning forward on her small, wooden stool. Her hand, famously steady, with the ability to draw inhumanly straight lines for up to one hour (before needing a ciggie break) shook suddenly and briefly before becoming still again. The sound of her machine whined hungrily for the naked flesh (good skin, excellent tone) now flat out on the floor in front of her. A tall, thin, punky girl lay face down, half of the outline of a pentagram etched into her spine, her skin still red and enflamed from the needle's incision.

What the...?!

Star suddenly sniggered. It was a snigger pitched somewhere between nervous and amused. She wasn't green, by any means. She'd seen it all over the years: big bouncer-type lads screeching like banshees as the letters 'F-U-C-K' were inked onto their knuckles; teenagers, with their pungent reek of hormones, giggling and sweating their way through having respective names burned onto each other's arms; sombre looking, menopausal women almost throwing orgasms such was their delight as a pair of hearts, or the words 'Bite Me', were branded onto their pelvic area. She'd watched people scream, cry, laugh hysterically, puke, faint, urinate, even leap from their seats with horror as that first sting of the needle bit into them, as that little taste of adrenaline surged through their arms/legs/backs/pelvis/neck/whatever. But she had never—not in the ten years she had been working as a professional tattooist—had someone fuckin' die on her.

This was new.

It wasn't like this client, this particular client, to be nervous. Punky Girl was something of a regular. Star had always thought she had the look and attitude of a student, probably from York Street Art College around the corner. Somehow sensing a quiet day, Punky Girl (was her name Melanie, maybe—or Melissa?) would often casually stroll in, A2-sized folder by her side, asking for more black (always black) occult symbols to be tattooed.

This was her first Sunday appointment, a slot normally reserved for regulars. Like a lot of regulars, the real serious tattoo addicts, Punky Girl never spoke much, staring into space as the work was done. Occasionally Star would have noticed her arm getting a slight bout of shakes when she was feeling the bite of the needle. But she had never made a noise, never complained, never even as much as winced until today.

Fuckin' weird...

And she was dead, all right.

Perhaps it was the shape of her body on the floor, almost hog-tied, arms and legs somehow having crossed behind her back and curvaceous ass (yes, Star had noticed; yes, she had leered) as she fell. Perhaps it was the stillness, not just a lack of movement, but an almost statuesque stiffness, no gentle rising and falling of the lower back, no rhythmic whisper of breathing—all things a tattooist, like Star, would be working closely with, and against, every day. Either way, Star was quite sure this bitch was dead.

Gone. Kaput. Fucked.

She reached across her workstation and turned the radio off. There was the distant sound of something colliding with something else, a hint of momentary madness, and then nothing.

Star looked back at the body on the floor. She still couldn't believe what had just happened.

She sat her machine down carefully on the workstation beside her and rose from her stool. She bent down slowly, studying the fallen girl's pentagram. What had been done so far was fine, a little frayed at the corner where Star was inking when the girl had suddenly fallen, but otherwise in good shape. She had got most of the outline sorted. She was just about to change to another machine for filling in colour. As it stood now, however, the pentagram was unfinished, incomplete, unprofessional.

On dead skin.

She pulled her latex gloves off and discarded them in a nearby bin. Running a hand through her dreadlocked hair, a habit Star had developed when thinking on some shit that needed sorting, she strolled over to the door of her gaff and slowly opened it. Lighting up her third ciggie of the morning, Star cautiously stepped outside, sweeping her eyes left, then right, as she took her first drag. She could see the crooked outlines of two fallen people nearby. A dog lay sleeping (*or dead?*), its lead twisting and turning to meet the hand of its collapsed owner. Along the long street, Star could make out more crumpled bodies. Just a few, what with it being early on a Sunday. But it was enough to reinforce what she already feared: this wasn't just some new, drastic reaction to the needle she was dealing with. This was bigger.

She left the shop, allowing the door to close behind her. She moved past the dog, past the other couple of bodies and on down the street. Star discovered a Sunday more quiet than any she had ever known. She had never been a fan of Sundays, for that very reason, but this was taking the Mickey. This was like a bad dream after some dodgy hash.

A handful of cars were stalled, untidily, across the city centre. More people were sprawled like homeless refugees on street corners and sidewalks alike.

Several birds lay like fallen confetti outside a nearby church building. This was powerful. This was *really* powerful. This made her pause, captivating her. She inched closer, studying their little corpses in turn; each was surrounded with pink, or the suggestion of pink, rather, where their bodies had struck the tarmac. They spoke to her. Their imagery spoke to the artist within; feeding, enriching. They told her what had happened. It was a language Star understood, a language that was graphic, explicit, hideous. She reached her free hand into the pocket of her combats, finding her mobile phone. She needed to capture this. Carefully, she called up the camera option, working with the natural light to take a series of pictures that would do the image justice. She stepped back, the artist within her momentarily content. She slipped the phone back into her pocket.

Star looked to the church. It stood tall and solemn, its heavy wooden doors lending a gothic feel that was less than welcome. She drew one hand to her lips, sucking on the remains of the cigrarette. It tasted good, steadying her. She took another drag, drawing the smoke in deeply.

"You can do this..." she whispered to herself.

She climbed the cement steps towards the church. Cautiously, she opened the gothic-looking doors, the sound of their creak ridiculously loud. She stepped inside, each Doc Marten footstep heavy on the tiled floor. There was a musty, nostalgic smell which she remembered from attending Sunday School as a child. She had referred to it, once, as the smell of God. She moved towards the inner doors, finding them open. Inside, neatly resting in the same seats they had no doubt sat in for years, an entire congregation slept the sleep of the dead. There were more people here than she could count.

Star shivered, a cold and tingling sweat breaking out across her body. A sudden feeling of anger rose up within her.

This shit would have to happen now, she thought, breathing the last drag of her ciggie in deeply, and then flicking it down the aisle of the cursed church. Why not last year, when she was living in a squat in London, snorting Charlie like sherbet, moving from one fucked up relationship to another. Not knowing whether she was straight, gay, artist or junkie. Why did this shite have to happen when she had finally got her ass in gear, finally made something of her life, found her niche, found her passion?

Quietly, Star slipped into one of the empty seats at the back of the church. She leaned her head on the pew in front, breathing deeply. An old man rested beside her, one hand shovelled into his trouser pocket. His bible sat next to him, an embroidered bookmark with an orange tassel peeking out from its pages. The golden lettering 'HOLY BIBLE' was inscribed across its leather front.

Star lit another cigarette and smoked indulgently, sucking the nicotine and tar out of the damn thing until she was burning filter.

"Fuck me," she whispered to herself.

Returning to the shop, Star walked decisively over to her stool. She sat down before reassessing her posture and choosing instead to sit cross-legged on the floor. She pulled on another pair of gloves. Settled and once again poised, Star retrieved her second custom-made iron from the nearby workstation. She inserted a new needle then revved the whole lot up again. She ran a critical eye over the half-completed pentagram on the dead girl's back, checking the line work. Her hands were shaking, nervous energy rattling through them. She breathed in, steadied herself then began.

She'd never left a job looking unfinished, and she sure as hell wasn't going to start now.

...

Several miles south of Starcrossed Tattoos, Tim Adamson helped Caroline Donaldson clamber out of the window of their stalled train. The ridiculous sight of a burning car, burrowed into the driver carriage greeted their exit. It felt more real from outside. He heard the girl beside him giggle, then cry mere seconds later. She looked at him, hoping for some sort of comfort, but he had nothing to give her. He was still trying to get his own head around it all. In fact, he felt like crying along with her. Instead, he ran a long-fingered hand through his hair, shaking his head and breathing out in one complete motion.

"Fucking mental," he muttered, staring at the car. "Did you see that?!" he added quickly, looking at the girl. "It was... I'm telling you, that's… like…"

He paused, realising he'd never find words to describe what had happened. He was trying to make sense out of nonsense. The rules had changed, and everything was different. Everything was dangerous. He needed to focus on what he *did* know. He knew the old lady on the floor of their carriage was dead. He had known it even before the girl told him, explaining all that happened when he'd briefly zoned out. He knew that a car had buried itself in the side of the train, now smothered in flames. He knew that his MP3 player was broken. He didn't know the name of the mousy girl who was standing, shivering, in front of him, although he had the sneaking suspicion that she was in his Biology class. Or was it Chemistry?

He pulled his hoody off and handed it to her.

"Here," he muttered.

"Thanks," she replied, meekly, sniffing back her tears. She took the hoody, pulling it close at first as if it were a cuddly toy, before throwing it over her head.

"I don't know your name," he said.

"Caz," she said in a low voice.

"I'm Tim," he said. "I think you're in my –"

But she wasn't listening. Tim watched as she turned to look around the Balmoral train halt. He followed her gaze, noticing several more bodies, each as peaceful looking as the old lady had been. Apart from the low crackle of flames nearby, he couldn't hear anything. There were no cars, no movement. Nothing alive stirred, neither from the streets below nor the bridge above. Nothing.

Tim slowly approached a nearby body. It was a young lad, not much older than himself. Bending down slowly, as if worried the dead lad might jump up suddenly (*BOO!*), he prodded, with one finger only. Nothing happened. The poor bastard didn't stir. Braver now, Tim cautiously placed his hand on the lad's shoulder, finally working with both hands to roll the body over onto its back. The lad's face was nonchalant, almost as if he were still tuned into the headphones on his head. Touching him was strangely a non-event to the teenager. Tim had thought that there would be some kind of definite chill to be gained from handling the dead. But the body was still warm. The lad might as well have been asleep.

"Is he…dead?" Caz asked him.

"Aye… Think so…"

Tim touched the body again, as if making sure. Still no reaction. Nonchalantly, he picked up the headphones, placing them on his ears. It was one of those portable radios, it seemed. Digital, maybe. Some granddad rock was playing, somewhere between country and Bryan Adams. Nasty stuff. But it would do.

"You're not taking that off him! What are you like?!" Caz barked, seemingly appalled.

Before Tim could reply, both kids suddenly jumped, simultaneously startled.

THE NEXT TRAIN FROM PLATFORM ONE WILL BE THE...

It was the train station Tannoy, an automated voice all too familiar. Its cold, pre-recorded tones rang out through the still train halt, slaughtering The Silence with an almost visceral shredding. Once the Tannoy had quieted, its mechanical fuzz snapping like an electronic twig, there was only the crackle of flames to be heard.

The two kids looked at each other.

Caz started giggling.

Tim joined in.

...

Professor Herbert Matthews sat up in his bed. He realised how late in the day it was on feeling the chronic rumbling in his belly (meaning he hadn't been served his Sunday morning fry-up in bed) and a precarious stillness in his head (meaning a heck of a lot of time had passed since setting his eighth glass of bourbon down the previous night).

His wife, Muriel, was nowhere to be seen, and the sun was not only shining brightly, but splitting through the partially closed curtains of his bedroom. In short, Herb had no hangover. Herb was hungry. Muriel was nowhere to be seen, and so, he surmised, something was most definitely amiss.

By all accounts, it seemed that Muriel hadn't joined him in bed on Saturday evening at all. There, on her dressing table, the Victorian one that she had fought tooth-and-nail to secure at auction one day (against Herb's better judgement and the good health of his bank balance), was the same dressing gown that his good wife had ironed just yesterday afternoon. It definitely hadn't moved since then. Not only that, but her book wasn't on her bedside cabinet, and the lamp (this one was the clincher for the good Professor) which Herb had neglected to turn off by his bedside table (because that was Muriel's job) was still shining uselessly in the sun-split bedroom.

Something was definitely amiss. Yes siree.

Feeling for his spectacles, Herb climbed painfully (*Damn arthritis!*) out of the four-poster bed he had shared with his wife for forty years, peering around for his own dressing gown and slippers. He frowned upon seeing that the aforementioned slippers still lay where he had kicked them the previous night, and the aforementioned dressing gown (not washed, not ironed) lay across the chair of his desk. His papers were everywhere, a half-drunk bottle of bourbon still sitting, bottle-top still removed, beside a half-empty glass.

The entire room stank of him, and not Muriel. There was no trace of her inane (yet easily missed, it seemed) need for tidying. There wasn't even a hint of her floral perfume in the room, or that pungent hairspray she insisted on spraying on her hair every morning, regardless of whether or not she intended to go into town for shopping. There was nothing of her here, no evidence at all that she had passed through their bedroom in the last twelve hours, and every suggestion that she hadn't. And, frankly, that more than anything else that Professor Herbert Matthews would see, hear, or think from that time onwards, was utterly terrifying.

Ever since retiring from his position as Head of Faculty (Engineering) at Queens University Belfast,

Professor Herbert Matthews had spent all of his time in this very house. He had figured the countryside would make a much better retreat for him, and Muriel (being something of a fan of solitude herself) had seen no reason to object. So lock, stock (four-poster bed, mauve suite of chairs) and barrel they had upped-and-away'd from middle-class Malone Road, Belfast, to the wilds of Ballyclare.

For Herb, it was an idyllic life. Semi-retired on health grounds, he had been trying to put the latter part of his career behind him. He had preferred to linger on the glory days in industry, refining the very nature of engines and propellers and any other bloody thing which had cogs and wheels and gears. Herb had made those things run almost magically, lending him the reputation of something of a mystic within the linear world of engineering. He had been trying to rediscover that creative part of him, the part that had earned him such a name for himself that even his signature at the bottom of a research paper would lead to its immediate publishing in any journal across the globe.

His latter days in academia weren't so glorious. At first the students loved him. His reputation had preceded him, meaning that you could have heard the grass grow at one of his lectures, such was the utter zeal of the young undergraduates that lapped up every syllable that came from Herbert Matthews' mouth. But times changed, and the students became more interested in partying than in an old school scholar like him. No longer did they remember the major feats of engineering he had pioneered. No longer did they care for his tales (dressed in pomp and ceremony for effect) of how much the mechanical world owed to Herbert Matthews. Soon, Herb became less of a pioneer and more of a drunk, his lectures losing much of their old vitality, out-of-date and irrelevant to an audience becoming increasingly less impressionable. Finally, he found himself in his office, drinking, instead of turning up for lectures.

Before long, questions were asked about Herb's mental health, and doctors were called in to assess his suitability for work. The result was a diagnosis of alcoholism and agoraphobia, leading the professor to review his whole lifestyle. Retirement to the country had been seen by his doctor as a helpful first step to defeating his demons, but for Herb it was to be the only step. For the last ten years, he hadn't gone as far as the garden gate of his house, relying heavily on Muriel (and a neat glass of bourbon) to look after his every need.

Until today, that was.

Gingerly, Herb crept down the stairs, his pace and posture dictated more by poor health and lack of exercise than any perceived need for stealth. The countryside, usually quiet, was unbelievably still this Sunday morning. Even the birds were on strike, the wind whistling, unchallenged, through the trees surrounding the Matthews' small, two-storey cottage. The sun shone magnificently bright through the front door's stained-glass window, casting a red and green glow against the pale walls of the hall and landing. Nothing could be heard. All was still.

Herb turned the handle of the living room door.

"Muriel?" he called. There was no reply. "Muri-eeel?" he tried, singing her name in that way he did when she was trying to ignore him.

There was still nothing.

He opened the door wider, allowing some of the flickering light, from what appeared to be the television, to catch his eye. The curtains in the living room remained closed. Light from the television bounced around the walls, courting the shadows.

"Muriel? Are you in there?"

As the door opened further, Herb could just about make out the familiar frame of his wife sitting on her favourite chair—the one opposite that bloody idiot box that seemed to entertain her so much. On closer inspection, Herb realised that the television was simply broadcasting a snowy picture, as if the channel hadn't been tuned in properly. Muriel remained in the shadows, the sunlight unable to get past the living room's heavy-drawn curtains.

"Muriel, do you know what time it is?" Herb asked, the shaking in his voice coming more from a state of nervousness than any kind of impertinence.

But Muriel wasn't listening. Her eyes remained fixed on the idiot box as if it were broadcasting something entirely revolutionary in the way of entertainment. Biscuit crumbs littered her lap, leading Herb to believe that her latest Weight Watchers diet (or whatever it was this week) had fallen by the wayside yet again. A cup of tea rested in her hand, some of its contents having spilled onto the mauve armchair, drying, unchecked, to create a dark stain. Yet Muriel herself didn't move.

Nor *had* she moved.

"M-Muriel?" Herb said again, this time his voice shaking.

...

Star packed only a few things to take with her. Her small cloth satchel, tattered through years of airport abuse, held her portable radio, a couple of hats—*never leave home without at least a couple*—and her ciggies. Just the essentials.

She paused at the doorway of her shop. She gave one last look around, wondering if she would ever return. A single bookshelf loaded with books and CDs leaned against the back wall. Flash art covered the other walls, mostly comprised of traditional imagery like anchors, hearts and pin-ups. It was what people were asking for these days, tattoo styles going in and out of vogue just like any other art. A few of her own paintings leaned against the front desk. She hadn't even got around to hanging them. Yet, even though she hadn't been in the shop very long, even though it barely spoke much about the things that made her feel at home, *really at home*, it still felt like she was walking out on her whole world.

She looked to the floor beside the workstation, finding Punky Girl's body still there. Star had dressed her finished black and grey pentagram tattoo, covering it with Clingfilm more out of habit than for any other reason. It had turned out okay, given the circumstances. It had been important for her to finish it for her own reasons, but Star found herself hoping the poor bitch would have liked it.

She could tell when someone didn't love their tattoo. Even when they made the right noises, cooed and fussed over their ink as if it was a new born baby, Star could still sense when someone didn't get the tattoo they had really hoped for. It was in their eyes, a dead look with no moisture, no glassy sheen.

Punky Girl had a dead look for other reasons...

Pulling on her beanie hat, Star stepped out of Starcrossed Tattoos, deciding to head to the city centre. She would stop at whatever shop she could find along the way which had a television. She wasn't sure why the radio was still playing music, but she knew that noon had passed by with no news broadcast. In order to work out just how wide-scale this whole PEOPLE-DROPPING-DEAD thing was, she'd be needing the use of a television.

A fuckin' telly, of all things.

She hated them. She didn't even own one. Music was her thing. Star would usually have her iPod with her, but this morning she had mistakenly grabbed her radio instead. It didn't bother her, because she quite liked that bloke who DJ-ed on Real every Sunday morning.

Music—*any* music, really—helped her work. It put her in the zone. It helped her focus on cutting those incredibly straight lines she was respected for.

She was going through a weird phase of listening to movie soundtracks, *Betty Blue* being the current favourite. This amused the gang who usually hung around Starcrossed, of course. She absolutely loved that film, but some of those philistines hadn't even heard of it—a veritable classic, a piece of cinematic history, and yet those jokers were singing *Groove is in The House* every time she mentioned it.

Fuckin' arseholes.

Walking along the death-stained streets of Belfast, Star suddenly felt grief for those a-holes at her shop. In their own way, they were the closest thing she had to friends in Belfast. Family, even. She had tried to call a few of them on her mobile. It was early on a Sunday, so most of them probably hadn't even got out of bed yet. Fuckin' alcos, the lot of them. She could imagine it, all right—those clowns had slept right through the end of the fuckin' world. A part of her smiled at that.

...

The two teenagers made their way into Belfast, the added thrill of walking on a rail track racing their pulses further. Their youthful hearts were dancing with emotion. They hadn't got to THE-WORLD-HAS-ENDED-AND-MY-MUM-IS-DEAD stage, although they were fast approaching OH-MY-GOD-THE-WORLD-HAS-ENDED. There was a difference: the former related directly to their own situation and the true horror of it. The latter, however, still had a certain Hollywood romantic notion to it. With the former, Tim and Caz were victims, but with the latter they were survivors. Different. Special, even.

They ventured off the track onto the nearby streets, crossing the Adelaide halt bridge to reach the Lisburn Road. Death was still heavy in the air, the normally bustling slice of student accommodation and coffee shops providing not even a whisper of life. Tall, early-Elizabethan houses seemed to take on a new, sinister quality when stripped of activity. Beer cans littered the streets, their collective rattle echoing through cul-de-sac after cul-de-sac, no longer smothered by laughter or spontaneous shouting, music or traffic.

Everything and everyone that had once brought life to these formal, stern-looking houses, with their high ceilings and angular roofs, had died, leaving the houses themselves as the only survivors. Weather-beaten, sombre and persistent, only brick and mortar remained, when all of life was spent.

An occasional car had mounted the pavement, paper spewed out of bins and glass splintered from nearby shop windows. A light breeze carried the remnants of several post-boozing take-aways.

The teens had been walking for about ten minutes, Caz at times calling out her throat-scorching *hellooooos* as she marched, tutting each time she didn't get a reply, Tim busy with his mobile as he dandered behind her, texting one minute, dialling the next, each time having no joy. Seemed no one was in, anymore.

They came across a few more bodies, Tim checking each of them for signs of life. He was getting braver the more he checked, now lifting and rolling them over if necessary rather than just prodding them. One of the bodies had made him a little curious. It belonged to a girl in her twenties. An attractive girl. She was dead. He was almost sure of that. Yet she still seemed very alive to him, almost radiant. She wasn't pale like the others. In fact, Tim wondered if she was just unconscious, if maybe this one had somehow, like Caz and him, been immune to—

What was it, anyway? Some kind of plague? An attack?

He bent down to touch her. Her body was hot. Not just warm, like some of the others, cooling as time passed, but actually hot. And there was something about her face. It wasn't peaceful. No part of it seemed content with death, like the other corpses they had seen thus far. Instead, this body—this small, petite female, with ginger hair and a faint peppering of freckles—seemed almost angry.

Tim reached his fingers towards a lock of her hair. It glistened in the sun, gently moving in the light, warm breeze. He ran each strand of ginger through his hand, almost expecting her to look up at him—a prince to awaken her from her still, angry sleep.

"Excuse me!"

Tim looked up to find Caz glaring at him. He had almost forgotten she was with him, such was his fascination with the corpse.

"Look… what are we going to do?" she blurted out.

"I don't know," he replied, turning away from her.

He started texting again, sending message after message. He'd worked his way through all of the guys in his band, anyone else he knocked around with. Everyone he knew. Everyone except his dad.

A part of him hoped his dad was dead. Another part of him grimaced at that thought.

A darkness suddenly surrounded him like a cloak. It wasn't just this whole END-OF-THE-WORLD thing. He was confused by lots of things, all that had gone on over the years, unsaid, unchallenged, unexplained—

how that bastard—that *hypocrite*—had come into his bed each night, when he was shivering and crying himself to sleep. How his mum had known about it, yet said nothing.

"Tim!" Caz persisted.

"What?!" he shouted back.

"I just think we should have a plan, or something… an idea of where we're going. I mean… are we going into town? Or to the police station? Yes… we should go see the police, shouldn't we?"

Tim laughed in reply to this idea, picking up a police hat lying on the ground right next to its owner. He placed the hat on his head and performed a mock salute.

"Oh, fuck off, Tim!" Caz swore, tears building again in her eyes.

He knew he was being a dick. He even knew *why* he was being a dick. He needed to be distracted from thoughts he didn't want to think, memories he wished he couldn't remember. But the anger, the confusion was now raw on him. He could almost taste it on his lips.

Throwing the hat to the ground, Tim bent down beside the policeman's body and studied the gun by his waist. For a few short moments, he simply stared. Then, somewhat in awe, he carefully removed the gun from its holster. It was a handgun; that much Tim knew. It felt heavier than he'd expected, and holding it gave Tim a sense of power he had never felt before. He liked this new feeling. He liked how it cleared his head, made the bad thoughts go away.

Rather than tucking the thing in his belt, like he'd seen cops do in movies, Tim put the gun in his shoulder bag.

He looked up to find Caz watching on without saying a word.

…

It was the less modern studio of the two in the Real FM building that Sean found himself in. Its walls were wooden, littered with old pictures of celebrities who had been interviewed there over the years. A large plastic clock kept silent watch over time, never out of synch with the hourly pips, faithful to the very second. A small window high up in the back wall was blacked out and soundproofed, designed to keep passers-by from peeking in and upsetting the flow of broadcasting. A yellow lamp shed a little light on the dark studio, providing just enough illumination for Sean to pour coffee and undress vinyl, with the effect that it always seemed like night-time. That's what Sean liked about this studio. It had a smoky, Memphis jazz-club feel to it.

As one disc played out, Sean lined up another, fading music in and out without as much as a cough for his adoring public. Even for a DJ as economic with chat as he was, five songs without a single word was kinda pushing it a little.

He tipped a little more vodka from his hip flask into his coffee. All this stress was getting to him. The twelve o'clock news hadn't happened. He didn't know why it hadn't happened, and with the sudden lack of producer or newsreader to ask, it didn't seem that anyone was awfully bothered about this monumental gaff.

And that just didn't make sense.

A part of Sean knew that something was wrong, that something had happened since the end of *Teenage Kicks* and the start of *Whiskey in the Jar*. He knew deep inside that something had gone badly askew, affecting more than just his playing list. He knew all of this because the twelve o'clock news hadn't gone out, and not one listener, not a single sinner from the twenty-odd thousand good citizens of Belfast he seemed to play to most Sundays had rung in to complain.

He stared at the mic hanging several centimetres away from him. It was one of the old school mics, its thick and heavy metal both familiar and comforting. He didn't know what to say, but he knew this shit demanded he say something. Maybe he should ask for someone to call in and let him know what was going on out there… or maybe that would make him sound like a daft git. Maybe he should let everyone know that he was still here, still playing good music like he always did, just to see if anyone would then get in touch.

Someone like your ex-wife... eh, Sean?

Maybe he should just leave the studio and go and check the staff room to see if the others were there. But he hadn't left his mic during a broadcast in all the years he'd worked the job. It was bad luck and downright rude, he reckoned. No, there had to be another way. Sean needed to think about things for a bit and then decide what to do. He poured himself the last of the coffee, adding another generous drop of vodka to help him concentrate. He put some thinking music on.

...

Herb reached for his bottle of bourbon, a cure for many ills.

He was still in his pyjamas and dressing gown, what with Muriel not having taken the time to set out his clothes for the day like she usually did. Instead, his wife remained perfectly still and lifeless on the armchair. The spare duvet lay rolled up on the sofa opposite. Herb knew what this meant; Muriel had spent another night away from him, another night on the sofa bed that she'd brought to the house only last week. Her last night...

The crumbs were annoying him.

Muriel would not like to be been found like this. It wasn't the Muriel that Herb had known and loved and shared his life with all these years. That was the Muriel that Herb really wanted to be with now, the Muriel who *didn't* sleep on the sofa bed, the Muriel who *wasn't* becoming increasingly tired and bored of life (of him?!), and so, based on this simple logic, he did something which didn't come naturally to him.

He tidied.

He started with Muriel herself. Carefully, Herb brushed every last crumb off her lap then prised the teacup from her stiffening fingers.

She never flinched, her listless eyes remaining fixed on the television, which was still flickering soundlessly in the corner of the living room. She didn't even so much as breathe as Herb continued with his mission, folding out the collar of her blouse, replacing her slippers with her favourite shoes and sliding on her wedding ring. (She sometimes removed it for comfort.) Herb wasn't sure why he expected her to move or breathe or talk. He knew deep down that she would never do any of those things again, but a part of him still expected it—*longed for it*—all the same.

Stepping back like some sort of artist, Herb examined his work. He looked at the corpse of his wife with the same critical eye that had won him a reputation for spotting the flaws in the blueprint plans of prototype engines all those years ago. And, as was the case all too often with the blueprint, he found the image wanting.

The crumbs were still there. They were all over the floor, and Muriel wouldn't like that.

And so it continued, Herb working out how to use a vacuum cleaner for the first time ever, in order to suck up the offending crumbs before moving onto every other thing that remained out of place in their home, every unseemly blemish that remained unattended to by the meticulous eye of his wife. He cleaned the small, two-story cottage from top to bottom, learning the uses of many machines and potions (that he had noticed Muriel using through the years) for the first time in his life. He did it for her, but also for himself, noticing (again for the first time) how therapeutic cleaning and tidying could be.

Once done, Herb sat himself down on the sofa opposite his wife.

There was nothing else left to do.

So he cried.

...

Barry Rogan woke with a start, smelling his hangover before he felt its nasty effects on his body. The room stunk of beer and dope, the smell mixing with the taste of last night's Chinese in his mouth. Suddenly he knew he was going to be sick, jumping out of bed and running to the nearby sink just in the nick of time.

"Jesus..." he muttered to himself, wiping the puke from his stubbly face.

Barry adjusted his eyes to the semi-dark bedroom. The curtains remained wisely closed, offering a little protection for him and his hangover against the cruel onslaught of daylight.

He made a move towards his bed again, thinking another couple of hours' sleep might be in order before he could face any of the remaining day. It was then that he noticed the shape of someone under the duvet. Closer inspection revealed the well-rounded body of a female..

Still have it in ye, boyo.

He had been feeling a little washed out since he'd graduated from Queens University. Barry wasn't quite ready for the BIG-BAD-WORLD yet, but was feeling like something of a hanger-on doing the student circuit. He had known this time would come, dreading it all the years of his degree (*BA Honours in English Lit. Waste of paper.)* But this little honey in his bed, this additional notch on his bedpost… well, it kinda showed him he still had his old mojo. He wasn't past it just yet.

Events were starting to come back to him now. That ninth pint of Harp had really nailed him but he was beginning to recall actually meeting what's-her-face. She had been sitting across from him, in his usual spot, to the left of the dance floor at local indie haven, The Limelight. *Going Underground* by The Jam had been playing, and Barry was just about to get up and throw some drunken shapes on the floor before she caught his eye. She was looking back, standing around a table full of her friends. Small, blonde, skirt up to her neck, looking slutty enough to be his type and *drunk enough for rock and roll* (to use one Barry-ism). She was ticking all the boxes in the Rogan list of essential criteria so Barry wasted no time in springing into action, grabbing his beer and casually strutting over to her table. He waded through her friends, some of them good *Plan Bs* (to use another Barry-ism), jumping right in there with a cheesy smile and some good chat. The rest was history, as they say.

Girls loved a lad with confidence. Barry was convinced of it. He'd learnt this single fact of life through trial and error over the years, suffering all too many hungover hours in the library or lecture theatre in the process.. English Literature meant nothing to Barry Rogan. 'How to pull' was the only subject he had ever taken seriously during his three years of mounting up student loans and beer cans. And yet again, he'd passed his exam with flying colours...

Slipping back into bed, his duvet cover still in need of a good laundering, Barry smugly threw one arm around the corpse lying beside him.

TWO

For the next few hours, before the rain came down, many of those who had survived WHATEVER-IT-WAS-THAT-THEY-HAD-SURVIVED found themselves in a sort of limbo. Shock was an odd thing, evoking a varied range of reactions to what had happened to them. Some found themselves screaming uncontrollably at dead relatives, their primal keens ripping through the pungent silence. Others seemed almost shell-shocked, staring at empty TV screens, or lifeless streets from their bedroom windows.

Some people started moving.

From the outskirts of Belfast, they cautiously made their way into the city centre, hoping that whatever help was going to be sent (sent from where?) would arrive there. Likewise, others outside of Belfast, from towns like Omagh and Enniskillen to the west, and even Lisburn and Newry to the south, made their way carefully up the motorways, driving around the dead and broken to reach The Big Smoke.

Some people found themselves unable to move.

Ken Fitzpatrick, recovering from a road traffic accident which had left him in traction, had spent the last couple of weeks completely immobile at Craigavon Area Hospital, thirty-odd miles south of Belfast. He was unable to wash, feed, piss, or control himself when the nurse gave him a bed bath. Ken had been completely dependent upon the staff to meet his each and every need, with only a short cord close to his bed to allow him to call for help. Help hadn't come even though he had been pulling that bloody cord for the better part of three hours.

Ken was on a heavy prescription of painkillers, and would have been for some time, had this whole END-OF-THE-WORLD thing not fucked things up for him. Four times daily, one of the nurses would come to give him both pills and a drink to wash them down with. The nurses would come at other times as well, brandishing a bedpan for him to do his business in. That hadn't arrived lately either, meaning that, with all this nervousness, Ken had soiled his pyjamas. The lack of painkillers was starting to have an effect on him. He could feel a mild tingle in his arms and legs. Within an hour, this tingle became an irritating itch, an itch he couldn't scratch, what with being strung up like a turkey in a butcher's window at Christmas. The itch soon gave way to a throbbing pain, growing in intensity until he was unable to stand any more, passing in and out of consciousness. Before long a fever broke on his brow, and his breathing intensified, this combination leading to violent nausea. Within twenty-four hours, Ken was dead, choking on his own vomit, his pain finally—and *eternally*—killed.

...

Quite a few miles above where Ken lay, the BMS26 flight from Edinburgh to Dublin passed. A Scottish lass by the name of Susan Stern had recently discovered herself to be the sole surviving passenger onboard. Forty-one bodies rested around her. Susan would have thought they were sleeping, save for the fact that they had all nodded off at *exactly* the same moment. And then there were the air stewards lying across the aisles. For Susan, the faint hope that someone alive was flying the plane would evolve slowly over the next thirty minutes or so, the autopilot taking her safely towards a runway at Dublin airport. That hope would eventually fade as a dead pilot failed to take manual control for landing, and the plane simply wandered south of Galway, using up more and more precious fuel. Although travelling at quite a speed and covering quite a lot of land, Susan was ultimately on her way to nowhere.

...

Sean Magee chose not to move, still spinning discs from his recliner chair in the Real FM studios. After exhausting the various emergency service numbers, Talking Pages, and his old hag of a mother—*none of whom answered*—Sean had spent the last hour lifting and replacing the phone, debating as to whether or not he should call his ex-wife. He definitely knew something was wrong. Very wrong—so very wrong that he wasn't sure he wanted to know what exactly it was.

Terrorist attacks? Chemical warfare?

His hip flask was empty. His play list was nearing exhaustion. There was nothing doing. He knew now that he had to make that call.

A couple of minutes' walk from Sean's studio was Barry Rogan's house. Barry also chose not to move. He'd spent the morning in bed, sleeping through both hangover and Armageddon (which was worse?), one arm slung around the corpse beside him. When he finally awoke, it took him a while to readjust before inspecting the shape in his bed more thoroughly. It was then that a good ol' slap of *WHAT-THE-FUCK?!* woke him up properly.

It wasn't the first time Barry had found someone incapacitated lying in his bed. Before he had learned how to charm his way into a girl's pants, Barry had used other, less noble methods. His mate, Dave, had got him into it, scoring him the drug Rohypnol. He'd only used it three times, only to see what it was like, and, as he'd said to Dave afterwards, the girls he'd used it on were dead keen anyway. But he'd never forgotten their faces. Each of them had burned a permanent stain on his life, occasionally leading to sporadic bouts of depression and self-reproach whenever dark, guilty thoughts wormed their way to the forefront of his mind. And so Barry lived in a constant state of denial, learning to reason his ever-creeping conscience back into its box each time it threatened to stab him. It was a mistake he'd made (okay, *mistakes*) but it was all behind him now, wasn't it? Just a part of growing up that he regretted. Everyone had regrets. These were his.

What did it matter now, anyway?

But fact was that the girl in his bed *now*, at this very moment, looked drugged. There was no denying it. This began to eat away at him. He felt the first wave of guilt wash through him, threatening to break down his well-protected dam. It was a familiar feeling. He looked, fearfully, towards the bed again. She looked just like the others had looked: peaceful, oblivious to what he was doing and where he was doing it, oblivious to his unprotected cock sliding up her leg…

No! That wasn't what happened last night!

More waves of guilt beat against his dam, stronger now and threatening to tear it down, but he knew—he simply *knew*—he hadn't used that shit, not for a long time now. In fact, Barry hadn't seen Dave in years, not since he'd decided to put that... part of his life behind him.

Barry gently shook the girl. He couldn't remember her name. He tried to search his busy mind for some clue, as if in remembering what she was called would make some sort of difference to what had happened. Yet it was lost to him now, with only the smell of her hair, of whatever product she had used, straining from the clammy air clouding his room. He could almost taste the guilt swelling in his mouth like an ulcer. He ran a single hand along her face. Yet with every caress of her dead cheek, every gentle embrace of her limp, dead body, he could find no release. He suddenly needed someone to comfort *him*, someone to stroke *his* hair and say it would be okay. But she wouldn't stir. He became angry with her, shaking her violently as if to shock her out of this senseless coma. But it was no good. Barry curled up in a ball beside her cold, still corpse. He closed his eyes, hoping it was all some bad dream, hoping that when he opened them again, it would be different...

...

Roy Beggs was one of the survivors who *were* moving, gradually working his way up the M1 motorway. He was travelling in his military Land Rover, packed to the brim with chemical toilets, canned foods, bottled water and other essentials. Hidden beneath his provisions was a small armoury, including a number of Browning 9mms and several SA80 assault rifles. Although recent years had seen him train fresh recruits for the Territorial Army, Roy was a veteran of the Royal Irish Regiment. He had been trained for such eventualities as whatever the fuck this was. He had taken action rather than just sitting back, sorted things out directly, the way things needed to be sorted out. That was his way. Always had been.

Sitting beside Roy was Mairead Burns, a staunch Republican who had spent more than a few hours in the back of one of these Land Rovers. Mairead was also a veteran—a veteran troublemaker for the likes of Roy, for the so-called security forces who had blighted her land for too many decades. She had spat, stoned and sworn at pseudo-soldiers like Roy, calling them traitors and murderers. She had stored weapons and explosives in her modest terrace house on the Garvaghy Road, hiding bombers and active members of the Irish Republican Army before and after operations. These weapons and bombs had been used to blow people like Roy to pieces as they investigated false emergency calls in Republican areas. That was *her* way.

An apocalypse was the only thing in the world that would bring the likes of Roy and Mairead together. These two were like oil and water, hated by and hating each other in a merry-go-round of misery, grinding Northern Ireland into a political quagmire that had proved a fucker to get out of.

Conversation between the pair had been limited, for obvious reasons. Yet ironically, they shared quite a bit in common. Both believed in their retrospective cause with a passion like no other. Both had broken the rules—broken the law—to further their cause. Both came from Portadown, described once by a key Republican politician as 'The Alabama of the North' (and neither Roy nor Mairead could argue with that). Yet, since Roy had picked Mairead up, somewhere on the Seagoe Road of said Alabama, hardly a word had passed between them.

Mairead had been in the car with her husband Mickey when the shit had hit the fan, managing to steer off the road when he had taken a nosedive for the dashboard. She had tried everything to wake him up, then cried heavy-hearted tears, rinsing out twenty years of marriage in a desperate and vulnerable keen that one wouldn't expect from a hard-nosed battle-axe like her.

Yet it wasn't the first time this morning Mairead had cried.

Dressed head-to-toe in black, she and Mickey had been on their way back from their son's grave. He would have been eighteen years old today, and for that reason Mairead's tears had been particularly heavy. They had dried quickly when Roy had shown up. She wasn't going to let one of his sort see her showing any emotion, any weakness, any humanity, so she clogged those eyes up quick-smart, slipping on her Easter Rising face as smoothly as changing gears.

She was scared and confused, and so, God forgive her, Mairead had taken help from the first person who had come along. Even if that person were the devil himself. Mickey would have turned in his grave, (were he to have had one) if he could have seen his wife getting into a Land Rover with a Brit Bastard like Beggs. But Mairead knew deep down that she had been left with no other choice.

Slowly and quietly, the pair travelled up the M1 motorway to Belfast. The signs of death were everywhere. Smashed cars, the bodies of their occupants cast out of bust windshields, littered the sunburnt tarmac. Roy navigated through the desolation with one eye on the road and another on what was happening behind him: a small convoy of cars tailed his Land Rover, perhaps of the belief that following a military vehicle might lead to help of some sort...

...

Stepping carefully over two corpses belonging to an elderly couple, Star pressed her hands and face against an electrical shop's window. Her dreadlocked head reflected in the large pane of glass, the piercings and random zips of her urban combats glittering in the sharp sunlight. There were a few people inside the shop, all dead, lying on the smoothly polished shop floor as if they'd simply got tired and decided to take a nap. Star was beginning to wonder if she were dead, too, the Great Leveller perhaps spitting her weathered corpse back into the city like some hard-to-chew lump of gristle. Maybe she was damned to be a ghost, destined to haunt these Godforsaken streets for all of eternity.

She was just about to turn away from the shop window when something happened. Her heavily blackened eyes narrowed as every television inside lost reception, giving up life as simply and peacefully as every corpse seemed to have done. Snowy screens washed over every set like some kind of fucked-up Mexican wave. Star didn't move from her spot, simply staring at the fuzzy nonsense through the window.

This was the stuff of horror movies.

...

Later, Star found herself sitting alone, nestling a cup of coffee she'd got from a machine. On the floor was her shoulder bag, containing the few possessions she'd taken with her. Beside that, a couple of Marks and Spencer bags, containing a few edibles and bottles of water.

It was there, the Marks and Spencer Food Hall in the city centre, that she'd seen it: a pram, dead mother draped over it like a fallen curtain. It was a powerful image and, like the dead birds before it, she'd captured it on her phone camera. Of all of the horror Star had encountered since leaving her shop earlier on, all of the bodies she had stepped over, walked around, even searched for valuables (*hell, it was the end of the fuckin' world; what did it matter?!),* only these pictures were etched permanently into her camera phone and mind. All the other bodies, all the other faces were like a sea of blanks, merging into each other.

But the birds...

That pram...

Like a tattoo, each image stung and itched whenever she thought about it. It brought home to her the seriousness of what was happening all around her.

Those little wings, static, immobile...

That little face, peaceful, silent...

She hadn't found *any* signs of life.. Only the hoarse crackle of flame, a radio playing Dead Air FM, those fuckin' televisions. Belfast's buzz had suddenly been snuffed out, leaving a messy and broken landscape. As she tiptoed through the dead streets, opening a shop door here, checking a crashed car there, Star couldn't help but think how similar this desolation was to the aftermath of IRA bombs from days gone by. Only difference was that bombs made a sound.

Perhaps due to her love of travelling, Star had made her way to Great Victoria Street. The Great Victoria Street Station was the centre of all travel from and to Belfast, hosting both bus centre and train station within its modern metal and glass structure. A small shopping mall greeted those entering the station's main entrance, but many preferred the side entrance, where the taxi depot serviced, close to the station's coffee shop. Countless times Star had caught the popular Airbus from Great Victoria Street to Belfast's International Airport. That bus had been the first step in many a journey to near-and-far. Now, of course, Great Victoria Street's constant hubbub was as dead as everything else, the bodies of queuing holiday-makers and businessmen sprinkled around its spacious interiors, cafe and shopping centre like spent dominoes. An occasional suitcase had fallen hard on the floor, spilling clothes and toiletries messily onto the well-polished, grey tiles.

Star ran her tongue over the back of the stud piercing her bottom lip, remembering for some reason that she had forgotten to brush her teeth that morning. But these things, these details from the old world seemed pointless now, mere echoes quickly dying as their value, their relevance became buried beneath The Silence.

A sudden, shrill noise of breaking glass snapped Star out of her trance. She turned to follow the sound, her eyes widening as they found two figures outside, moving towards the station.

...

Sean picked up the phone, this time with surety. He was going to ring his wife—

Ex-wife, Sean; don't forget the EX.

—and find out what just what the hell was going on. It had been hours now, but the phone was still working. That was a good sign, wasn't it? He dialled the number, a number he hadn't rung in five years, not since that Christmas she had told him there was no need to call anymore.

No need?!

Yet still he knew it off by heart.

A panicked voice answered quickly. "H-Hello?!"

It was her. He'd never forget her voice.

"Sharon," he began, the vodka in his coffee having slurred his speech a little, "it's—"

"Sean!? Oh, Sean... everything's wrong!"

"What? Slow down, Sharon… where are you?"

"At home," she cried, her despair ripping through the phone as if electric. *"T-there's no one left outside! I-I was at church and..."* She crumbled, a long and high-pitched whine taking over from where her voice left off.

"What?! Sharon, you've got to calm down..." She wasn't making any sense to him.

"Everyone's dead!" she yelled at him, angrily, as if whatever was happening was his fault, to be laid at his

door along with everything else that had gone wrong in her life. A part of Sean became defensive. He felt his guard rise automatically, but then she softened, repeating her words in a calm, quiet voice. "*Everyone's dead.*".

"Sharon," he sighed, wishing she were beside him in the studio, within reach of him. "Just tell me what's happened. Is it a bomb?"

But she ignored his question.

"*They're... dead...*" she repeated, eerily, as if she couldn't quite believe it. As if the logic of what she had witnessed was utterly foreign to her.

But there was something else.

"*Sean,*" she said, her voice changing gear, as if everything that had happened was suddenly forgotten to her, "*I'm so very sorry... but I can't...*"

Sean's eyes widened, his hands starting to shake. He'd heard those words before. It had been eight years ago, just before they'd broken up. He'd phoned home one night just to check up on her before he started work. He'd been doing the evening slot then, his show having been moved during yet another one of the suits' shake-ups. When he rang, Sharon was in weird form, talking a lot of bollocks and generally not making sense. Then there was that voice, those words—an ethereal and lifeless whisper. Half in the world, half out of it.

Drugged.

Sean had been able to get an ambulance to her just in time. She had taken enough pills to kill an elephant, but they were able to pump them all out of her stomach. Ironically, after saving her life, Sean lost his marriage. By the time the shrinks had picked Sharon's bones and brains, session after session of whys and wherefores, there was nothing left for Sean. Depression, she'd told them. A feeling of disenfranchisement. And Sean had been the reason for all that, of course—the late nights, the morose, subdued lack of conversation, the bad sex.

The bad sex?!

She needed more, she'd told them. And then she told him that she was leaving, that it was part of her recovery to put behind her all the things that were wrong in her life. Things like her marriage…

"Sharon, listen to me... Are you okay? Did you take anything?! Sharon?!"

There was no response.

"Sharon!"

There was the sound of a phone falling from the other end of the line. It rattled through his ear like change spitting out of a slot machine. Then nothing.

(Nothing was the new something.)

"Sharon! Sharon!"

The last song had ended, perhaps minutes ago. Sean hadn't even noticed. It had been *Don't Fear The Reaper* by Blue Oyster Cult. Later, Sean would see the humour in that. Later, he'd remember every last song he'd played in those final hours, the hours when the world had ended, when everything had changed.

But now…

Now only The Silence ruled the airwaves, The Absence… The Lack… It seemed to overpower everything. It started with the radio going QT, every electric radio and ignored alarm clock throughout Belfast now gently humming. Even static became a thing of the past. Then the power stations gave up, no longer able to hold out to the demands of a dead city's indulgent waste of electricity. Unmanned and uncared for, computers simply stopped telling machinery what to do. And then came the blackout. Like toy soldiers falling, the lights throughout Belfast dimmed one by one until there was nothing but shadow. Heaters and television sets around the country powered down.

Electronic billboards gave up their relentless campaign of marketing, whilst arrival and departure times at Belfast's two airports finally dulled. Everything and everyone was officially pronounced deceased within seconds. In the dipping sun of the late afternoon, Sean buried his head in his hands whilst Belfast became a new city.

A city without power.

A city without Sharon.

...

"Shit!"

Caz stepped away from the broken glass at her foot. She was lucky not to have sliced herself.

"You all right?" Tim asked her.

"Fine," she replied. "Never even noticed that."

"You have to be more careful," he snapped back.

(Me Tarzan, you Jane.)

Caz smiled, surprised at how much she welcomed his concern, no matter how badly expressed it was. She would have liked to think of herself as an independent girl, someone who could look after herself from day to day. Even her parents had stepped back as she got older, allowing her the run of their entire attic conversion as her own, self-contained flat. It surprised her, therefore, to find herself not only fancying Tim Adamson but needing him, as well. He had become something different to her. Something better. She wanted him to protect her, look after her. She felt safer because he was around.

Her sudden neediness was probably more to do with circumstance than constitution. Everything around them was broken and dangerous, like the glass at her feet. They had been together for the last few hours, wandering through the torn city centre, avoiding the bodies and wreckage like skittles from some twisted game. A strange and foreboding sense of exactly what was happening was fading in and out like summer rain. But even in silence, even when she didn't know what

Tim was thinking, to be going through it all with him by her side made things that little bit easier.

She didn't know why they had chosen to come to the station on Great Victoria Street. Maybe it was because they had met on the train, where everything had gone to hell. Maybe it was because they had heard that automated voice over the Tannoy.

(THE NEXT APOCALYPSE WILL BE LEAVING FROM....)

Regardless of the reason, they had found themselves drawn to this place—a place of transition—a place where journeys began and ended, yet rarely felt completed. In that way, it made perfect sense to come here. This was the place of the disenfranchised. This was where you waited for something else to happen, somewhere else to go.

Star watched both kids as they approached the side entrance. The young lad held one large, glass door open as the girl made her way through, before following her. Star lit up another ciggie as she watched him bend down to search through the contents of a split-open suitcase. He moved away, empty-handed, choosing instead to rummage through the coat pockets of a nearby dead body, picking a few things out and shoving them into his shoulder bag. Star waited until they had walked a few metres beyond the entrance. Then she stood up, moving her chair away with her foot. She took another drag, smiling wryly as the two teens stopped in their tracks, studying her as if they couldn't believe their eyes. The dreadlocked tattooist was used to people looking at her in that way, her colourful image both shocking and attractive to Belfast's conformed-looking majority.

"Hey," Star called.

The two kids looking back at her were the first living people she'd laid eyes upon.

"Hey," the lad replied.

THREE

Then came The Rain.

It came down like cats and dogs. Torrential. Sombre. Purifying. It put out every fire, every little flicker of flame. It wiped clean every bloodstain from where the fallen had hit the ground, sterilising the pavements and roads as if Baby Jesus were trying to clean up his mess before Daddy got home.

The now sizable convoy of survivors behind the Land Rover mostly had their headlamps on. All except Steve Marshall, who hadn't bothered replacing a broken headlamp since his shambles of a car failed its MOT. Steve was making do with one headlamp, straining against the poor light and rain-stained vision in order to follow the military vehicle in front.

In the front seat of Steve's car was his dead wife, Kirsty. Her corpse was surprisingly radiant. Steve could still smell her perfume, mixing with the smell of shit coming from the cot in the back seat of the car.

That's where their son Nicky lay.

Kirsty was wearing a simple white blouse and short mini-skirt, allowing a generous view of her long legs. Even with the rain coming down, Kirsty's tan still glowed, her legs resting slightly to the left of the gear stick. Steve felt the hairs on the back of his hand brush gently against them each time he changed gear.

They were setting out for a Sunday drive when the madness struck, sending the light traffic on the Lurgan Road wayward as Steve skidded to an abrupt stop. His wife and son were suddenly quiet. There was no impact. Even the cot remained fastened into the back seat. Yet he couldn't wake either of them.

He remained in the car for some time. Hours, maybe. There was no movement outside. The other vehicles on the road remained motionless, their drivers and passengers slumped against the grip of their safety belts. He was too frightened to get out of his car, too frightened to do anything apart from shake Kirsty, trying to rouse from her sleep.

(It was just sleep, wasn't it?)

With time, Steve realised it *wasn't* just sleep. It was something different from sleep. But he couldn't give up on them. This was his family, and it was his responsibility to care for them. He had heard of all types of situations, over the years, where people fell into comas, almost to the point of seeming to be dead, only to be revived hours, days, weeks or months later. *This thing could be curable*, he told himself.

Steve remained focused on the task at hand, maintaining his place in line behind the military vehicle at the front of the convoy. He hoped the police or the army would know what to do in a situation like this. He hoped they would bring him to a doctor, or a hospital, no doubt set up to deal with whatever had just happened.

They can do anything these days, those doctors. Anything.

...

They were about ten miles shy of Belfast, but the torrential rain and choking darkness was making the difficult enough job of driving through sporadic wreckage very hazardous indeed.

Roy figured they needed to find shelter for the night.

He heard Mairead speak, maybe for the first time since getting into the Land Rover.

"What are you doing?"

"Pulling into Lisburn, love," he replied, eyes still on the road, windscreen wipers going like the hammers. "It's too dangerous to go on."

"But, what if they send some help to Belfast, and we're not there? What then?!"

"Well, just you leave that all to me, love. Nothing to worry about."

Roy checked the mirror to make sure the other vehicles were still following him.

"And besides, don't you want to meet all of this crowd?"

He smiled over at the stern look on Mairead's face before adding, "Never know… may even be a few more Provos in there for you to chat with, eh?"

He could see Mairead seething at his remark, finding it difficult to hold back her anger. Provos was slang for the Provisional IRA. He was having a dig at her and he was enjoying her reaction. That's the kind of man Roy Beggs was.

He knew Mairead Burns. He'd dealt with her before, back in the 80's, when they had been investigating a lead from one of their grasses. The deal was that the little fucker told Roy and his boys about any local IRA weapon stores in the area. Striking gold would slice a good five years off the little toe rag's life sentence.

Sure enough, they struck gold.

Mairead and her husband had been hiding a shitload of mortars in the greenhouse of her council house, just off the Garvaghy Road in Portadown. She had pleaded innocence, of course, when they had kicked her door in one night. Spat, screamed and scratched at the soldiers who threw her into the back of the Land Rover, her young child crying uncontrollably as he stood in his pyjamas, watching the scene unfold.

But she didn't recognise Roy. He had just been another Brit Bastard, no doubt, tearing her house apart. Another camouflaged goon. The Enemy. It made Roy laugh. That was twenty odd years ago, when both of them were a lot younger and even more bitter and entrenched. Yet even now, her face was hard as Roy continued driving down the slip road, trying to do the best for all of them by finding somewhere to rest up for the night. Somewhere for them all to be comfortable. Somewhere where they could maybe even wash or grab a bite to eat.

Somewhere, of course, without dead people.

Before long, Roy had found the perfect spot, straining against the poor light to make out a signpost nearby. It signed towards a primary school, just off the slip road, close to the motorway. Roy pulled over next to the school's gates, using his indicator lights to let those behind him know what he was doing.

Home sweet home.

...

Sean had to get out of there.

He was still shell shocked from the phone call with Sharon. He couldn't sit anymore in that damn room, surrounded by his ever-growing collection of vinyl and CDs, in a radio station that could no longer broadcast. With the lights now down, he was virtually sitting in the dark, surrounded by useless equipment. It was pointless to sit by the mic any longer. After more years than he cared to count in the business, his job was over. He had finally retired, making the transition from crowd favourite to has-been a lot quicker than he previously thought possible.

Plus, he badly needed a piss.

In the sombre twilight, the rain's constant and furious drone being the only soundtrack available, the once popular Real FM DJ shoved the bottle of vodka into his pocket and left the Godforsaken studio. He walked through the small corridor, stopping off at the toilet. He relieved himself before continuing through to the staff room. There he found all of those he had missed. The newsreader and production team. The receptionist, the cleaner. Some of them were resting on the floor. Others were slumped in chairs, bodies draped messily across the dining table like discarded dolls. The producer's coffee had overturned, its contents evaporating into the humid studio, leaving a dark, dry stain on the poor bastard's opened newspaper. Sean couldn't go near him. He couldn't go near any of them. He knew they were dead, even though he'd never seen a dead body before. They looked empty, void, and he couldn't bear to be in the same room as them.

He moved through to reception, opening the door to the outside world. He found himself in the street. The Rain beat down upon him, unacknowledged. Trickles of moisture ran down his expressionless face unchallenged. He was a shadow of a man now. He could sense the death. He thought he could even smell it. It was all around him, spreading throughout Northern Ireland like poison. He knew the vast majority of his twenty thousand listeners lay dead. But only one of them mattered to him now.

He walked with purpose, defiant of the dark, the rain and the few bodies he passed along the way. He was seeking closure, and in a world which seemed to have completely closed down, his quest seemed ridiculously ironic. Yet for Sean, it wasn't just closure from the phone call that was needed, but closure for his entire marriage. Closure for everything since that fateful night she had taken those pills.

He'd treated her well. Never hit her, never left her lacking anything. She had had everything materially that she could want. As long as Sean had a few quid every week to spend on CDs (hell, most of them he got for free, anyway) he was happy. The rest of his pay packet (which, let's face it, wasn't too bad after all his years at the station, and his pension was mounting up nicely, too) had been hers to spend as she pleased. Clothes, books, things for the house, whatever. She had it all, in his eyes.

But she didn't have him.

Eventually he reached Sharon's house. He'd driven past it a few times in the past, sometimes pissed up, intending to call in. But he'd never had the balls to see it through. Now, he had no apprehension at all. He opened the door quickly and assertively, quite confident that no one indoors would mind all that much.

From the inside, it didn't look anything like the house Sharon had shared with him all those years ago. He wasn't sure whose taste it was decorated according to, but it sure as hell wasn't Sharon's. Well, not the Sharon he knew, anyway. The walls of every room were white, almost blending into the ceiling, like a sea of blandness. Random and abstract artwork cluttered the place, a painting here, some weird sculpture… *thing*… there.

In the living room, he found a photograph. It was Sharon and some arty-looking bloke. Smart pinstripe suit paired with trainers. Fancy Britpop haircut. Bit of a poncy looking fucker for a man of his age. Sean guessed it was this dude that Sharon had shacked up with. For how long this had been the arrangement, he couldn't tell. He realised, suddenly, how little he actually knew about Sharon since *that Christmas...*

Turning the handle of the kitchen door, noticing the phone missing from its hands-free base in the hallway, Sean found the closure he was looking for. There, sprawled on the chequered-tile floor, still in her pyjamas, the phone resting in one hand, lay the only woman he'd actually ever cared for. On the kitchen table near where she lay, a tub of pills had spilled. Sean didn't need to read the prescription label on their side to know what they were.

Sean pulled a chair out and sat himself down. For long moments he simply stared at his wife's corpse, one hand over his mouth.

"Oh, Sharon," he muttered, his hand muffling the words. "Sharon, Sharon, Sharon..."

...

"Do you know what's happening?" Caz asked the tattooed woman.

They were sitting at the small coffee shop within the station's mall. They'd exchanged the basic pleasantries—names, etcetera—but little else. It seemed to Caz that this wasn't a woman who enjoyed talking much. The constant patter of rain kept a steady, sombre rhythm to an otherwise silent tune. A single candle burned in defiance against the ebbing blackness of nightfall.

"End of the word, doll," Star replied. "The way this place was going, I'm just surprised it didn't happen sooner."

"But how?" Caz persisted. "Maybe it's just something that's happened in Belfast?" She hadn't travelled that much in her sixteen years, but she knew the world was a big place. Who was to say what was going on in, say, Portadown or Ballymena, never mind Melbourne, Australia.

"Television's gone," Star replied, drawing on that damn cigarette again. "Not a single channel broadcasting. BBC, RTE, Channel bloody Four, Sky... even the fucking shopping channels. None of them are working. No TV... no world." She snubbed the cigarette out in the ashtray on their table. "Much as I hate to admit it, television's our window to the rest of the world. It tells the news. Only thing that beats it is the internet." She searched through her pockets, finally producing another cigarette. "And the internet's fucked too. Not a dickie-bird about any of this on there. Some sites aren't connecting at all."

Caz looked over to Tim. He was playing about with Star's lighter, striking flame, then blowing it out. Striking flame again, then blowing out. It was starting to irritate her.

"Tim, *don't*," she scolded, before turning to the other survivor again.

"Why are *we* still alive, then? This disease, virus, gas attack—whatever it is. Why hasn't it affected us?"

Star laughed. "Who's to say it hasn't?"

"Well, we're still here, aren't we?"

"For now, yes." She lit up the other cigarette after grabbing her lighter back from Tim. "But how do you know we're always going to be immune to—well, whatever the fuck it is we're immune to? We could drop dead at any minute."

"You might, if you keep smoking like that," Caz snapped.

The other survivor laughed, blowing a cloud of smoke into the teenager's face. It was enough to push Caz over the edge. She stood up, kicking her chair away in anger.

"Star!? That's your name, isn't it?! I thought a star was a symbol of *hope*," she hissed, then walked away, sniffing away the tears.

She stood, looking out at the rain-stained streets to an empty void of Belfast.

Hope?

...

That first night was difficult.

The seats at the bus station were not so comfortable, but they were roomy enough to use as beds. They stretched generously in rows, offering plenty of legroom for even the gangly frame of Tim Adamson. A cold finish offered a hard, yet firm, mattress. It wasn't exactly The Ritz. Sure, the Europa Hotel was just next door, a mere stone's throw away from the bus station, but none of the three really fancied dragging dead guests out of bed before lying down in more comfortable surroundings. They weren't quite there yet, so here they remained, in this huge, glass building. Clinical-looking. Minimalist décor. Its inoffensive, polished floors and pale walls perhaps providing the serenity that the three needed. In a way, staying at the station, sleeping there like travellers waiting for the next bus or train helped them feel alien to this new and strange, dead world. Separate from it. Just passing through. In the courtyard outside, as if in response to the survivors' sub-conscious meanderings, lines of buses were parked neatly beside each other.

Neither the teens nor Star had come prepared, so they just used their coats as blankets. Comfy duvets had seemed unimportant, somehow, during their retrospective scavenging throughout the city centre earlier that afternoon. Sleep had been the last thing on their minds.

Whilst the night drew in, the torrential rain seeming to make the skies look even darker, the three survivors made the best of their makeshift beds, sleeping on adjacent seats. No one spoke or said goodnight to each other. And although all three were utterly exhausted, sleep didn't come easy to them.

FOUR

Sean couldn't bring himself to get up. To leave. This was not the closure he was hoping for. He had dreamed of being in this house, had gone over in his head what he would have said to Sharon when she would have answered the door. But here he was. In her kitchen, staring right at her. A corpse. Just like all the others. Only whatever had got everyone else, in the end, hadn't been pills.

It would have been better for Sean if she'd died like all the others, taken away without rhyme or reason. Unpreventable. Completely random. Yet this—*this again?!*

A noise. Creaking of a door. Was it locked? Had he closed it when he'd come in? Sean couldn't be sure. Maybe it was just the wind. Or a cat. Did Sharon own a cat? No. There it was again. The noise. Footsteps. Someone else was in the house, moving towards the kitchen.

Carefully, Sean rose from his seat. He felt scared, aware of having broken into the house. Worried about being found.

Slowly, he moved his hand to the rolling pin sitting on the draining board. As the intruder made their way down the hall, Sean readied himself with the makeshift weapon, hiding as best as he could behind his dead ex-wife's fridge. Slowly the door opened, revealing a soaking, yet familiar face. Sean remembered him from the photo. The only difference being that the man (Sean didn't even know his name, and that seemed odd to him all of a sudden) seemed a lot more distressed. The once-perfectly-styled hair was glued to a furrowed forehead by cold, sickly-smelling sweat. His skin was pale, as if he'd just seen a thousand ghosts. His eyes hung out of their over-exerted sockets, a crude display of fear and loss damp on each pupil.

As he entered, he caught sight of the corpse, sprawled out on the kitchen floor.

"Sharon," he gasped, weakly. "Oh… my god… Sharon…"

Sean followed the other man's eyes, seeming to illustrate what he himself was feeling.

Sharon...

Sean began to miss everything about her. All those phone calls he had cut short. The endless number of nights he had left her in the house, by herself, while he was out pretending he was still twenty-one at some random club. Sean longed for every one of those wasted seconds to be available to him again. He resented the time he had lost. Wasted. Squandered.

A sudden tearful choke gave Sean's position away. As the other man turned sharply, hearing the noise, his sullen face changed.

"Bastard!" he screamed in a posh accent. It was perhaps the poshest version of bastard Sean had ever heard.

He lunged for the DJ, a fiery vengeance in his eyes. This whole END-OF-THE-WORLD thing obviously wasn't sitting well with Sharon's hunnykins, the man she had shared her life (and bed) with for the best part of five years.

He looked like a man who had snapped, the sight of seeing his girlfriend dead on their kitchen floor perhaps adding to whatever horrors he'd already been dealt thus far. Sean didn't know if the guy had recognised him, or knew who he was. He couldn't tell if his attacker knew that he had once been able to make his partner happy.

Make her cum...

But the way his hands locked around Sean's throat, it sure felt like he had.

Sean swung weakly at him, grabbing his damp, slick, poncy hair with one hand and punching him with the other. It hardly seemed to affect the crazed attacker. He probably didn't even feel it, such was his fury. A string of incomprehensible obscenities and abuse spat constantly in Sean's face. The words were becoming lost to him, swimming away as if part of a dream. He began to feel his own grip on the attacker go limp. His throat had dried up, starved of air. It began to numb against the onslaught of pressure. He couldn't breathe, couldn't move, couldn't shake this son of a bitch off.

This is it, Seany-boy. Say your goodbyes to your dead wife.

The room was going dark, spinning. The noise of the man yelling at him was fading in and out.

Ex-wife, Sean. Don't forget the EX.

His mind began the slow-but-sure journey through life. His eyes began to blur, stars shimmering and dancing all around him, his lungs giving up the fight against the pressure of the man's grip. Sean could feel the tightness in his chest intensifying, years of heavy drinking seeming to kill him that little bit quicker, that little bit sooner.

And then came the jolt. A sudden and almighty halt to proceedings. As if the pause button had been pressed, the words stopped attacking him, spit stopped soaking him. The grip loosened, his assailant's eyes becoming still and startled.

Another jolt. Then another.

Sean grabbed his moment, kicking out with a desperate burst of energy. The other man's body fell to the floor beside Sharon, Sean landing immediately on top, spitting and coughing, recovering his breath.

As his eyes regained focus, the dizziness gradually clearing, giving way to nausea, Sean was able to make out the profile of a young man staring down at him, bloodied kitchen knife in one hand.

...

Roy stepped out of the Land Rover and gestured to the cars pulling up behind him that he wanted them to stay put.

He pulled a raincoat out from under the seat. Sliding it on, fighting against the aggressive rain, he moved towards the school's front gates, keen to check the place out before allowing anyone else in. He unlatched the gate, opened it, and jogged the few metres across the playground to the school's front doors. His considerable beer belly meant he was out of breath by the time he had covered even that short distance.

The gates were locked. Roy gave them a good shake, but they held tight. He would have to find another way in. Squinting against the heavy rain, he pulled out a torch and snapped its beam on. He was going to have to go around back, and the Land Rover's headlamps weren't going to illuminate anything for him there.

The heavy-set soldier stepped carefully, lighting his way with the torch as he took each step around to the other side of the school. If the back door weren't open (and why would *any* door of a school be open after midnight on a Sunday?) then he might have to break open a window. It was locked tight, just as he thought.

Following the walls leading back around to the front of the building, Roy searched for a suitably-located window to bust through. He hadn't banked on one already being broken.

Someone had got here before them.

...

He opened up the Land Rover door, passenger side. "Come on. Get out."

The torrential rain invaded, soaking her like a car driving through a puddle. Mairead Burns stared back at Roy Beggs, part incredulous, part surprised.

"Thought you said to stay here!" she shouted over the wet din.

Roy laughed. "You think I'd really trust you to stay here by yourself?" He opened the door wider, stepping aside to let her climb down. "Look, Provo… I changed my mind. Come on. I want you where I can see you."

Mairead climbed out, coat in hand. Fuming, she watched Roy go around to the back of the Land Rover and pick something out. He seemed to take ages, rummaging through all the gear he had stocked. She pulled her coat on. The rain continued to hammer down, and Mairead was growing impatient. She was also growing scared. Was he going to shoot her? A part of her really didn't give a fuck whether or not he did, yet another part—the fighting part, the soldier within—was already hatching out escape routes.

"Come on," Roy gestured, pointing to the school across the forecourt-cum-playground.

Mairead felt his eyes lingering on the back of her head as she walked through the school gates, Roy following closely behind her. They made their way through the splattering puddles until they reached the front doors of the school.

Roy showed Mairead the broken window.

"Listen," he said, speaking in a low voice, "I know we're very different, you and me… Very, very different. But we're similar, too."

Mairead looked back at him, bemused. "Look, where is this going?" Nervously, she watched Roy take a handgun out of his pocket.

"We're both soldiers, you and me," he replied, his face taking on a deadly serious expression. "That's what I mean."

Mairead laughed.

"You're not going to get all love-thy-enemy on me, are you?"

Her eyes fell back to the gun. It seemed more like he was going to shoot her than hug her. Give some bullshit speech about honour, then shoot her. His face seemed forlorn. For the first time since they had met, Mairead realised that he was talking straight with her. And it scared her.

"Don't think I don't know what you are and what your kind have done to people like me in the past," he spat.

His hand gripped the gun tightly, and it looked for a second as if he were going to use it, right there and then.

"But there's no law here, not anymore."

For a few static moments, they stood poised on the stark, rain-stained tarmac. The elements continued their brutal assault. Roy's hand was still clenched around the gun, Mairead's eyes stuck to it like glue.

It was an ironic choice of venue, given what was being said. It was where it had all started for adults. The playground. All their politics and bullshit opinions about themselves. All their rules and regulations. All their games. But none of that mattered now in this broken-down world. Stripped of people, society's conformities and structures seemed pointless. No politics. No borders.

There was only this window. This school. A crowd of frightened people huddled in their cars, waiting for someone to help them. A man standing beside a woman with a gun which he may or may not use against her.

It was Roy who broke the stalemate.

"God only knows who or what's inside there," he said, eyeing Mairead, "but they got here before us, and I'd prefer to have back-up before I check it out."

Mairead stared back, trying to work out if any part of him were talking shit. His rugged, yet not altogether unattractive face strained against the rain. Water had dampened his thick moustache, making it look heavy.

She went to snatch the weapon. Roy held onto it tight.

"Can I trust you, Provo?"

Mairead glared at him, her hand firmly gripped around the gun's barrel. The two of them looked for a second as if they might suddenly struggle for it. In days gone by, they almost certainly would have.

"You can trust me," Mairead replied, finally.

She wasn't lying. They needed each other. Both realised it. He hated her as much as she hated him. Fuck, the way he talked to her was as if she was dirt on his shoe. This peace between them wouldn't last forever, but it was needed now.

Roy Beggs relaxed his grip, allowing the Browning 9mm to be taken from his grasp. As his eyes remained fixed on her, Mairead Burns dropped its magazine, checking it held the full thirteen rounds. She slipped the magazine back in then pulled the topslide across before nodding back at him. It was a series of motions so fluid, so calculated, that she knew he'd be unnerved. Hoped he'd be unnerved.

A part of Roy Beggs, she reckoned, regretted giving her the gun right there and then.

Another part of him would regret it later.

...

She squeezed her small, stocky frame through the broken window, helped by Roy, dropping down onto the tiled floor below. The room she landed in was dark, and it took her eyes a while to become accustomed to her surroundings. In the poor light, Mairead couldn't make out much, short of the room's shape, a doorway and little else. However, she worked out fairly quickly that she must be in a locker room of some sort. The smell gave it away.

Sweaty socks.

It brought her back several years, just before her son, Pat, had got too big. Just before he had started washing more than his face, combing his hair more often, asking for whatever trainers were fashionable at the time. Just before he had left school, got himself in with a bad crowd, found himself in more trouble with the pigs than even Mairead would have liked.

—Just before he blew himself up.

Mairead put the thought out of her head, sliding it into the same box her dead husband was currently residing in, unchecked, unmarked. A box that would have read 'Briefly Mourned', had someone the time to mark it such, but everything had happened so quickly that such a box hadn't even been built yet. Thoughts circled freely around her broken mind. Nothing had settled. She felt almost dizzy with the chaos of it all, yet fought to steady herself. This was the first time she had been alone, the first moment of solitude, and it didn't bode well for the future.

Mairead had to focus, concentrate.

She snapped on the torch that Roy had given to her and slowly moved towards the exit from the locker room. Leaning back against the wall, she held her torch with one hand as the other moved to slowly open the door. It creaked obnoxiously, causing her to freeze. She held her breath, listening for signs of life or alarm.

None. Nothing.

(The new something.)

Mairead crouched, sneaking her way out into the school's main corridor. It wasn't far to the back entry, which she had agreed as her rendezvous point with Roy. Finally she reached her destination. A door stood, solidly. A key was resting in its heavy-set lock, thoughtlessly left by a caretaker who was probably dead now. With little sound or trouble, Mairead undid the latch, turned the key, and opened the door to the somewhat rain-soaked and bemused face of Roy Beggs. Without even as much as a nod to her, he crept in, pulling the door quietly shut behind him.

Together they moved along the school's main corridor, checking each door they came to for signs of life or death. It was Sunday, so the classrooms normally stocked full of screaming children were empty. Each chair was stacked neatly on top of its respective desk for the cleaner. Yet the floors remained as they had been left the previous Friday. Specks of glitter from the afternoon artwork glistened in the poor light. Desks remained unpolished. A thin veil of dust hovered in the musky air. The cleaner, a Miss Evelyn Johnston, currently lying dead in her bed, had a similar attitude in death that she'd had in life. Do as little as possible—as little as you can get away with.

She hadn't even bothered to wake up in order to die.

A sudden noise. Something falling or tapping against a table stopped the two unlikely allies in their tracks.

Roy drew his own 9mm and prepped himself for action. He looked to Mairead.

She shrugged her shoulders, signalling to him that it was the first time she had heard the sound. Taking the lead, Roy inched his way back down the corridor.

Mairead followed, suddenly thinking how easy it would be to shoot Roy in the back, were she to take the notion.

There, again. Same sound.

Roy glanced back, his eyes straining against the darkness, no doubt finding the frame of Mairead, gun ready, several feet behind him. She fought back a smile. He was clearly freaking out. Hers was a profile that would ordinarily have struck terror into him. A profile that could have meant his death, were it to have been several years ago, in the heart of West Belfast.

The noise, again. This time louder.

The door to a classroom further down the corridor gently swayed open, almost invitingly. Roy stared at the door's movement, pausing briefly, before looking back to Mairead. She shook her head in response. She felt just as apprehensive as he looked.

Roy gestured to her that he was going to make a move. Mairead nodded back, indicating that she understood. She was prepared to back him up.

This time.

As the door to the classroom flapped gently in the draft, the heavy rain seeming to drown out any sound it was making, both soldiers caught an earful of that noise again. It was like tapping, a nervous rhythm being drilled out on wood. It hummed within the still, lifeless corridor of the school, darkness cloaking every painting, every photograph and every trophy lining the walls. This was their guy, Roy seemed sure of it, and Mairead readied her gun in agreement.

Following close behind, Mairead watched Roy darting through the door, handgun raised. His voice rang out, aggressive and full of venom.

"On the fuckin' floor! *Now*!"

Sprinting in from behind, Mairead could see that he'd almost pulled his trigger, stalling at the last second and lifting his gun high into the air, almost as if surrendering.

What the fuck is ...?!

And then, with the pale moonlight spilling through the classroom's opened curtains, Mairead could see the reason for Roy's bizarre about turn. The small profile of a child, terrified, looked back at her. Alone at a desk. Her hand holding a pencil, as if it bore the meaning of life itself.

For a moment, there was silence. The child had stopped scribbling with her pencil.

Instead, she screeched on seeing Roy's large frame, on catching sight of the gun that had been aimed at her only seconds ago.

The sudden, shrill noise of the child screaming startled Roy even more than being met with a fully-grown threat could have. Mairead watched, agape, as the heavy-set soldier almost tripped over himself like some kind of big green clown, dropping his weapon in the process.

Mairead set her torch and gun on a nearby desk. She made a beeline for the distraught child. With the desperate, maternal instinct of a mother robbed of a child in its prime—

(*"There's been an explosion, Mrs Burns ..."*)

—Mairead wrapped the girl's small frame in her arms. She looked to Roy with even more disgust in her eyes than he was, no doubt, used to.

"For fuck's sake, Roy, she's just a child."

...

Sean sat himself down at the kitchen table. There were two bodies on the floor now, lying in almost romantic proximity to each other, as if part of some kind of Sid-and-Nancy scene.

Yeah, Romeo and fucking Juliet.

He went to speak, realised he couldn't, and instead poured himself a drink from a jug of water on the table.

He drank half of it down before offering the rest to the other man..

"Oh, fuck," came the reply, the young stranger staring at the corpse he had just created. Huge terror-stricken tears filled his eyes. "I… I didn't mean… I tried to shake him off you…" He turned to look at Sean, desperation in his face. "*I had to*!"

Sean stood up, pulling another chair to the table. "Don't look at it. Here. Sit down a minute."

The other man went to sit down, then, seeming to realise he was still holding the blood-stained kitchen knife, jumped back up again. He threw the knife to the ground, as if it were a hot coal.

"Fuck!" he yelled.

"Listen, the guy was a nut," Sean offered. "You had to do it, just like you said."

He looked at Sean. It suddenly seemed to click with him just who he was talking to, just whose life he had saved.

"You're that DJ, aren't you?" he said, somewhat inappropriately. He ran one shaking hand through his lank, wet hair. "Fuck me… I used to listen to your show..."

Sean was about to answer when the lad jumped back to his original train of thought, launching himself into another full-on keening session. The DJ watched on, powerless, as he bawled like a child..

"What… the fuck… is going on here?"

Sean insisted he sat at the table. He fixed them both a proper drink from the fridge. Two cold beers. For several long and much-needed seconds, the two men sipped at their drinks, shivering.

Sean told the lad everything that had happened to him. Every event in detail, from the minute he had put on *Whiskey in the Jar* to now. He told him about there being no news bulletin, about the sudden and unmistakeable silence that descended. About the vodka and coffee he had consumed. About the dead newsreader and his ex-wife's phone call. About the music he had played.

(A lot about the music he had played.)

He told him about the bodies he had seen on the streets and the quiet carnage. About the rain and the madman who had attacked him. He told the lad everything, because he reckoned the lad deserved to hear it all. He thought it might calm him down. Hell, calm them both down.

When Sean was done, they both sat quietly, glaring at the two bodies on the kitchen floor. It was as if they were watching something on television, drinking beer and shooting the breeze. Father and son. Watching the footie on the box.

"What's your name, by the way?" Sean asked, setting his beer down and offering the lad his hand. "Figured I should really shake hands with the guy who saved my life."

"Barry," replied the young dark-haired man, shaking Sean's hand limply. "Barry Rogan."

FIVE

The Preacher Man stood bathing in the moonlight, a lone figure amongst the dead and rain-beaten streets. He was soaked through. Heavy, solemn breaths filled his lungs. His heart was despondent. His brow furrowed, although that was nothing new. Daily his brow would furrow, as he stood where he stood now, in Cornmarket, near Belfast's busy Victoria Centre, preaching the good word. His voice would carry across five streets of sinners, some cursing him to his face as his campaign of blood and thunder was waged. He had toiled, mostly in vain, people these days being more interested in what they could buy from the high street than in saving their souls from eternal damnation. Clothes, jewellery, shoes, games, DVDs. All manner of shiny, sparkly things. The devil's grip on Belfast was strong, that was for sure.

The Preacher Man had often warned of what was now happening. *The Second Coming. Judgement Day. Armageddon.* His well-worn Bible provided proof of how hard he had worked to save sinners, some of whom were now lying dead around him. (*For the wages of sin is death.)* But he failed to see why he, himself, had been left behind to suffer along with them, why he hadn't been snatched greedily away in the Great Rapture by his Lord and Saviour, Jesus Christ.

He had been preaching when it all happened, standing at the wooden pulpit of a small gospel hall over on the east of the city. It was the place he had worked at for the last five years, ever since he was relieved of his duties from one of the larger denominations. His congregation was modest. Ten or fifteen regulars, mostly older people. But they were loyal, dependable, hard working Christians. Suitably, the title for today's sermon was 'God's Wrath', and that hadn't gone unnoticed by The Preacher Man. But that wasn't his only message. Over the years he'd also told the good news of God's mercy—God's love for those who were faithful to him. *His rod and staff to comfort them as they walk through the valley of the shadow of death.* Yet here he stood in Cornmarket. Alone. Broken. Rejected.

Why me, Lord? Why? He had stood in this very spot many times. Microphone in hand, his brothers and sisters in Christ around him. They had sung the old gospel hymns, their voices joining together in worship of their Saviour. Yet the only song he could find it in his heart to sing now was one of sheer desperation. Numerous doubts wormed their way into his mind. Hadn't he been faithful enough? Hadn't he preached enough, won enough souls for his Lord Jesus? Hadn't he himself been blameless? Or had he let the Devil get under his skin and bowed to temptation?

He remembered the day that he himself had been saved, standing in line under the crude shelter of a mission tent twenty years ago. The rain had beat upon the canvas then as it did now. He remembered thinking it was The Devil, pounding against the fabric, calling out to him. Warning him, lying to him in order to distract him from the Word of The Lord. It was one of his co-workers who had invited him to the mission. There he heard the good word delivered with incredible passion and angst. Like him, the preacher that day was someone who was touched by God, someone who could literally feel every sinful urge and vice, the grip of The Devil getting stronger with every passing day. He had been reduced to tears, crying and begging the Lord Jesus to enter into his heart and wash it clean of all the vile and sinful thoughts and desires he had. He wanted to be sober; he wanted to be pure. He wanted to be forgiven.

God knows, he had done some terrible things in the past. And now, he found himself wondering if he had somehow slipped up again. He knew that some people would backslide, falling away from God's love and mercy as The Devil's influence once again dragged them back into the sinfulness of the world. He struggled daily, prayed incessantly every time the persistent little bastard tried his damndest to reclaim his soul. The Devil was everywhere: on the radio, on the television, on the internet. In bars and clubs, the filthy underbelly of the city, drug infested dens of iniquity. He was in computer games, worldly magazines and papers. He was in the filthy books that The Preacher Man had once found his wife reading - *romance novels,* she called them. Love stories that said nothing of the real love he experienced from Jesus, his Lord and Saviour. But he had fought valiantly against such influences in his own life. He had fasted and prayed, beat himself, even, whenever Ol' Nick's grip had tightened around his heart. And he thought he had won, thought that he had repelled the forces of Satan

But he hadn't won.

The Preacher Man searched desperately through his well-oiled Bible for clues as to why he had been abandoned, left to rot amongst the damned—*a sheep amongst goats*. As he cried out to God, his voice rasping into the blackness of the night like a ship's captain in the throes of a storm, the incessant rain continued to fall.

...

The survivors from the cars gathered in the school's assembly hall, strangely silent despite their impressive number. Roy was busy herding them, showing them where to get some water, helping to open up the larders and free some tinned foods, tasking some of the more 'together' survivors with simple jobs, such as wrapping torches with masking tape, creating makeshift lamps to illuminate the dark corridors, canteen, and hall. For the most part, they seemed happy to be led, content to be occupying themselves with small responsibilities, striving to keep their minds from dwelling on individual tales of woe.

Except for Mairead. She was still fussing over the child she and Roy had discovered a short time ago, sitting in the dark at the very desk at which she had spent most of her third year at Primary School. Her school uniform had been sloppily hanging around her tiny frame, back-to-front, so Mairead was fixing it for her, helping her look smart.

She was called Clare McAfee. She was from the area, mere minutes away from the school. Clare had told Mairead that she didn't know what to do when her mummy had fallen asleep. She had forgotten that it was a Sunday, worrying that she would get into trouble for not going to school. So that's where she went. She had washed, made herself some cereal and dressed, before hurrying out into the dead world.

The school gates were locked. She told Mairead that she thought they were locked because she was late, so she climbed over them. The doors were locked too, so Clare had broken the window, climbed onto the bin and clambered through. She didn't remember that part, probably due to the shock, but Mairead noticed her arms were scratched where the glass had sliced her, leaving her white blouse slightly stained by blood. Luckily, apart from that and a few bruises from dropping down into the changing rooms, Clare was relatively unharmed.

It seemed that she had sat all day at her desk, in the classroom where she had spent the best part of the last year, scribbling nonsensical words into her homework jotter. When the jotter filled up, she started on the desk. That's what the noise had been—that insidious scratching that had freaked Roy Beggs out, almost leading to...

(*"There's been an explosion, Mrs Burns..."*)

The poor child. Zoned out, catatonic with fear and loneliness. Half dressed and hungry, her clothes soiled and her tiny heart broken. Sitting at her desk, scribbling as the night drew in and the rain opened up.

"I think it's still okay…"

Mairead looked up from where she and the child were sitting to find Roy offering Clare a glass of milk. A friendly smile filled his red, puffy face. Mairead hadn't seen it before. It suited him. It made him look more approachable and less like the fucking Brit thug he was.

"You can smell it, if you like," he added.

Clare obediently took the glass and sniffed it, smiling up at Roy to let him know the milk was okay.

He smiled back, producing a chocolate bar from his back pocket like some kind of bargain-basement magician. He whispered, conspiratorially, as he offered her the chocolate, "Don't tell anyone I gave you this, all right?"

The soldier's voice was gruff, but heavy with affection. His large-boned, poorly exercised profile seemed bear-like compared to the tiny frame of the child.

"Say 'thank you'," Mairead encouraged, more for the child's benefit than for Roy's.

"Thank you," Clare repeated, parrot-style.

The hungry-looking child made very short work of the milk and chocolate. Her innocent little face swallowed the bar in a few bites, her cheeks filling up like a gerbil. She gurgled the milk down loudly, with both Mairead and Roy watching her every move as if it might be her last.

Mairead reached one hand into the pocket of her jacket, feeling the handgun Roy had given to her earlier. She gripped it tightly. Its cool, smooth metal now represented a duty to protect as opposed to a means to fight. With a child's life in the balance, Mairead's mindset was changing. She had seen Roy as her enemy—in many ways, her captor. The 9mm had made her an equal to him, perhaps even a threat, and she wouldn't have hesitated to use it against him. Yet now, as she watched the burly soldier fuss and gush over the child he had literally tripped over himself to save, Mairead realised that, at least for now, they both wanted the same thing: To protect the innocent.

The very definition of innocence.

It remained to be seen who or what the new threat was, but as her hands curled around the familiar shape of the Browning, Mairead knew she would be ready, waiting to take out any bastard who threatened her child's safety.

(*"There's been an explosion, Mrs Burns..."*)

(*"...an explosion."*)

(*"...an EXPLOSION."*)

"How's she doing?" Roy asked Mairead, interrupting her thoughts.

"She's okay. Probably still in denial."

Roy shook his head.

"I'll get her a camp bed made up, so she can get some sleep. It's after midnight, so we should all rest up here anyway. At least for tonight."

Mairead agreed, smiling over to Clare as the young child drained her glass of milk.

Looking around, the two ragtag leaders could see groups of survivors working together to make the assembly hall as comfortable as possible. It was to be the birth of a new community. One, perhaps, without colours or flags or murals on walls. One simply about survival and the struggle for such, both emotionally and physically. Mairead wondered if it were possible, even in their situation, to build a community like that.

"Finished!" Clare suddenly exclaimed, proudly offering her empty glass to Roy.

His eyes welled up as he took the glass back, walking away without so much as a word. It touched Mairead. Roy Beggs, a man not unlike herself, roughened around the edges by the hard-dealt hand of the so-called Troubles and their self-fulfilling bitterness. Someone who wasn't normally accustomed to displays of emotion. Yet even he was melted by the total innocence of this little child and the sheer hell she'd been through.

"Good girl," Mairead said, embracing her.

...

Roy wandered out onto the damp tarmac playground, finally grabbing a minute to be alone and take a few breaths. He often felt claustrophobic whenever conditions were cramped. And boy, were they cramped, now, in the school's small assembly hall. He needed to get away.

The rain was still hammering down, and Roy took shelter under a nearby bike shed. He looked over at the convoy of cars and other vehicles parked throughout the school grounds, near the trees.

These people were his people now. They looked to him, obeyed him whenever he asked them to do something. And now there was this child, Clare. Christ, she was just a baby. Not normally a man given to self-doubt, Roy Beggs suddenly began to feel every ounce of the responsibility resting on his shoulders. In his heart of hearts, as his mother would have said (God rest her soul), he knew—he simply *knew* that there were no helicopters waiting for them in Belfast. No ships at the docks, full of British troops—*Real soldiers, Roy, not glorified TA like you*—ushering hordes of survivors onto boats to be shipped over to The Mainland (RULE BRITANNIA!) where everything was just hunky-dory. No, Roy knew that this was their lot. Small groups of survivors gathering. Rebuilding. Restoring what was left of an over-saturated world.

Taking in another long, deep breath of air, Roy thought about these things. Breathing out, he caught a glimpse of movement by one of the cars. Squinting against the poor light and pouring rain, Roy was able to make out the figure of Steve Marshall, one of the survivors.

Steve had driven behind Roy's Land Rover in his beat-out Fiesta, with the one headlamp. Roy remembered his car, like a one-eyed bandit, battling defiantly against the downpour of rain. He had met Steve earlier, the two of them having recovered some canned food from the school's kitchen. Roy had found him uneasy company, but put it down to the catastrophe rather than any other factors. Hell, they were all uneasy company today. But now, whilst the others thrived on being together, comforting each other, quietly, in a shared hour of need, this guy was just sitting in his old, beat-up car.

"You okay over there?" Roy called out, back on duty again.

"I'm dead on, mate," Steve replied, smiling back. He stuck his head out of the open door of his car. "Rain's still holding up, I see."

"Yeah," Roy muttered, half-heartedly. "Guess it is."

It was the first time someone had mentioned something as trivial as the weather to him. Small talk didn't seem appropriate anymore. It didn't fit. Didn't mean anything. But, sure enough, the rain of earlier was still holding strong. Despite this, the clouds had cleared a little, peeling off their grey skin to reveal a small treasure of stars. For Roy, seeing the stars offered some kind of hope. Some kind of reassurance that whatever God was up there still had his hand in the game. Still cared enough to make the moon and stars come out at night.

...

Steve Marshall sat in the driver's seat of his car. He had the radio on, but only a dull-pitched static could be heard playing over the tip-tap of the rain's constant beat. He watched, carefully, as Roy Beggs turned back, the heavy-set soldier jogging the short distance from the old bike shed to the poorly lit school building. He closed the door of his car, blotting out the rain.

Steve leaned back, looking over at the body of his beautiful wife, Kirsty. Her blonde locks glimmered in the fading twilight. Goose pimples rose above the smooth silk of her legs, an oblivious reaction to the crystal chill of the star-filled night.

"I think we're going to make it," he said. "I know we've had it tough, what with Nicky being born and all, but I just know, somehow, that it's going to be all right."

He smiled, stroking her usually rosy cheek with one hand.

She said nothing, still staring into the ether as if daydreaming.

It was one of the things that Steve had loved about her—yet feared. Those Wonderland eyes, an ethereal quality that separated her from just about every other woman that had ever been in his life. It made Kirsty all the more mysterious to him, all the more beautiful.

It was as if she were an angel or some other otherworldly creature, one that had been sent to enchant him, to love him—and, ultimately—to leave him. A creature like this couldn't be held by one man for too long. He knew that. Still, even now, he held onto her. He loved her and held her, even in death.

Steve turned to the back seat of his beat-up Fiesta, picking up the little bundle carefully wrapped in blankets. He peeled the blankets back, finding the lifeless eyes of the dead child staring back at him..

"Wake up, Nicky," he whispered. "Come on, son."

SIX

The glare of the early-morning sun broke through the bus station's huge glass windows. As she opened her eyes, Star yawned loudly, wondering whether she had slept at all. She couldn't remember sleeping – just her eyes closing and the busy static behind her eyelids.

She looked to the seats opposite , finding the two kids still flat-out, layered by the coats of strangers. Dead strangers, their bodies still littering the station's mall as if they, too, were dozing, as if they had all been part of some sponsored sleep-in for the homeless or the blind or the starving children in Africa.

Star rubbed her eyes, the charcoal from her eyeliner staining her hands. She dreaded to think just how she looked now, purposely avoiding the no-doubt panda-eyed reflection in the glass of the building's walls. She strolled in the direction of the station's little cafe. A coffee machine sat behind the counter. She fired it up, marvelling that the damn thing still worked. She fixed herself a nice strong cup of the black stuff. A line of chocolate bars caught her eyes, and Star felt a pang of hunger rumble through her empty and knotted belly. She had forgotten to eat yesterday, what with that whole WORLD-ENDING shit happening. Star shook her head, smiling at her own wry thoughts. She was expecting to wake up to a different world where an apocalypse hadn't happened, where people would still want tattoos and those a-holes at the shop were still hanging around to take the piss out of her. But it wasn't how the day was going to roll. Mother Nature had other plans, bless her callous heart.

Star noticed movement from the corner of her eye. There was something outside. She slowly lifted her coffee and chocolate, carrying both towards the back exit from the station, leading to where the buses were parked. Taking a sip, she checked in on the kids as she passed the seats, both still sleeping soundly. She caught the movement again, looking out into the forecourt, finding a bus. The sun's assault on the rain-stained tarmac was growing intense, and she struggled to make out anything beyond the bus' windows, but she could have sworn that she saw a shadow or something or someone moving from inside. There was another glint of the sun, another dancing shadow, and Star eased herself cautiously out of the shelter and perceived safety of the building to draw closer to the bus. Its doors were closed, but it wasn't parked like the others, the large wheels turned a little on their side as if the vehicle had stalled mid-manoeuvre. The sign on the front read 'Belfast International Airport Airbus'.

Another movement. Star moved closer to the bus, finding the shadows and glints were not mere play by the sun but rather the signs of life. Someone was locked inside. A man, probably middle-aged, shaking and banging the bus door. He was panicking. His white shirt was stained with blood.

"Jesus..." Star muttered to herself.

She felt around the door, looking for some way to prise it open. It was useless. Fucking thing was locked up tight. The stupid bastard was glaring out at her now, banging at the door as if to get her attention, eyes filled with fear or rage or madness.

"I hear you..." she said, again more to herself than to him.

She raised her hand as if to calm him, then added, this time louder, "You'll have to open it yourself from the inside."

But he wasn't listening; even when she slapped her hand on the glass, he refused to listen. He was wired, completely out of it. And who could blame him. God knows how many bodies lay in the aisles in there with him, the festering smell of death as the sun rose. Star suddenly felt the guilty urge to take a picture of him through the glass, to capture his rabid emotion and add it to her growing collection of their new grim reality. She even reached into her pockets, finding the camera phone, before catching herself.

"Forget it," she said, turning to wander off.

It was then that she saw the others. At first count it looked like around twenty people, dotted between the other buses as if lost. Some of them looked at her, others looking up into the sky. They unnerved her. Something was wrong with them.

"H-hey," she said to them. "You lads... okay?"

But they didn't speak. They didn't even blink; even the ones staring up at the sun seemed somehow immune to its glaze, their eyes wide-open like white china saucers.

One of them suddenly lunged at her. It shocked her, and she moved to side-step him.

He fell over, hitting the ground hard.

She barked at him, "What the fuck's your problem, mate?!"

But he didn't say anything, pulling himself, clumsily, back onto his feet as if learning how to walk again.

Another came at her from the other side, blindsiding her. He managed to grab her arm and was leaning his face in as if to kiss her. She'd met creeps like this before and knew how to deal with them, quickly bringing the full force of her knee into his groin. A hoarse yelp escaped from his mouth as he stumbled back, saliva spilling from his bottom lip in a long, shiny drip.

"What the fuck's the matter with you lot?!" she screamed at the others.

They were still hovering around her like a pack of horny dogs. Star backed away from them, walking quickly towards the station. Once inside, she closed the door behind her, one eye still fixed on the crazies. She moved one of the sturdy metal bins up against the door. It wouldn't hold if they tried to get inside, but it made her feel better, and in today's world, that meant something.

Turning, Star looked to find the two kids still asleep on the benches.

Or were they asleep?

Her heart seemed to swell in that very moment, the rush of blood flushing her cheeks. She brushed a dreadlock away from her eyes and swallowed hard, the taste of cigarettes and the MORNING-AFTER-THE-END-OF-THE-WORLD heavy in her dry, raspy throat.

"Guys?" she said, walking slowly towards the benches.

They both lay completely still. She moved towards Caz, noting her glasses resting between her fingertips. Star reached her hand over to tap the girl's shoulder.

A movement from behind startled her and she turned sharply to find Tim on his feet. She was just about to say something to him, something smart and quippy, something to make her look like she was holding together instead of falling apart. But something about him wasn't right. His head bent to one side, heavy bloodshot eyes staring into her face as if he were stoned.

"H-hey," she said, "What's the ma_"

A sharp pain from the back of her neck interrupted her. Her hand reached to the pain. There was a moistness there, dampening her skin like heavy sweat.

Turning, Star found Caz staring back, her pretty little eyes narrow and angry. She snapped at her, teeth catching Star's tattooed hand. Star tried to shake her off, but Caz held firm, gripping all the more tightly, the sharp pain of her vice-like bite breaking skin.

From behind, Star felt the other kid's teeth sinking easily into her already torn, wet skin.

She heard herself scream.

She woke with a start, reaching for the back of her neck as she bolted upright. Her eyes swept over the station. The kids were nowhere to be seen, but a nearby body, a middle-aged woman with a very poor idea of colour coordination, reassured Star a little. The dead were still... dead.

"Jesus..." she whispered to herself, shaking her head and smiling.

A fucking nightmare.

It seemed weird to wake from one nightmare, only to find herself in another. But that was the way of things, now.

She stood up. Her back hurt, stiffened through years of bad posture while tattooing, aggravated by the hardness of her makeshift bed. The building she was sleeping in was modern, its exterior comprised of little more than metal and glass. Great Victoria Street station, encompassing rail and bus travel (the old Europa Bus Station) stood beside the most bombed hotel in Europe. Yet its design and architecture were an expression of Belfast's new era of peace, the post 9/11 era, when the familiar gun and balaclava combo seemed to no longer have a place in Belfast.

She found Caz and Tim sitting in the station's café with an orange juice each. They seemed subdued, Caz in particular wearing all the body language of someone whose world had fallen down around her. But she wasn't dead, and she wasn't a fucking zombie, and she should be grateful for that. A scattering of corpses littered the tiled floor throughout the station.

"We need to do something about these bodies," Star said, without even as much as a good morning. She could hardly bare to look them in the eyes. "I don't know about you two, but I'm starting to notice a nasty smell around here."

But they didn't reply..

As Star drew closer to them, she noticed that Caz was crying, her young face raw with fresh tears.

"What's wrong with you?" she asked, coldly, pulling up a chair and searching her pockets for cigarettes.

"What's *right*?!" Caz replied, sniffling. "With *anything*?!"

"Sun's up," Star remarked, lighting up her ciggie.

(and you're not a zombie)

Caz suddenly flared. "Our families are... dead! Our friends are dead!" She looked at Star incredulously. "How the hell can you just sit there smoking, as if it's just another day?!"

Tim rubbed his nose, but added nothing.

"Well…" Star began, leaning back in one of the café's comfy chairs, "I haven't got any family. No significant others, and all my mates are probably as happy in death as they were in life." She looked at Caz's tear-stained cheeks without even a hint of emotion in her own eyes. "I wasn't much of a people-person, shall we say."

Caz buried her head in her hands, emotion once again taking its toll on her. Star studied her face, pretty as it was, all blotchy and bubbling. She had the sudden urge to paint it.

It seemed the younger survivor had reached that stage of grief where denial was out the window, no longer the crutch it needed to be when the shit smashed into the fan. Not only had the world ended, but here she was sitting with some punk who didn't seem to care. To top it all off, she was making a prize tit of herself in front of the boy.

Tim was handling things in a different way. Yeah, he seemed nervous, but something within him, something Star couldn't just put her finger on yet, seemed a little more hardened to this whole world ending thing. He looked to Star, and then to Caz, perhaps unsure of what to do or what to say. He still seemed lost in a daze, perhaps well used to burying shit like this—*Like this?! What could be like this?!*—deep within. While that couldn't be the healthiest way of dealing with things, normally, Star reckoned it might be an attribute in this situation.

She watched as he placed one hand on the shoulder of the girl.

"It's okay," he said.

He probably knew it was a lie. Yet Star liked him, almost immediately, for at least trying to make things better for his friend. He was a good kid. That much she knew, from the start.

Dragging on her ciggie, Star watched the little drama unfold before her tired, blackened eyes. She wondered why she couldn't jump right in there. Create some sort of group-hug, like you might see in an episode of *Friends* or something. She entertained the idea that she and these two kids might be the only people left in Belfast. Perhaps the whole fucking world. And that was a bad situation, bad enough to warrant a little display of emotion.

But things were going to get worse for them.

...

"So what was she like, then?" Barry asked. "When you were together, I mean."

The two men had sat up all night, drinking every last drop of booze in Sharon's house. They didn't move from the kitchen, where the two bodies lay side by side on the floor. In a sense, it helped to get used to the dead, two at a time, before going outside.

Sean gave the question the consideration it was due.

What was Sharon like?

He remembered mainly the bad times perhaps as some sort of defence mechanism dictated by his brain (and heart) to help put their sorry marriage behind him, to allow him to move on the way *she* had so very obviously been able to. Running a hand through his receding mane of hair, the ageing DJ shot a glance around what used to be *his* kitchen, *his* home with Sharon. Yet now, sitting at the table, his dead wife at his feet, he barely recognised the place.

"She was..." he began, hardly knowing how he could end his sentence, "*funny*, I suppose."

"Like, funny ha-ha?" Barry offered.

"Well, yeah," Sean continued. "We did make each other laugh. In the early days, anyway."

"But then it all went sour, yeah?"

Sean could see that Barry's mind was only half on what he was asking. But half was good enough, given their particular circumstances. 'Half' was also bloody apt to describe his relationship with Sharon. A woman he loved. Yet, a woman he had only given 'half' of himself over to.

"*Sour* wasn't the word for it."

A couple of moments passed between the two. Sean realised that there was no music playing. They had sat for hours in complete silence.

Barry spoke next. "I had this girl once, right? She wasn't half bad-looking either." He smiled, probably thinking back on his misspent youth and a girl that was more than likely dead now. "Thing was, she was one for flirting with other blokes, and stuff. She'd be grand when she was sober, talking to me, kissing and stuff. But then she would get pissed and become a real bitch."

Barry stopped short. Sean noticed he was staring at Sharon's body while he talked. He seemed fascinated by her stillness and maybe her beauty, her long brown hair gleaming in the virgin light of the new day.

"Thing was, Sean, this girl had Eczema. You know that disease that makes all your skin peel off?"

Sean was beginning to wonder where Barry was going with this story.

"Well, I think she should have been happy with any fella looking at her twice, never mind the whole fucking bar! But she was, like, always looking for attention. Always looking for someone else's eyes to give her the once over."

He swigged at his beer again. His speech was slurring, his eyes completely bloodshot.

"It was because she was insecure," he continued. "I realised that later. I guess I just couldn't understand why my eyes weren't enough for her."

Sean rubbed his own eyes, the feeling of tiredness and drunkenness seeming to wash over him simultaneously.

He looked at Barry, nodding. This was an odd character. Couldn't be over twenty-five, with a face somewhere between angelic and demonic. The kind of guy who would live life to the full, riddling his body with every last narcotic and vice known to man in order to chase the dragon. He was probably the very nemesis of Sean's own nerdy youth, pissed away in independent music shops and mild-mannered prog-rock gigs.

Barry drained his can of beer dry before finishing his spiel. "Anyway, at the time I just ignored her when she was like that. Walked out and left her to walk home on her own. But this is the thing; I could have sworn, mate, that the longer we spent together, the more circles we spun in that bullshit merry-go-around, the more fucking skin she shed with that Eczema shit… It was like being with me was literally wasting her away."

Sean said nothing, but he knew exactly what Barry was talking about.

He had ignored Sharon, his greatest love, cheating on her with his music. The music was safe. It made no demands. But his wife was dangerous. She demanded to know him, inside as well as out. Sharon didn't have Eczema, and she certainly hadn't wasted away visually. Even now she looked radiant, her skin still rich and soft-looking. Her hair still shining and glittering, like some kind of movie star's. But as the years of their marriage rolled by, the very essence of what she truly felt for Sean had wilted away to nothing.

...

The survivors at the school gathered in the canteen for breakfast. It was a sombre-looking place, gray and depressing from crudely polished floors to damp-stained ceiling. Roy began to think back on his earlier days in the barracks, where downbeat mess halls would be the norm. Somewhere to grab a cup of tea and put your feet up between patrols. Somewhere to talk about the fucking mess going on outside that you were expected to deal with, a shelter from the ever-present threat of bullets and fucking bombs that IRA terrorists like—

He was reminded of earlier. He had searched the hall for their newest addition—the child, Clare, the wee girl he had very nearly put a bullet through. He found her at a table across the canteen. She was sitting with Mairead, the two of them getting on like a house on fire. Mairead was plaiting her hair, stroking and petting her as if she were a puppy. And that didn't look right. To see someone like Mairead, so cold, so hardened—so fucking *dangerous*—getting on like a playschool teacher was odd. Roy wasn't sure if he liked it. He might have preferred the old Mairead. At least you knew what to expect.

One of the older survivors, a large, ever-smiling bear of a woman by the name of Sylvia Patterson, helped organise a simple meal of juice, cornflakes and tinned fruit. The juice was lukewarm, the fruit sugary, but those gathered were very grateful. Almost everyone ate hungrily.

They were spread throughout the canteen, sitting in groups. The survivors seemed to need each other's company. Safety in numbers. Conversation was sparse at first, but eventually people began to talk, everyone telling their stories. In a way, it was cathartic.

Steve Marshall sat beside Roy. He finished his meal, leaving only a spoonful of cornflakes in his bowl. His eyes glazed over, a thousand-yard stare that didn't bode well for conversation. To Roy, the younger man seemed lost in his own world, whistling and tapping his fingers to an unknown tune.

"So where're you from, Steve?" Roy asked, more to break the silence than out of genuine interest.

"Portadown," Steve replied. "Killicomaine direction," he added, perhaps knowing that a man with a name like Roy Beggs wasn't going to be from the *other* side of town.

"Oh, right," Roy replied. "I have a cousin lives around there. Just near the high school."

The younger survivor looked at him.

Roy realised his mistake, and corrected himself. "*Had* a cousin, I mean. Funnily enough, I don't think I've chatted to her in a while. She mightn't even live there anymore, to tell you the truth." Again he corrected himself. "Fuck's sake. She *definitely* doesn't live there now, let's face it."

Steve smiled, clearly uncomfortable with Roy's forced and clumsy attempts at conversation. Within seconds his eyes glazed over again, that inane whistling and tapping returning.

Another moment passed. Roy noticed the cook, Sylvia, looking at the two of them, an uneasy expression on her face. Theirs was the only table where no one was talking or crying—or, weirdly, laughing. It looked odd.

Roy tried again, this time more out of suspicion. "So had you any family, Steve?"

The soldier's question was as insensitive as you could get, given what had happened to them all. Yet, unknown to Roy, it hit an even rawer nerve that most with Steve Marshall. The young survivor thought first of his little son Nicky. He recalled the wonderful cocktail of emotions he had gone through when Nicky was born only a couple of months ago. Joy, fear, love... the panicked sense of responsibility. It was a difficult pregnancy with his wife, Kirsty, eventually giving birth prematurely.

He remembered holding her hand as she screamed and cried, her relatively small belly seeming so strained that it might explode. Steve loved her more that night than ever, her face blotchy, her nose and mouth glistening. It felt primal to be with her during the birth. As if a part of them were to be joined together, forever, through the experience. Now, the corpses of Nicky and Kirsty were in his car. His son's corpse cooked in the cruelly indifferent sun. His beautiful wife still sleeping, oblivious to it all.

Steve looked up to see Roy's face staring back at him. He realised that he hadn't answered the question. He knew that he needed to be careful with these people. Sure, they might be his only hope to find some help for his family—some *real* help— but they might not understand him, might not see the bigger picture. They might try to take his family away from him. He needed to play his cards close to his chest.

His mind drifted back to the first time he met Kirsty. They were at some student dive, and she was part of a larger group of friends, and friends-of-friends, drinking together. It was pound-a-pint night, so everyone (regardless of how little of their student loans were left) was able to get pretty tanked. His favourite song was playing, *Cannonball* by The Breeders, and Stevie-Boy was all primed to go wild. He made for the dance floor, and there she was, standing on her own like some kind of mannequin. Tall, elevated above all of those around her. Moving, slowly and dreamily, as if the music was flowing through her like water, washing her long, lithe body.

On that first day—just like her last day—she was without blemish, her eyes lighting up her pale face.

Her eyes.

"Steve?" the soldier beside him persisted.

Careful, Stevie-Boy, careful.

"Em… Sorry, mate," he muttered, suddenly getting up from the table. "Gotta take a piss. I'll see you later, right?"

Roy watched as Steve shuffled out of the canteen towards the bathrooms. From another corner, Sylvia watched too. Neither of them could work him out. At times Steve seemed a little too bright and chirpy, and then he'd freak out like he'd just done now. Roy wasn't sure whether he liked a man like Steve Marshall being around. Inconsistent. Jumpy. Someone he couldn't read. But grief took its toll on them all in different ways. The more generous part of him settled on that, calling check on his gut instinct. For Roy, grief was something to be avoided, and that made someone emotionally raw like

Steve Marshall unsavoury. He saw in Steve the kind of pent-up fear and insecurity that he felt within himself. Yet, Roy wasn't ready to face his demons. There was too much needed doing, and doing was proving to be a great way of avoiding the real dangers of thinking.

He watched the survivors at the other tables continue to console each other, some crying, others comforting, before switching roles, everyone getting a chance to tell their stories. People of all ages, all religions, men as well as women, were shedding tears for themselves, their loved ones and one another. They were bonding, building a new community, a community with a shared grief, shared history, shared loss.

Roy looked over to where Mairead and Clare were sitting. Mairead's eyes were looking right back at him. Stern, cold, and unforgiving. It was as if she blamed him for everything that had happened, refusing to move on from her petty resentment, to recognise how everything was changing, even things between them.

Fuck her. She isn't worth the hassle.

He looked away, not bothered by whatever the hell her problem was. He'd more important things to think about, like what their next move would be.

...

By 10.00am, talk amongst the tables had moved on to what had caused the disaster and how widespread it was. Different people had different ideas. For those still crying, it was too much to think about, so they drifted off to the assembly hall or out into the school's grounds. For others, the very act of talking about what had happened helped deal with it

"It's got to be them Arabs," commented an older man named Trevor Steele, his face rough like dried mud. "Probably one of them gas attacks or something."

John McElroy, slightly younger but equally as bigoted as Steele, joined in. "Too many foreigners running around these days."

A young Egyptian woman named Aida Hussein shook her head. In days gone by, she'd suffered several racist attacks on her home in South Belfast. It grieved her to think that even at a time like this, racist attitudes were still rife.

"For fuck's sake," snapped a young, studious-looking girl beside the two men, noticing how uncomfortable Aida looked, "have a bit of tact, would you?"

"Well what do you think happened, then?" Steele protested.

The girl sighed heavily. "Well, I'll tell you this, Trevor," she began, "if it was a gas attack, you'd fuckin' smell something, wouldn't you?" She laughed, sarcastically, before whispering under her breath, "Or maybe *you* wouldn't, you sweaty ol' bastard."

Roy had to laugh at that one. A few others who'd heard the quip joined in. The noise seemed to echo, almost inappropriately, around the room. It felt like laughing in church. Someone looked at Roy and smiled. Suddenly, they were all laughing, even Aida. For the first time since the disaster hit, it seemed to Roy that people were beginning to loosen up a little.

As talk continued, the survivors seemed to look to Roy, as if for reassurance or permission to continue. But he said little, simply listening as they bounced back and forth through various theories. Chemical attacks, nuclear meltdowns, bird flu, food poisoning, something in the fucking water. All the clichés were present and accounted for. One man, an austere-looking bloke with eyes that would bore through you, suggested that this was the wrath of God. That humanity had got too big for its boots. Although not a religious man, Roy thought this was probably one of the more believable theories.

Yet, regardless of what had caused it, everyone seemed to take for granted that this disaster was nationwide, perhaps even global. One survivor, a young fellow who had joined the convoy of cars fairly late in the day, commented about how the internet seemed to go a little askew shortly before the power shut down. He was online at the time, trying to contact people through e-mail, message boards, social networking. To his surprise, however, one of his message boards, a huge online community of sci-fi and horror fans, displayed a worrying lack of active members. Those who were signed in didn't seem to be posting. The young lad told the others how he watched as, one-by-one, all those signed-in were logged out, their names dropping off the screen. Soon his own power shut down, logging him off permanently, too.

Another man, an Eastern European with a relatively poor command of English, explained how he'd tried to phone his family and friends back in Riga, Latvia. He'd only been in Northern Ireland for a month, working in a meat factory in Portadown. His first purchase on getting his pay cheque was some new clothes. His second was a flashy new mobile phone. He'd spent the whole journey to Belfast, sharing a lift with a co-worker from the factory (they'd been on the same overtime shift when it all went south), ringing everyone on his 'contacts' list. None of them—not a single one of the twenty-odd numbers he rang—actually answered. The man, a large, burly giant named Peter Stokenbergs, started crying as he told his story. As the others silently watched on, Sylvia, (the group's emerging cook and maternal type), immediately comforted him.

SEVEN

Regardless of the occasional bickering and outbursts, the survivors appeared to be making themselves at home at the school. No one seemed to be too keen on moving, perhaps craving the security and comfort this little haven provided. It made sense. The school had been deserted when things had gone belly-up, meaning there were no bodies lying around. Even the school's fairly spacious grounds, consisting of the playground, some gardens, a football field and gravel sports track, were relatively untouched by signs of death, a couple of dead birds and a hedgehog being the only casualties in sight.

The assembly hall's polished wooden floor was large enough to provide the survivors with adequate space to set up makeshift camp beds, piling their few belongings next to such. From what Roy could tell from overhearing something Sylvia Patterson had said to a group of similarly-aged women and the Eastern European man, talk was already moving towards what could be rustled up for lunch.

"So what's the plan, then?"

The voice came from behind him, and he was quite sure who it belonged to. Turning, Roy was met by Mairead, the young Clare hanging off her arm shyly. She still possessed the 9mm Roy had given to her, tucked neatly but noticeably inside a pocket of her jacket.

"Seems everyone's happy here for a bit."

"Here?! But didn't we agree that help would come to Belfast? That we should gather in the city?" Mairead lowered her voice, not wanting to upset Clare. "Roy, if anyone comes, they're not going to find us here. We're over ten miles from Belfast."

"Who's going to come?!" Roy snapped back.

"I don't know… Emergency Services? Rescue? Helicopters?" A scowl drew across her face as she added, "God knows we had a shit load of helicopters here in the eighties when they damn well *weren't* needed. Surely they'll send them now they *are*?!"

She was referring to days gone by, when the British Troops had pulled out all the stops to deal with the terrorist threat in Northern Ireland. To Roy Beggs, a comment like that was like a red rag to a bull.

"*Typical*," he sighed, turning and walking away. He stopped, looked back at her, then shook his head. "Fucking *typical*."

She followed him, defiantly, Clare still hanging onto her arm.

"Whenever something goes wrong, there you are, rabbitin' on about what the Brits did or didn't do. Never anyone else's fault, just the Brits." Roy laughed sarcastically, "I bet you think this whole thing is some British or loyalist conspiracy, don't you?"

"Don't be fuckin'—"

"*No*! You listen to me!" Roy yelled at her, "No one's going to fucking come! Not the British! Not even the fucking *Americans*! No-fucking-body! Alright!?" His face was purple with rage. He noticed Mairead stepping back, Clare cowering close to her. "This is it," he stressed, firmly. "This is our lot. And we stay here until I say otherwise. That clear?!"

He felt Mairead's eyes burning into him. The sleeves of his camouflage uniform were rolled up, and he noticed her looking at his tattoos, proudly boasting affiliation with loyalist paramilitary groups. What he'd said earlier had been right. They weren't too different from each other. They had been fighting the same war, just from different sides. But she couldn't let it lie—couldn't show him some respect—and that angered a man like Roy Beggs. A bitter man, a man not used to backchat. Especially from a woman. He was no stranger to showing a woman who was boss, especially a woman like Mairead Burns.

"Fuck you, Roy," she said before turning and walking away from him.

"You Provos are all the same!" Roy called after her, still seething.

Without even turning around, Mairead graced his last comment with a one-fingered salute.

He couldn't have hated her more.

...

It took Caz, Star and Tim the better part of an hour to clear the sixteen bodies out of the small mall at Great Victoria Street, Star somehow able to haul them on her own, whilst the teens worked together. They didn't drag them far, just out to the courtyard where all the buses were parked. A few fire blankets were used to cover some of the dead, whilst a large waterproof canvas sheet (discovered in the storeroom of the little newsagents in the station) could cover the rest.

In a huge, plastic mass grave, the bodies began their final rest.

Their sunglasses, iPods, and handheld game consoles littered the floor, Tim and Star ransacking every suitcase. As Caz watched on, disgusted, arms folded and face like thunder, the two built a pile of technological treasure.

After the clear-out, the three survivors found some cleaning materials and gave the place a freshen up. The clinically-pale tiles shone after being mopped, reflecting the gleam of the sun through the huge glass windows quite beautifully. A railway-cum-bus station was a strange place to call home, and each of the three saw each other as strange bedfellows to share it with, but they could relax a little better now the bodies were gone. The clear-out had been a release of sorts, so at around noon they treated themselves to yet another junk food lunch of potato crisps, chocolate and Coke to celebrate a job well done. They dined at the same cafe in the station, where they'd met.

Each of the three were starting to talk a little more now, mostly banal stuff at first. Talk came around to what everyone had done before the disaster hit, with Caz and Tim laughing about teachers and classmates they both knew. Star listened, quietly, smoking her way through yet another box of ciggies liberated from the newsagents. It was one of the benefits of being at the station. Plenty of smokes on stand-by.

Despite herself, the tattooist was glad to see the two kids livening up a little. A part of her felt a little guilty about not doing much to console them. It was a lot to go through at any age, this whole END-OF-THE-WORLD thing, but to go through it as a teenager, with all those hormones popping off at the same time? It must have been fucking *gruesome*…

"So what did you do, Star?" Caz asked, smiling for the first time since they'd met.

Her face was pretty. Innocent, a little bookish, maybe, but with a certain quirky appeal that Star couldn't help finding attractive.

"I scar people, make them bleed," Star replied, smiling mischievously.

Caz looked back, confused and a little scared, but Tim's eyes widened as it clicked with him what she meant.

"Shit… I knew I recognised you! You're that tattooist chick, aren't you?" He leaned forward, beaming. "My mate Andy went to see you a couple of months ago. You know Andy? Goth lad, with eyeliner…"

For a brief moment all three were quiet, sharing the same realisation that Andy was probably dead now.

"I always wanted a tat myself, but my ma wouldn't let me," Tim added ruefully, breaking the silence.

Star took another drag, winking at the lad with a mischievous look in her eye. "Still want one now?"

"Fuck yeah!"

It was the first time Star saw the lad really animated. Tim Adamson reminded her of many of the young kids who came into her place in the past to get tats. People like Andy, no doubt. Quiet, awkward, skinny. They would sit sweating whilst she got her stuff ready, stinking the place out. After three of those wee gits in a row, Star would have to open the windows wide to get rid of the stench. But Tim was nothing but excited by the notion. Even Caz, the stuffy little bitch that she was, seemed to be encouraging him.

"Yeah! Go on Tim!" she egged, showing more of her playful, teenage side.

Star saw a new dynamic come into play. It was obvious to her, even if not to Tim, that Caz was besotted by the lad.

"What would you get?" Caz whispered, as if it were a sin they were talking about—a secret, adult sin.

Tim's smile seemed to fade. Like a lot of kids that would have come to her, Star reckoned he had never taken the idea any further than 'how-cool-would-it-be-if'. His face furrowed as he, no doubt, thought about all the things in the world he could get tattooed. It struck

Star as pretty funny. Although, ironically, he had all the time in the world to make up his mind, it seemed very important for him to make a decision right now.

"What can you do?"

Star laughed. This kid was cute. She liked him.

"Not a lot here, that's for sure... We'd need to go back to the shop. I'd need all my gear."

Suddenly, the idea of getting tattooed became about as realistic as grabbing the morning paper. Or watching television. Or making fucking breakfast—or anything that people used to do to pass time in the world before... *this*. The faces of the kids seemed to echo this dawning realisation of Star's. No one was getting a tattoo today. Not here, not anywhere else. It was probably the first day in a hell of a long time that no one got tattooed.

The finality of what they were all facing continued its journey towards hitting home, pushing along the queue with the fallen birds and the dead church, the little pram from the supermarket and the punky girl nose-diving to the floor. Normal, everyday stuff had changed. Everything was fucked-up.

Star glanced up at the blank, petrified faces watching her.

These people—these kids—seemed to be looking to her, hoping she would be able to offer something to blot out the inevitable smack of reality threatening to spit in their tired eyes. Each of their faces was steeped in denial and all-consuming fear. Yet she had nothing to offer them.

Without another word, Star simply got up and wandered out into the courtyard. The Great Decay across Belfast whistled through her nostrils. She remembered her dream; the dead having risen like something out of a cheesy horror flick. It seemed almost familiar.

...

Sin. Everywhere.

It was all The Preacher Man could see. Billboards with their whoring sluts flaunting themselves. Dancing with the devil, selling their ill gotten gains. (SALE! Buy Now Pay Later! All Items Must Go! New Season's selection in Store!) And what did it all mean *now*? Where was the rush *today*?

Corpses lined shop floors, their flesh having dried somewhat in the early sun. A few cars crisscrossed over five sparsely-filled streets.. Fallen pedestrians sprinkled randomly, meeting at the entrance to the Victoria Shopping Centre, as if struck down before reaching its shelter.

The Preacher Man made his way past the bodies, on through the quiet shopping centre. The structure rose up around him, a modern-day Tower Of Babel. He reached the other side, where he found the bandstand in its new location, away from Cornmarket. In days gone by, the ornate, Victorian structure had been a focal point for Belfast's amateur street theatre. Music, mime artists, buskers, charity collections and protesters all gathered there. It was a stage for all the wares of Belfast's wannabe thespians, quasi-musicians and wheeler-dealer types. It was also The Preacher Man's pulpit. His Rock Of Ages, his Anchor From The Storm. Now, however, the bandstand was nothing. No meeting place. No stage. No storm and sure-as-fuck no anchor. The post-apocalyptic bandstand was but a focal point for death.

He could sense something. A feeling of movement around him, drawing in towards him. Closing in on him. Coming to take him. Like Job in the Old Testament, infamously stripped of his entire world in a wager between The Good Lord and Satan, everything had been taken from The Preacher Man. Gone were his friends, his family and (most importantly) his audience. He was left with nothing. Even sin was dead, its dark memories splashed over billboards, and glittering like fool's gold from shop windows. No more voices to battle against, no more insults to suffer. It was difficult to find a purpose. But surely he had been left behind for some reason. Surely God hadn't just abandoned him to rot in the scum-infested world with all the sinful.

The movement took form. With his poor vision, the Preacher Man could only make out shadows. Maybe demons coming for him. But God wouldn't dump *him*, a faithful servant… and leave him like a dirty ragdoll to be tormented by the forces of darkness?! The shadows were almost upon him, swirling around like a cloak. As they drew closer, their bodies and faces now tangible, The Preacher Man realised they weren't demons. They weren't forces of evil, sent to snatch him away. They were people. Broken, scared and hungry. In need of a leader, a prophet, a shepherd.

Here was his purpose.

Here were souls who needed saving.

…

Tim was in the station's bathrooms, the large steel urinals providing more than enough space for him to aim. He took a piss, too self-consumed to give a thought to how the plumbing continued to work, washing away his urine and spat-out gum with its usual flush.

He was staring in the huge mirrors behind the sinks when the tears came. They came hard and fast, like the rain. They poured down his face, rinsing out a bucket load of pent-up grief. Family, friends… the whole world… all dead. It finally hit home. He mourned his mother, his sister, his friends, the other guys in the band. The loss burned a sharp, flaming blade of grief down his chest, choking him, stabbing him again and again, as if to make sure he was well and truly dead—well and truly finished off. He mourned everyone he ever knew in that mother of all outbursts, everyone he would meet in his daily routine. The stony-faced bus driver, Bertie the caretaker at his school, his teachers, the girl with the cute arse, who worked at the newsagents near his house—all of them were finally pronounced dead and given their send-off.

Yet when it came to his father, Tim Adamson spat out a more complex cocktail of emotions. Those nights spent in his daddy's arms as a small child. Love one minute, abuse the next. Such memories had receded deep into Tim's young mind, peeking out briefly and dangerously on occasion, only to be hammered back in with angry music or violent video games. It literally took the end of the world for them to finally flood his young mind.

Tim didn't know he had been screaming and wasn't aware he was on the bathroom's hard floor. Everything was a blur, suddenly. Voices were straining to be heard above the shriek of his polluted heart...

(*his mother his sister friends and bandmates the girls he had fondled clumsily behind walls at school those who had rejected him those he had rejected teachers uncles the bus driver the girl at the newsagents*)

He put his fist through the large mirror above the metal sink. Again and again he bashed, splitting both glass and skin, crunching against bone, shredding fingernails like dried glue. Glass burrowed into his fists, and blood sprayed over the broken mirror, sink and tiled floor. He couldn't feel any pain. He couldn't feel any shame, either, his aching heart having burst through the thin veneer dividing what he *really* felt from what he wanted others to *think* he felt.

But Tim *could* feel himself being held, the small arms of Caroline Donaldson gripping around his broken body with desperation and love.

She had sprinted quickly to the bathrooms on hearing the screams. She held Tim with passion, her own tears erupting as if inspired. And there the two teens remained for the best part of an hour. In the brutal honesty of that time, no words were spoken or needed to be spoken.

...

She smiled. Star actually *smiled*, lighting the last candle of the thirty-two she laid out around the bus station to fight off the black of the incoming night. She lit a joint to celebrate, having realised that she still held a scrap of weed in her pocket. Good stuff, too. Scored from her old mate Stumpy, an odious-looking little toe rag who used to hang around her shop. Yet, like a lot of that motley crew, Stumpy had eventually grown on Star, becoming part of the furniture. Now the poor fucker was dead. (Doped to his eyeballs, but dead nonetheless.)

She had liberated the candles from the craft shop in the station's small mall. It seemed a shame to use the boring ones, so Star used different types, colours and scents to create a pungent (but not altogether unpleasant) aroma, and distinct mystical glow against the evening sky.

The tall glass walls of the station came alive with the light, almost radiating. From quite a distance, the station's illumination stood out amongst the clouds, a single expression of life and hope amongst the darkening backdrop.

Star sat cross-legged on the floor, at one of the station's side doors, looking out onto the courtyard. The buses looked back, as if taunting her, reminding her of the dream she'd had. But the makeshift graveyard consoled her, weirdly. She didn't need to be sleeping to suffer a bad dream. It was all right there under her nose. Hidden, but still there.

Somewhere in the station she could hear crying—or was it laughing? The smoke was really beginning to take effect, numbing her brain, yet opening up her imagination like Pandora's Box. From somewhere else, another voice carried in the light breeze, almost audible. It didn't matter where these voices or cries or laughs were coming from. In the cheerful moment of draw, nothing really mattered much.

"Hope, eh?" Star whispered to herself, thinking of the words Caz had said to her, taking another drag of her joint.

Smiling, she leaned back, feeling the night air blowing in against her face with the first pitter-patter of The Rain.

...

Roy Beggs took a minute to listen to the same pitter-patter on the school's high windows. It was always something he liked to do, listening to the rain beating off the roof of his car or windows of his flat. Once upon a time, when the world was alive, he enjoyed that simple pleasure with his wife. Now he simply saw the bucketing rain as another element to take into consideration when securing the Lisburn school where he and his followers had gathered.

The group would have been lost without him.

Although the toilets in the school still seemed to flush, Roy feared they would start to really smell if the survivors continued to use them, the sewer system no longer being maintained. He insisted that everyone use chemical toilets, which could then be disposed. It was a small thing, but all too important when trying to maintain hygiene and prevent disease.

Piss and shit were the least of his worries, though. Roy was coming to realise that with a breakdown of society came a breakdown of law. There would inevitably be looters, rapists, and opportunists only too willing to prey upon a community such as theirs. Preparation was needed, and—as with all preparation—security was imperative. Roy had been busy working alongside some of the men. They had blackened out most of the windows of the school, erected some simple tripwires on the football pitch and gravel track, and moved most of the cars outside the grounds. They couldn't remove all evidence of their presence, what with that ever-present silence highlighting every little whisper from each of the mouths assembled in the school, but they could minimise signs of life and prepare themselves, as best as possible, for anything untoward.

The soldier spent the remainder of his day planning his defence strategy, showing some of the more trustworthy and balanced-looking survivors how to use firearms such as the Browning 9mm handgun and SA80 assault rifle, part of the basic armoury stored in the back of his Land Rover. Later, he drew up some rules for the community, some basic laws that they could all follow. He posted these rules on the canteen wall, the assembly hall – anywhere people seemed to gather. He carried a set himself in his pocket and gave further sets, scribbled untidily onto pieces of lined, file paper, to anyone he trusted to carry a gun.

Except Mairead, of course.

Avoiding his nemesis hadn't been that difficult. Mairead took herself off to nearby shopping centre, Bow Street Mall, to get some supplies. That was what she had told the others, anyway. He suspected differently. For Roy, the main reason for her excursion was to bond with Clare, her newly adopted daughter. Roy shivered to think how the former IRA operative would corrupt the youngster.

Start them young.

Tired from all of the day's grafting, Roy was now sitting quietly with some of the other survivors, enjoying a cup of tea. One of them, an older man named Tom, had been an electrician before he had retired. Working with an engineer named Fred, and a shitload of fuel from the garage down the road, Tom kick-started an old generator they'd found around the back of the school. The result was a little electricity, enough to comfortably power a cooker, a water heater, and one or two lights. The first thing they heated was a huge flask of tea. Sylvia Patterson brewed it for the men, washing out a whole sink of mugs to make sure they all had something clean to drink from. Even though they didn't have any fresh milk, and the extra sugar made the brew taste saccharine, Roy was still enjoying his caffeine hit.

A flash of spontaneous lightning suddenly illuminated the door to the canteen. It was unexpected, making even Roy feel edgy.

He sat his tea down.

There was a man by the door, staring in through the square panes of glass.

Roy squinted against the darkness outside. Lightning, again, affirmed what he was seeing. His eyes narrowed. Shushing the suddenly panicked survivors around him, he reached for his rifle, some of the other men following his lead. Soon Roy's makeshift army were all armed, fingers searching clumsily and nervously around the metal of their firearms.

The doors burst open as another sudden blast of lightning preceded a gruff and stuttered roll of thunder. Like a scene from some fucked-up fairytale, the sorry silhouette finally revealed itself to those gathered. There, in the dimmed down light stood Steve Marshall, dripping wet from head to toe. In his arms was the small, clearly dead body of a child.

"I tried…" Steve said, half to himself and half to those gathered. "I tried everything. I sang to him, bounced him on my knee, kissed his beautiful face. But no matter how much I talked to him, how much I rocked him…" Steve looked up, pulling the dead child close to his chest. "I just couldn't wake him…"

…

"Wash me!" screamed The Preacher Man. "Wash me in your blood!"

The Rain hammered down, its righteous fury decontaminating the sin-stained streets of Belfast. It was Judgement Day, and The Preacher Man had one last mission before heaven would sing out in celebration of Christ's new reign.

There was still time.

He had to prepare a path for the Lord. He needed to cleanse and baptise any sinners who remained (hidden and ashamed) in the shadows, before God's beautiful Angels came down to reclaim him, to lift him to Glory, where he would reign with all those who prophesised before him. This was his mission, his gift, his privilege. His congregation surrounded him, heads stooped and hands clenched in front of them. They were penitent. They were empty vessels, wide open to receive showers of blessings. Whilst the rain carried out its cleansing work, the blood of Jesus spilling once again onto the earth to fill their hearts, their souls, The Preacher Man stepped out into the drawing evening, Bible in hand, and began to preach. His voice once more echoed through the streets of Belfast.

PART TWO

"...from so simple a beginning endless forms most beautiful and most wonderful have been, and are being, evolved."

(from *The Origin of Species*
by Charles Darwin)

ONE

At first The Silence was stifling. Washing across Belfast like a tiptoeing tsunami, it shushed everything and everyone in its path, sweeping all evidence of life under the carpet. Battery-powered radios and automated streetlamps, ignored, eventually powered down. Most of the dead decayed slowly and quietly, their deaths more like a curious sleep, their bodies hoping to blend into the earth just as apathetically as they had given up on life, simply and without protest. Occasionally, though, more explicit sights of trashed cars and broken people could be seen mangled together. Even then, what was left of crash-test human faces was generally expressionless.

On the whole, it seemed, the human race died without caring. After a post-millenium sway away from devil-may-care diets, towards a more holistic way of life, after an almost feverish obsession with all things environmental, all things organic, the human race had finally thrown in the towel. Mother Nature, like the Great Divine Whore She is, had simply fucked humanity without rhyme or reason. In her trail, even the early signs of devastation gave up.

At first, flames and smoke bellowed out of engines. Before long, even that died away. A foul stench of barbecued flesh and petrol seeped into the quiet night air. All that could be heard was the pitter-patter of daily evening rain and the whistle of a gentle summer breeze.

More survivors crawled out of the woodwork as time went by. Some were cowering in their homes throughout the city, staring deliriously at dead relatives and failing TVs. Others remained for days and weeks in a deep, dark depression, caring little for anything or anyone, including themselves.

Eventually, they moved. Short trips around their estates or apartment blocks soon gave way to longer trips into the city centre, to see what, if anything, was happening. They were mostly unsociable, eyeing each other up suspiciously. Some gathered in small groups, feverishly gathering supplies as if a nuclear winter were on the horizon. Most, however, remained in the shadows. Alone. Scared. Barely alive. Barely seen or heard.

The Silence, thick and foreboding, discouraged conversation. It was as if the world were one giant library—or church—where talking was seen as disrespectful. Random mad people, largely ignored, shouted, laughed or cried in shadowy street corners. They were despised for their candidacy. Their public nuisance would last only so long before a random shot in the night, or curious scream, spelled their sweet demise.

No one questioned it. No one cared.

Occasional fights would break out, sporadically, seemingly over nothing. It was probably more to do with frustration than anything else. But even these were largely ignored, reaching their conclusion within a very short space of time, one brawler lying bleeding alone in the street. Sometimes they picked themselves up again. At other times, they didn't. Fresh bodies were ignored as much as the older, staler ones. What was another body in a world now fortified with death? It was meaningless, like another leaf in a forest, another blade of grass, another cloud in the rain-clogged sky.

The Preacher Man was doing good business, his religious doomsday writ now believable in a world reeking of apocalypse. One by one, tearful and repentant sinners had seeped out of the shadows to join him. Some were simply unable to think clearly for themselves, needing a strong leader to help make sense of things. Others were terrified that God would shit upon them the same way He had shat upon their friends and family.

Great Victoria Street was largely avoided, Star's laissez faire attitude and solo boozing sessions unnerving most of the sombre majority. Days, then weeks, passed by. The same routine kicked in for Star, almost as if the apocalypse hadn't happened. By day, she inked. By night, she drank and smoked dope.

It was not her intention to invite others to join her and her two compatriots… but that's exactly the impression that her nightly routine of lighting candles gave to Barry Rogan and Sean Magee. Or maybe they just smelled the dope. The eclectic twosome arrived one night, sick of moving from one pub to the next. With hardly any need for introduction, the two lads and Star bonded, wasting no time in setting a precedent for how they were going to deal with the End Of The World. They partied endlessly, blasting out angry music from a pilfered, portable CD player, defiantly pissing all over The Silence's morose parade. Before long, even Tim and Caz could stand no more, moving next door to the Europa Hotel and finding a room without any of those pesky bodies to worry about. Alas, the three amigos followed their lead, stumbling drunkenly through the hotel doors, seeking out rooms with mini-bars and king size beds for their insatiable campaign of hedonism.

And so it continued, life finding its own sub-niche amongst the ever-rotting death thickly coating the streets. Unlike Lisburn, where the school's community continued to evolve and develop, few in Belfast tried to take control. Few tried to build anything amongst the nothing. Instead, pockets of survivors carried on living their own lives, ignoring those—alive or dead—around them, simply making do.

...

Trevor Steele peered through one of the school's front windows, his eye focused on a small patch of flames and glass just by the main entrance. Slung across his shoulder was an SA80 assault rifle, the weapon he had been recently trained how to use by Roy Beggs. Steele sighed , allowing the single Venetian blind he held open to fall closed. He counted at least four strangers out there, but there were probably more of them. They had no visible weapons, apart from petrol bombs, but that had been enough to keep the likes of Roy Beggs busy of a Saturday evening back in the day. Steele really didn't like the look of this.

"How many?" It was Roy's voice. Steele slowly turned around to face him. The soldier was as formidable-looking as ever, his rolled-up sleeves flashing ageing tattoos that all but sang of his past association with loyalist paramilitaries. That suited Steele just fine.

"Four that I can see. But there's likely to be more of them."

"Weapons?" Roy asked, studying Steele's face in a way that was slightly intimidating. As he spoke, the soldier continued to play around with a small two-way radio. Steele hadn't seen it before.

"Nothing visible, apart from the petrol bombs. But I couldn't be sure."

"I want everyone in the assembly hall. There are only a few windows there, so it'll be fairly safe. If things go badly wrong, there's always the fire exit nearby."

Steele nodded before heading off to get everyone together.

"Oh, and Trevor?"

"Yes, Roy?"

"Tell Mairead that I want her."

...

Roy walked through the school with all the importance of a headmaster, yet none of the finesse. He carried his portable two-way radio in one hand and a small gun in the other. Fear was heavy in the air. These people had suffered way too much to have to go through a situation like this.

The soldier helped to herd survivors into the assembly hall, aided by other members of his freshly-trained militia. He tried shushing those who seemed the most scared, the most audible, but it was no good. His patience was wearing thin.

He was about to move on towards the main entrance of the school, at least happy that everyone was safe in the hall, when he noticed the child, Clare, hiding under one of the tables outside the assembly hall. He paused, leaning down to look under the table.

"You know, it's very naughty for little girls to hide," he said.

"I'm not a little girl anymore," came the reply.

"Well, then," Roy began, thinking how true her words were—how very poignant and true, "maybe you should join all the adults in the assembly hall. How about it, eh?"

The soldier offered his hand. After a moment or two, he felt her small fingers grip it tightly, allowing him to gently pull her out from under the table. A sudden burst of gunfire rang out, and Clare pulled Roy close, the fear causing her small body to shake.

"Now go into the assembly hall like a good girl," Roy said in a stern voice.

He felt in his pocket for the Mars bar he had been saving for himself.. "Go on, now."

She took the chocolate bar and smiled, no doubt happy to get a little attention from the burly soldier who she was beginning to see as something of a daddy figure. Tears were welling up in her eyes, yet she seemed reluctant for them to escape, perhaps trying to maintain her composure in front of him. Roy felt for her. She was so very innocent. He watched her walk into the assembly hall, where the group's cook, Sylvia, was waiting to look after her.

He turned and walked briskly towards the main entrance of the school. The door was open, Trevor Steele and John McElroy having exited like the inexperienced idiots they were, firing wildly into the air as they sought cover behind nearby undergrowth. One petrol bomb had landed by the open door, the carpet in the hall already having caught fire, but Roy was able to quickly stamp the flames out and close the heavy door again.

Retreating to the window, Roy peered out at the carnage outside. Steele and McElroy were pinned down near one of the trees now, taking pot-shots wherever they saw a flash of gunfire emerge. Several spent petrol bombs littered the grass nearby, the large tree shielding the two men from the worst of their threat. From where Roy was, he guessed that there were probably ten of the fuckers out there, working together with a shitload of petrol and at least one gun. It was probably a semi-automatic from the sounds he was hearing, likely stolen from the body of a member of the security forces. That made Roy seethe even more. He didn't care why these bastards were attacking them—although he guessed it was to steal their powered-up base—but the thought that they had stolen weapons from men like him, men who dedicated their lives to protecting people, really riled the soldier.

He sat his two-way radio down and lifted the SA80 rifle leaning against the wall. Carefully, he fitted it with a scope and then, lifting one of the blinds, opened the window slowly, allowing both nuzzle and scope to slide out under cover of the Venetian blinds. He slid a fresh thirty-round magazine into the magwell then pulled the cocking handle back, placing one eye against the scope. He picked his first target, a twenty-something male with a football scarf covering his mouth. Roy squeezed gently on the trigger and then watched his bullets tear through the man's chest, blood spitting into the air as he fell.

One down.

Now he had to act fast.

Roy repeated the action, adjusting his aim, seeking out a target and firing. This time he found the skull of a thirty-something fat bastard, spilling his brain over the bonnet of a nearby car.

Another man was hiding there, and this one had a shooter. Roy ducked quickly as the man stood to fire. The bullets were well-aimed, suggesting some training, and Roy was forced to cover his head as pieces of glass from his window vantage point splintered around the room. Further shots and then a petrol bomb followed, taking advantage of the destroyed window, landing just behind the table. He crawled out of the room, cursing as he went. He had only time to grab his two-way radio before the heat from the licking flames soared. He closed the door, retreating down the corridor to relative safety.

As he retreated, Roy passed another survivor who was moving in to tackle the flames, armed with a fire extinguisher.

"Keep your head down, for fuck's sake!" Roy barked at her, ducking in behind the main corridor wall.

He caught his breath before raising the radio to his mouth. "Mairead, you there?"

...

Mairead Burns was sprawled out on the school's rooftops, drinking up the splendour of the action on the ground. She had been waiting for Roy's word before opening up with her own rifle, resenting the fact that—yet again—he was calling the shots, but respecting his ability as a soldier enough to play along. She needed to protect Clare, and working with Roy Beggs, in this case, was going to be the best way to achieve that. But it didn't mean she had to like him.

Testing her scope, Mairead picked out her future targets, shaking her head at the mess that McElroy and Steele had got themselves into. Not a bad thing. It provided Roy and her with an excellent decoy to distract these rank amateurs before they mounted the main offensive.

Two shots, almost in succession, and Mairead noticed how two men that she had hoped to take a pop at hit the deck, dead.

"Beggs, you're a damn good shot," she muttered to herself. "Even if you are a complete shit."

Another man jumped up, suddenly, from behind a car and sprayed the school grounds with semi-automatic fire, providing cover for a third fucker to let go with another petrol bomb. This one struck gold, Mairead watching as it glided through the air toward the school's entrance.

Come on, Roy, just give me the word.

A moment passed before she got what she was looking for.

Pzzt. "Mairead, you there?" *Pzzt.*

Picking up her two-way radio, the former IRA operative answered.

"I'm here," she said. "Looks like you're knocked out of the game, though."

It was a cheap shot, and she knew it. But it gave her pleasure to put Roy down at every opportunity.

Pzzt. "Just take the remainder of them out. There's a wee bastard behind that car with a shooter. Take him out first, and then we can see how many of them have real weapons." *Pzzt.*

Mairead didn't bother to reply. She set her radio down and retrieved her rifle. It was the Brit SA80, not the infamous AR18 she had been used to firing. Nicknamed 'The Widowmaker', the AR18 had been the IRA's most notorious sniper rifle of choice. And it packed a lot of punch, shattering the human skull from an admirable distance. But Mairead felt dangerous with any rifle. From her bird's eye vantage point, she picked her targets with ease. The silly cunt who was cocky enough to come out from behind his cover, firing wildly towards the hapless Steele and McElroy, was first to go. One shot from Mairead took him out of the game, sending him sprawling across the pavement. Another idiot was making a beeline for the first man's weapon, but Mairead caught him in her sights before he was even able to pick it up. A shot to the back of the head put him down, too.

Mairead watched as the remainder of the posse upped and legged it, pouring out of the various hiding holes they'd taken for themselves around the school grounds. She smiled as she watched them run, picking up her radio again.

"It's clean-up time, Roy. Let's get busy."

...

Roy listened from inside the school as the two shots from Mairead rang out, signifying the end of the road for another two of their opponents. Her next message, delivered swiftly after the shots, was all that the soldier needed to hear. Pulling a 9mm from his belt, Roy bolted for the door as quick as his heavy build would allow him. The front lawn of the school grounds was charred from the petrol bombs, and Roy was careful not to step on any patches that were still smouldering, fully aware of how easy it was to catch fire from those bloody things. Smoke was heavy in the air, providing Roy with some cover, yet also making it difficult for him to see.

"Steele! McElroy!" he yelled as he ran, "Move out! Let's finish this!"

The poorly-prepared militia grabbed their rifles, huffing and puffing towards the school gates, following Roy's lead. As they moved out into the open, the smoke cleared, and all three men were able to make out a small group running towards Lisburn's town centre.

There was another shot, dropping one of their number to the ground. Roy knew it had come from Mairead, picking the exposed fleeing men off like the chicken shit they were. As Roy gave chase, he, too, fired at will, cutting down another guy. His screams sounded brutal, Roy's smaller calibre bullets tearing through various parts of the man's anatomy before silencing him for good.

Steele and McElroy took cover behind a car. Noting this, Roy ducked behind a lamppost, worried more about the wild shooting of his militia than that of their fleeing opponents. Both men opened fire, their own semi-automatic gunfire cutting through the air to take down another runner. Another burst from Mairead took down yet another man who was trying to force a shop door open, leaving only one young woman in flight.

Roy waved to the others, signalling that he wanted her for himself. He made good his chase, catching his opponent due more to her tiredness and fear of being gunned down than his own athletic ability. She put her weapon down and sank to her knees, facing Roy with both hands on her head. She was crying, and a stain spreading across the front of her combat trousers suggested that she was in the process of pissing herself.

Roy paused to catch his breath before speaking. "How many of you are there?"

The woman sniffed away her tears, trying to compose herself. "There's only me, now. Everyone else is gone."

"You're lying," Roy said.

"I'm not!" she screamed. "Please don't hurt me."

"What, like you wouldn't do the same to any of my lot?" Roy said, incredulously. "I've got people who depend on me. People I need to protect. If I were to let you go, I wouldn't be doing my job, now, would I?"

"Please, I—"

"Just shut up and listen to me," Roy said, his patience all but dried up. "I'm going to need you to do something for me."

"Anything!" she begged. "Just say it and I'll do it."

The woman remained on her knees, looking up at him. She was in her thirties, Roy reckoned. Nothing especially remarkable about her. Just another drop-out, trying to make her way in the broken-down world. Dirty hair, hunger about the face. Slovenly clothes and skinny, malnourished arms. Possibly a drug user or hooker, working for some Big Man in order to get whatever reward she'd been promised. He knew she was playing along with anything he said. Fear was making her tremble all over, but the soldier (Protector? Leader?) couldn't feel anything but anger for her.

"Here's the message," he said.

But where there should have been words to follow, two bullets pierced her forehead, a jet of blood and brain spewing from the back of her skull as she fell, dead, to the ground.

Roy couldn't be sure that she was lying about there not being others, but that didn't bother him. The real problem was that she couldn't be trusted not to seek some kind of revenge, even if on her own. And if there were any others nearby, cowering in the shadows, the fear of God pissing out their dicks, they too would have witnessed how Roy Beggs deals with anyone who crosses him. It would set an example, a precedent that would show how those who prey upon his community end up. And that was the kind of rep he needed to be a leader.

He started back towards the school, his heavy boots echoing out throughout the dead, grey backdrop of Lisburn. A few flames flickered around him, the remnants of the various petrol bombs that had been thrown. A distant sound of a barking dog shattered the stillness. He spotted the face of a beautiful woman on a billboard, advertising perfume. Despite the colourful-looking bottle cradled in the palm of her hand, the soldier could smell only death. Death and more death.

He didn't see the point of covering over the bodies of the attackers. There were dead scattered throughout the whole world now, it seemed. Some of them reeked of too many days in the sunshine, as could be predicted. Others, Roy noticed, were better preserved, perhaps even as fresh as the day they had fallen. And that didn't make any sense at all.. He had to admit that this whole broken-down world was like the start of a horror movie. Yet he'd also seen enough nightmares come true in the real world, through his years of soldiering in Northern Ireland...

For Roy, it was simple. As long as people stayed with him, protected inside the school grounds, none of this would matter. The smell of death—*or undeath*, as the case might be—would be hidden from them. They didn't need to know about it. It would only freak the survivors out even more. Others, perhaps, would crack under the pressure, like Steve Marshall. And God knew they didn't need another fuckin' case like Steve Marshall. Roy would be there for them. No matter what creepy, horror-movie bullshit came to get them, Roy would take care of it. That was his job, after all.

The soldier walked slowly back towards his base—their haven. A glint in the distance gave away the position of Mairead Burns on the school's rooftop, and, for a moment, Roy wondered whether or not she would fire upon him, taking him down with the same precision that had spelled doom for their attackers. But she didn't.

TWO

Days had gone by, maybe weeks, and still Herb Matthews remained in the pyjamas and dressing gown he had woken up in on that fateful Sunday. He kept the kitchen clean, along with the rest of the house, simply filling the outside bin with the remains of every tin of Spam he left half-eaten. He even kept Muriel clean, giving his wife's corpse a bed-bath from time to time to keep her looking her best, but he never even as much as splashed water over his own unshorn face. It just didn't seem a worthwhile thing to do.

Perhaps it was the shock, or his condition (that's how the doctor described it) that kept Herb from checking to see what was happening in the outside world. He just couldn't physically do it. Sure, he did ring for an ambulance at one stage (although thinking back on it, he couldn't be sure if he had done that on the first day… or even the second) and he did flick around the television, getting nothing but fuzz from every channel, but even then he hadn't considered for an instant that there might be something wrong with the rest of world—only *his* world, the world which had begun and ended each day with Muriel.

A part of him didn't want to be found, didn't want to have to give her up to the doctors and the funeral directors who would, no doubt, need to take her away.

He didn't want to have to welcome all those strangers into his house (their home) and entertain them with cups of tea and grateful smiles, the way those things needed to be done. Herb didn't want or need any of that (and he was quite sure that Muriel didn't either).

Yet, another part of him was growing fearful of The Silence.

The Silence was everywhere. It was in the house. It was in the garden. (Which he gingerly breached in order to kick-start the generator when the lights went down. Was that the first day or the third?) It was in his shed, where he kept all the things which he had been playing with over the years—motorcycle engines, the amateur radio which he used to tinker about with many moons ago, its aerial still erected by the cottage, and that old, double-barrelled shotgun which Muriel had always been begging him to get rid of. The Silence—that goddamn *Silence*—was everywhere, and, after God knows how many days or weeks, it was starting to grate on Professor Herbert Matthews. It was haunting him, tearing at his very fabric—his very *essence.*

He needed to get out. He needed noise. He didn't realise how much he could miss it until it wasn't there.

Herb walked to the front door. He held his breath, opening the door with relative ease, stepping onto the garden path leading to the world outside for the first time in almost ten years.

There. That wasn't so hard, was it?

The old white van that Muriel would have driven remained parked in the driveway. The garden gate (a little rusty from the last time Herb had seen it) was firmly closed. Fields nearby were littered with what appeared to be sleeping livestock. Or were they dead? It was all enough to give Herb the shivers. This was a strange and barren land. It felt foreign to him, strange and exotic and dangerous. He wasn't dressed for the outdoors, either. It hardly mattered. He didn't make it much further.

First came the heavy breathing, then the palpitations. Soon the professor had a full-blown panic attack, complete with dizziness and swirling stars in his eyes. Finally, he passed out, waking to find himself half in and half out of the front door.

He crawled desperately back inside. He closed the door for what he thought to be the last time, locking it defiantly.

Shan't try that again, that's for sure.

...

Gavin Cummings sighed quietly before launching yet again into another rendition of El Shadi. A sizeable crowd, men and women, stood stoically by the Bandstand at the Victoria Square shopping centre, some with tears in their eyes, others with hands raised to the sky, as the twenty-seven year old's gentle acoustic accompaniment oiled over the fact that most people were singing out of tune. Gavin's eyes still followed the *Church Hymns and Chorus* book that The Preacher Man had proudly presented to him on his baptism. Even though he played the same songs twice daily, as The Preacher Man's campaign gathered serious momentum, Gavin just couldn't get the chords into his head. Deep down, he hated this banal shite he was playing. Yet after only a couple of weeks under The Preacher Man's charge, Gavin felt guilty even about that.

He looked over at a small child standing with a young woman. The child wasn't singing. He was staring at Gavin, as if knowing what he was thinking, what he was *really* thinking. Gavin looked away from him, suddenly embarrassed. He struck the wrong chord, turning back to the book resting on the stand in front of him. He flicked the page, hands shaking, feeling the eyes of The Preacher Man burning into him.

"Sorry," he mumbled, finding the right page.

He thought of his life before all of this. The clubs he would have frequented, the friends he'd had. Religion was never meant to be part of his life, and yet here he was. A believer of sorts. Unable to think of any other reason for the world to end than the supernatural, he'd turned to the one man who seemed to have purpose, a man he would have laughed at in the old world.

Before long the song was over, the congregation quietly setting their chorus books down on the ground beside them. Some of them sat down on the paving; others remained standing. The Preacher Man, himself, rose up into the bandstand, having made it his pulpit. To Gavin, the bizarre structure looked not unlike a birdcage, the Preacher Man some overgrown bird, and for a moment he thought he might start laughing. He remembered wanting to laugh before, in church, when he was young. It was the nature of the place, the nonsense of it. Too serious for its own good. Indulgently out of step with normality. He remembered feeling so nervous that he once started to laugh while a funeral was taking place, quickly dragged out of the pew by his mother and given a good ticking over. He couldn't even remember what he was laughing at.

The Preacher Man's words were lost to Gavin. He could never focus on what he was saying, mostly because, although it was heresy to admit it, none of what he said *really* made sense. There were familiar themes and sound bites throughout, mostly things he'd heard or seen scrawled across sandwich boards and church billboards before, but it all seemed to lack cohesion or relevance to the real world. Gavin knew he shouldn't be thinking like that – maybe it was his failing? Maybe he was blinded by the devil, cursed with the lack of vision needed to truly understand and accept The Preacher Man's teachings. This made him afraid.

Again, he caught the eye of the little boy. He was smiling over at him, his little face full of mischief. Gavin smiled back. The boy suddenly stuck his tongue out, more playful than cheeky. Gavin found himself laughing.

But The Preacher Man wasn't laughing..

"Demon!" he suddenly screamed, pointing the child out as if he were a wolf among sheep. "There's a demon amongst us!"

Panic erupted, people looking at those beside them. The boy's mother grabbed him close, shielding him from the fearful and angry eyes that suddenly surrounded them.

"No!" She shouted, trying to shuffle through the pressing crowd, but a couple of men were fighting to peel her arms from the boy.

"DEMON!" screamed The Preacher Man, still on his birdcage perch. "WE MUST CAST THE DEMON OUT!"

The boy was now crying, all trace of mischief drained from his face as two men were struggling to spread him across the paving, one holding his arms, the other holding his legs. A third man was babbling in what seemed to be another language, lost in some kind of trance as he pressed his hand against the child's forehead. His mother screamed, held back by two others. The scene was terrifying to watch, yet Gavin Cummings couldn't stop staring. A part of him was frightened for the boy, another for himself. Perhaps he, too, was possessed by a demon? Was that why he couldn't understand? Was that why he felt like a stranger here?

"Demon!" some were chanting. Others were shaking and screaming, as if they too were possessed. Several more enlightened believers lifted their hands up to the heavens, crying "God have mercy!"

Pandemonium was building, The Preacher Man anchored to the bandstand like the conductor of the bizarre and frantic orchestra before him. He looked to Gavin, as if to say, *Do something. Play something.* Gavin felt his hands reaching for the guitar, coming down hard on the strings the way they used to when playing in his metal band. He strummed down with power chords, their normally dramatic effect less powerful when played acoustically. Yet he belted them out, enjoying the feeling it gave him, the energy the music afforded him. Soon he was on his feet, chanting with the others as he continued to hammer out the powerful chords, The Preacher Man standing both hands held high, eyes closed.

The exorcism continued, the little boy kicking and screaming as the believers continued to work their purifying magic on his corrupt soul. The man performing the exorcism became even more frantic, his enthusiasm turning to aggression as he proceeded to bang the boy's head against the paving. The boy's mother, unable to take anymore, sank her teeth into her captors' hands, breaking free to run towards the man who was on his knees, still babbling and banging the boy's head against the stone. Gavin continued to play, his hands bleeding with the force he was unleashing against the strings. As he watched the scene unfold, the boy's mother pulled a small knife from her coat pocket, drawing the blade across the throat of the incoherent man on his knees. The cut man, aghast and suddenly lucid, fell back, holding his bleeding throat.

"Cast them out!" screamed the Preacher Man, several others grabbing the woman and shaking the knife from her hand.

Another woman, older than the boy's mother, reclaimed the knife and proceeded to stab the young boy with it repeatedly. The boy's cries were ear-splitting.

His mother was catatonic, the man she had stabbed stumbling around the bandstand as blood flowed freely down his white shirt.

"GOD HAVE MERCY!" cried The Preacher Man, others joining him as blood continued to be shed around them.

But Gavin still felt the power rage through him. As he continued to bang his guitar, the pain from his bleeding hands brought him to a new level of understanding. Laughter left his mouth. But it wasn't irreverent; it wasn't demonic. It was joyous laughter. He felt part of this. He felt at one with The Preacher Man, with those around him. He felt close to God, to himself.

He believed.

...

Sweat was building on his forehead as John McElroy stepped out of the school's mobile classroom. He looked left then right, his eyes alert like a schoolchild sneaking home before the bell rang. John had done some bad things of late.

It wasn't his fault. He was left alone in this world, without his wife Shauna and that bint, Glory, from work, who he fucked on a regular basis. And Roy shouldn't have given him the job of cleaning up after that whole Steve Marshall thing. They'd both been in the canteen when it happened, the crazy fucker bursting in with that foul little bundle in his arms. It was shocking, nothing short of it, lumps of dark, yellow skin peeling off the child like it was a plastic doll buried, then unearthed. The putrid smell, attacking the senses like a wave of sick.

But the other corpse in the car—that of Marshall's wife—hadn't been so foul...

He had made it to the makeshift grave where Roy had asked him to bury the bodies. The grave contained the child (and fucking hell, he couldn't bury that thing deep enough...) but he neglected to bury the woman, Kirsty. She had been Steve's wife, a young thing about half McElroy's age. And damn, even in death she was still pretty. McElroy kept her hidden, buried under old junk that the survivors cleared out of the school and threw into the mobile classroom. No one was ever going to find a black bin liner containing the body. Oddly enough, she didn't smell. In fact, she hadn't deteriorated at all, it seemed. And much as that thrilled John McElroy—night after night over the last week—it was starting to freak him out now. He was beginning to worry that she wasn't dead at *all*.

McElroy knew of comas that were so intense that even doctors couldn't tell if the person was dead or not. He recalled urban myths of bodies being buried alive, their coffins unearthed by grave robbers to find claw marks on the inside of the lid. But this was different. This was fucking out there...

He didn't feel any guilt. Not in the New World—a world within which McElroy had witnessed Roy Beggs—their champion—murder an unarmed woman in broad daylight as she begged and pleaded on her knees before him. A world where almost everyone had fallen dead within minutes. In a world where the shit well and truly *murdered* the fucking fan, it hardly mattered what John McElroy, ex-civil servant, was up to.

Did it?

The black bin liner was heavy, and it took all the strength in his squat frame to drag its bulk across the lawn. Yet he worked hard, pausing only to take a breath, mop his brow and keep an eye out for anyone who saw him. It looked all clear.

Most people slept well now, what with Roy having made things more secure, scaring the hell out of any would-be attackers, and Sylvia sourcing some comfortable sleeping bags and blankets from the school's main store room. The two of them were like mummy and daddy to the survivors, meeting their every need in a way that quietly secured blind obedience and allegiance. No one questioned any of their authority, whether it be the quiet, maternal power of Sylvia—the hand that feeds them—or the military presence of Roy Beggs—the hand that smites.

Once at the grave, McElroy dug hard and fast, still keeping a sneaky (and guilty) eye out for anyone watching. Before long he struck the sponge-like body of Marshall's son, catching the sickening gust of death off the child's unearthed corpse. He rolled Kirsty Marshall's corpse into the grave beside her son, throwing the earth back over the two bodies with as much haste as he could muster.

Out of sight, out of mind.

There. That was it done. No more temptation.

Looking left and right again, John McElroy wandered back to his sentry duties, another job sorted out.

THREE

Alan Gibson replaced his glasses with a slight sigh. It was no use. Yet another hour spent without getting a single word from the bowed head sat across from him.

Steve Marshall (the bowed head sat across from him) hadn't spoken a word since Roy Beggs roughly prised his hands off the rancid body of his young son, Nicky. At least the tears, then, had formed some sort of reaction. A release, perhaps, of pent-up emotion and delusion as the man tried to ignore the fact that his hopelessly deceased wife and son were gone forever. But every day since then, there had been nothing. Marshall simply stared out of the small classroom window, his eyes growing heavier, his shoulders sinking lower. Countless meals and drinks had been largely ignored, occasionally picked at with an almost autistic fascination, before Marshall returned to the business of staring out the small, cell-like window of his classroom abode.

"Steve, is there anything I can—"

Gibson didn't even bother finishing the sentence. There wasn't any point. This was a man who loss had hit, and hit hard. His mind was blank, refusing to allow even a single moment of lucid reflection. Post Traumatic Stress Disorder. As far up the scale as it could go. With no medication to help him, God only knew what chaotic thoughts were distracting Steve Marshall from reality, or what he made of the calm tide of words from Alan Gibson's mouth. But one thing was certain: the counsellor was getting nowhere with his patient.

Rubbing his own tired eyes, Gibson got up, moved toward the classroom exit, and slipped out, taking care not to slam the door behind him.

Roy Beggs stood waiting for him in the corridor.

"How is he today?" the soldier asked.

Gibson removed his glasses, cleaned them, then replaced them in a move developed more out of habit than necessity.

"Same," he replied. "Still doesn't want to accept his family's gone. It's as if his whole world has caved in. He just can't cope with it or deal with it, so his mind just shuts down. It's what we therapists call—"

"Everyone's world has caved in," Roy interrupted, looking sternly through the classroom door's window at Marshall's glazed expression. "We just have to pick ourselves up and get on with it, don't we?"

"Some people can't do that..." Gibson said.

He looked, again, through the window. Although Roy couldn't see it, he was the best chance Steve Marshall had of finally letting go of the dead family he'd kept stashed in his car. Buried though they may now be in the school football field, the bleak and embarrassing funeral having lasted only ten minutes before Roy called time on it, their faces still remained extremely vivid in the psyche of the man.

But Roy wouldn't see it like that. A mentally ill man was an unpredictable man. Not good for any community. Not good for morale. And in a place where everyone was hovering on the brink, still smarting from their own fucked-up worlds, morale was all too important.

"There's people in here who'd be much happier if he wasn't around at all..." Roy said, his voice loaded.

Gibson knew whom Roy was talking about.

He noticed her large frame lingering in the dimly lit corridor. She was listening in on his conversation with Roy, even though she feigned mopping the floor. Sylvia Patterson was whom Roy was talking about. She didn't say as much. She had a more gentle way of winning over the survivors' respect, and therefore a much more subtle way of manipulating the vulnerable community. But manipulative she was.

Gibson had her sussed. His mind built her profile. A mother of seven, and grandmother to ten. Harassed husband that scuttled to her every whim before the disaster hit. Sylvia simply couldn't deal with not being in control. She needed to be needed and so fell very easily into the role of provider within the school's ecosystem. Daily she toiled, washing and cleaning, dusting and wiping, cooking and gathering for all those resident. A solid oak of strength, mother to everyone—except Steve Marshall. A man like Marshall, a man who wore his broken heart on his sleeve (and his dead son in his arms until recently) would scare someone like Sylvia Patterson.

Gibson rubbed at the temples, where his hair was receding. "Roy," he said, smiling. "Locking Steve up is not going to help him work through this. He needs freedom, support and encouragement—if he's allowed these things, I'm quite sure we can make significant progress."

But Roy wasn't having any of it. He waved his finger in Gibson's face. "You see, that's precisely what's wrong with the whole fucking world", he said, grimacing. "People are too soft, putting up with sickos like rapists and child molesters wandering the streets. A tighter leash is what's needed. *Especially* now."

"Oh, come on, Roy!" Gibson said, laughing. "Steve Marshall isn't like that!"

But Roy didn't look amused.

It wasn't the first time that Roy had been over-zealous with his law-enforcing. Gibson knew his story, even before meeting him; he'd read his file. Back in the hey-day of the eighties, a young Roy Beggs stood with his regiment, supporting a police checkpoint on a well-known hotspot in West Belfast. The cops were looking for a white car which they believed to be transporting plastic explosives.

A member of Roy's patrol had fallen foul of the same type of explosive just a week prior, losing both his arms and half his pelvis after opening the lid of an industrial bin. Roy watched as the doctor broke the news to the poor bastard that he'd never walk or fuck again.

The night was cold and icy, Roy's patience wearing thin with every obscene comment and spittle hurled at him from the passing motorists. So whenever a Peugeot 205 failed to slow down when signalled by the cops, instead gathering more speed and bursting through the checkpoint, Roy's trigger finger wasted no time in shredding glass with lead, killing a small town pot-dealer, Gerard, and his cousin Kath almost instantly.

The car wasn't even white, and Roy knew it. But a pro-loyalist judge, anti-narcotics jury, and testimony from a cop who couldn't quite remember how much of a warning Roy had given before opening fire was enough to exit Roy from court smelling more of rose petal than toilet paper. Not that it mattered what the judge said. To Roy, justice was served, regardless of the outcome of the court case. It was eye-for-an-eye and to hell with anyone who thought differently.

But the boy's mother knew differently. Called Sadie by her friends, although christened Sarah at birth, she was a hardened and weathered woman who spent the whole time during the court case welling up tears behind her bone-dry eyes, as the coroner explained just how badly mutilated Roy's ammo had made her son's body. The boy's sister, Chris, herself only a child, sat beside her mother, holding her arm with a grip so tight it permanently marked the woman's skin. It was their icy stares that Gibson recalled from the pictures in the file, even today. The young girl's eyes were particularly memorable. Deep, deep blue. Slightly crossed, but still beautiful.

"We keep him locked up," Roy said, finally, to the bespectacled counsellor. "I don't care what your hippy feel-good books say about what he needs; I don't want Marshall wandering free, when he's capable of God-knows-what."

Gibson frowned but nodded.

Roy turned to walk away, then stopped. He slowly turned around. Shaking his head, as if disappointed with himself, Roy reached into his pocket and took out the bunch of keys that he'd found in the school's principal's office. He frowned, as if disappointed with himself, before pulling off the key to the classroom that Marshall inhabited, handing it to Gibson.

"I want him kept away from the others, Gibson. You can feed him, water him, clean out his shit and talk all the psychobabble you want. But mark my words: If I ever see him outside of that classroom, I'm holding you personally responsible. Got it?"

Alan Gibson took the key, smiling at Roy in that amicable way that he had.

"You're the boss, Roy."

Gibson knew that Roy wasn't a man to fuck with, but he had a responsibility to his client. Christ, that's all he had now.

...

It was early afternoon, and the sun was sitting high and mighty in a deep blue sky. Mairead Burns and Clare

McAfee sat on the swings in the school playground. Clare was sucking on a lollipop that Mairead had picked up from a nearby newsagents. It was the first lollipop she had enjoyed since that fateful Sunday when her mum hadn't woken up. Mairead couldn't believe that that was almost three weeks ago now. It seemed like only yesterday that she had met this little princess, this child that appeared so innocent in the heart of these new, sinister uncertainties. Yet it also felt like years ago that her life had been normal, when she had a husband, two sisters, an annoying mother, a living son...

"They don't ring the bell anymore," Clare said suddenly, swing moving to and fro in the delicate summer breeze, lollipop almost devoured.

"They don't need to, sweetie." Mairead said, ruffling the child's thick, curly hair, wondering if she should perhaps have a go at cutting its split ends, or even asking around to see if any of the other survivors had some experience in hairdressing.

Hygiene and vanity were a thing of the past for many. Yet Mairead kept herself and Clare reasonably clean, even if only for the sake of the child.

"Aren't we going to do anymore sums? Miss Stranney had been doing money with us, and we all had to bring in some shopping so we could make our own supermarkets. I brought in two packets of cornflakes and a tin of peas, but Miss Stranney said we had to bring in empty boxes and tins, not full ones." Clare looked up at Mairead, her lips toxic-orange with the lollipop. "Do you think Miss Stranney will come back to school?"

Mairead smiled, taking out a tissue to wipe the child's mouth clean.

"Why don't I teach you all about money? We could go to the shops and have a look at the money machines at the counter. Would you like that, love?"

"Yeah! I like going to the supermarket! I used to go with mummy. I'd pack the bags for her. I put all the tins in first then used another bag for the cold things, then another for the smelly things, like soap and stuff." Clare wiped her nose with her sleeve. "That's how mummy likes to pack things. She never puts things that don't go with each other together."

Mairead was worried about Clare. She seemed to talk about her mummy as if she believed she would see her again, yet never actually asked when that might be. She was perfectly content with Mairead—that much was obvious. The child rarely left her side, even for a second. Whilst other survivors talked to her or gave her sweets, it was Mairead that she came to whenever she needed something. Even just a cuddle. And that suited Mairead just fine. She adored Clare, counted her very much her own now. It was her second chance to raise a child the way it should be raised.

(*"There's been an explosion, Mrs Burns..."*)

A surrogate daughter.

"Mairead?"

"Yes, sweetie?"

"Could I call you mummy? Just for now, I mean?"

Mairead's eyes watered. She lifted the child up into her arms and hugged her tight.

"Of course you can, sweetie," she whispered into her ear. "All the time, if you like."

FOUR

The old DX-401 HAM radio hadn't been touched in years and a lesser-minded man than Professor Herbert Matthews may not have had the patience that was required to breathe new life into its old circuits. But a machine like this was always going to be a joy for Herb, giving him the opportunity to play God again. He knew precisely how to get this old boy working, just what was needed to resurrect it to become his sole link to the outside world. And he loved every minute of the challenge.

Once Herb had worked his magic with the internals, teasing his soldering iron around the heart and guts of the machine in an almost flirtatious manner, he turned his attention to the old, rusty aerial leaning against his house. It hardly seemed fit to be the courier of Herb's desperate SOS signals, but it was all he had, short of a washing line, that could do the job. Of course, Herb knew that with the transmitting and receiving power within the surprisingly small box now resting on his coffee table, the aerial wouldn't need to do much. Herb's magical add-ons had made his modest HAM radio ten times the machine it would have been on rolling off the production line.

Still have it in you, sir.

Within a few short hours, Herb was ready to fire up his rig. He worried about the fact that his sole energy source was a small generator at the back of his house as opposed to the power station up the road. With his homemade generator's limitations (even Herb couldn't create power out of thin air) it was going to be necessary to ensure that everything he had was channelled to the radio alone. Especially since receiving its 'special' add-ons. This baby could burn.

Herb returned to the house and sat himself down by the kitchen table, where the radio was rigged up. From the corner of his eye he could see Muriel watching him from the armchair, her eyes as lifeless and expressive as ever, her beauty still unspent. How long had she been like that? Time was a mystery to Herb now. His clocks seemed to spin around day-in-day-out, going nowhere in particular. Telling him nothing. Meaning nothing. All that meant anything to him now was Muriel and this radio. The only things of any value in the whole house—one dead and the other…

Pzzzzt.

Alive! Herb knew it would work, the electronics of the thing providing him with little challenge at all. Yet he still felt a little skip in his heartbeat as he turned the dial.

The airwaves were his now. He could tune in to and listen—*and please, God, talk*—to anyone who was broadcasting, whether they be on a private channel or not. Such was the genius of this machine. Such was the genius of Herbert Matthews, a man whose engineering prowess had led him onto many a confidential conversation in the early 80's, when these babies first came out. A few twists and turns of the dial, listening to the vibrations of sound like a doctor listening for a heartbeat, and Herb would be there. He flicked through the main frequencies first, listening carefully for any sign of life from each one he passed through. It took some time, what with the sheer number of them, but he knew how important it was to try the main frequencies before going all Herb-magical on it.

Pzzt. Pzzt.

The sound was musical to Herb, and he was almost tempted just to listen to an empty channel for a while, perhaps attracted to its sweet serenity. But he knew that enough time had passed giving into his almost carnal longing for solitude. He needed to talk, now, no matter how painful it would be for him. He needed to find out just why it was so quiet, why the phones and television and FM radio and Muriel had all died on him. He needed to find out before he decided what needed to be done about it.

Pzzt. Pzzzzzzt.

Each channel breathed the same as the last. Each a desert of activity, a barren soundscape where nothing more than Ballyclare's fresh country air whistled through. Nothing more than the wind and the slight rustle of leaves. Nothing more than the sun-parched clouds evaporating into the skyline, the heavier clouds spitting out their obnoxious belch of rain to create yet another heavy shower at night.

And then it came.

Pzzt. Pzzt. Pzzzzzt. "Ter..." Pzzzt. "airfield... calling all..." Pzzzt.

Herb was dumbfounded. His jaw dropped, the horn-rimmed spectacles falling, unchecked, off the end of his nose. He reached for his glass of bourbon and then realised the last of it had been drained dry hours ago.

"Sweet Lord," he croaked, all moisture seeming to have left his voice.

It was contact. He knew it. And what Herb couldn't believe was the channel he had found it on. Channel 40. The most common channel on any Citizen's Band radio.

Scrambling to pick up the mic, Herb cleared his throat before saying his first words in the Brave New World.

"H-hello?" he said, simply. "H-hello?! This is Professor H-Herbert Matthews. T-to whom am I speaking?"

...

Another piss-up.

Ever since Barry and Sean had arrived, there had been nothing but drinking, smoking dope, and partying at the station on Great Victoria Street, Sean spinning a few discs in some rig he and Barry somehow powered up. Star disappeared from time to time, going God-knows-where, to retrieve some weed and a shitload of booze. Repeat ad nauseum. Literally.

Together the three of them lived *la vida loca* drinking by night at the station, bopping around drunkenly to Sean's bizarre mix of dadrock and metal, then sleeping it off at the Europa Hotel the next day. Many of the rooms were now free of bodies, so the three revellers would often rest there to get away from the bright sunlight that would shine in through the high glass walls of the station next door. Light, as every self-respecting Irish drinker knew, was the arch-enemy of hangovers.

Tim and Caz took one of the rooms in the first floor of the hotel, still looking grand despite having been the most bombed in Europe. Its red carpets and ornate stairways screamed elegance even in the recent downgrading of the entire world. She and Tim lay on top of the gloriously comfortable bed in one of the hotel's executive suites, listening as Barry, Star and Sean came rolling through the doors, proceedings well underway for yet another night of hedonism.

"They're early tonight," Tim muttered, eyes closed, lying slightly to the left of Caz.

"Think they started earlier today," Caz reasoned. "I saw Star skulking about the place at about eleven this morning. It's been weeks now. How they keep drinking like that amazes me. Especially Sean. He must be, like, fifty, that bloke."

"The dude's a legend," Tim laughed.

"Yeah, he's old enough, anyway."

Caz looked over to Tim, sneaking a glimpse at his long, skinny frame sprawled out on the bed. They were both fully clothed, and neither had dared dip below the sheets. She fancied Tim like mad, and her young hormones were racing now that they were finally sharing the same bed, but she couldn't bring herself to make a move. That was his job, anyway. Boys did that, not girls. It was, like, the dating law, or something. Yet Tim looked about as far away from making a move as Belfast was to Tokyo. He was wearing that same nonchalant expression that he wore most days, whether he was pouring himself a coffee or strolling to the toilet. Reading Tim's emotions was like trying to read Braille when you weren't blind. Difficult and bloody frustrating.

"Tim?"

"Yep?" he answered, still keeping his eyes closed and body completely still.

"You know when you were… you know, upset and stuff, the other week?"

Tim's eyes suddenly opened. . His body seemed to tense all of a sudden, his feet moving up toward a fetal position. Caz hadn't mentioned that day since it happened. It was an unspoken rule, it seemed, to leave that day where it was. Spent. Clocked. Dealt with. Never to be discussed again.

"Well, I just wanted you to know that I'm always here to listen to you."

For a long and agonising moment, Tim didn't reply. She thought she could see tears building in his eyes again, and for a horrible moment Caz thought she was about to witness a repeat of that day.

But then he turned towards her.

"I know," he whispered, almost inaudibly. "You too."

He turned away again. Another awkward moment or two passed. Caz felt very aware of her breathing and how loud it sounded all of a sudden. The Silence from outside seemed to leak through the windows and creep into bed with them. Even The Rain seemed to shush, its constant pitter-patter gingerly hovering by the window, waiting for something to happen. Something important.

And then it began. At first, she felt Tim's ankle wrap slowly around her own. The mere touch of his socked foot sent ripples of euphoria through her, and Caz's heart started to race like that day, weeks ago, whenever she had watched him walk through the door of her train car.

With all that had happened, she almost forgot her crush on Tim Adamson and how he made her tingle every time he walked past her in school. Caz allowed a smile to cross her face. His ankle seemed to draw closer, cuddling her own. She began to wonder what colour his socks were, stifling an unexpected giggle at the thought.

"Seahorses," she heard herself whisper.

"What?" Tim replied.

"Seahorses," Caz said again, her smile beaming quietly and excitedly, her face reddening. "They're one of the few creatures that mate for life. They swim about wrapping their tails around each other, as if holding hands." Caz reached her hand behind her as she spoke, soon finding Tim's own waiting for her. "I always thought it was cute."

FIVE

Sylvia Patterson sat at the canteen table, sleeves rolled up, soiled apron still clinging to her waist. Having taken it upon herself to prepare all of the survivors' meals, helped by the delicate hands of Aida Hussein and the burly strength of Peter Stokenbergs, it seemed she was spending every waking minute in this bloody kitchen. Once one meal was finished and the dishes cleaned and tidied, it was almost time to get things sorted for the next. There was barely time for a cup of tea in between, never mind a walk around the school grounds or jaunt downtown to get any supplies.

She watched Gibson enter the canteen, probably fresh from another session with Steve Marshall. Marshall wasn't popular with her. Never had been and—since his little sicko revelation—he never would be. Sylvia had lost grandchildren in the WHATEVER-THE-FUCK-HAD-HAPPENED. When word spread about what Steve Marshall had been up to with his child (the actual details of the story taking a few twists and turns along the way) he become some kind of paedophile. Worse, even. Sylvia had been right about him all along.

Yet, were Sylvia to be completely honest with herself, the Marshall incident was more of a shocking reminder of what had happened to her, of what had been snatched from her, and how very sorrowful that made her feel.

With everyone in the community caught in some kind of trance, busying themselves with the very basics of survival in order to forget or detach themselves from what they lost, a stunt like Marshall's seemed all the more grotesque. They had endured their time of grief, comforting and consoling each other that first day, and daily for the ensuing week. They had exorcised those demons in a very tidy way, no one spilling more tears than were absolutely necessary. No shredding of raiment or gnashing of teeth. But now that time was past. The box was ticked, and they owed it to themselves, and the human race in general, to rise from the ashes. They needed to build something from which society could grow, and they needed to do it sooner rather than later. It was as simple as that.

However, like some form of fungus thriving in their very dampness, Steve Marshall's tears threatened to seep through and destroy the necessary foundation that the school's community was built upon. The façade that everything was getting better, that death was behind them all now. That suffering was in the past, alongside mourning, the present being a time only for rebuilding. Grief had no place in that mindset, especially a grief so brutal. Marshall was a huge gaping hole in their plans. His rampant emotions needed locking away. The less the survivors saw of him, the better.

That was Sylvia's opinion and, so, was also the popular opinion.

And then there was the threat of Gibson, Marshall's long-suffering counsellor and sole ally. Sylvia watched him walk into the canteen, whistling nonchalantly to himself. She cursed under her breath as he spotted her.

"Hello, Sylvia," Gibson said, flashing a toothy, white smile.

"Alan," she replied, guardedly.

"So how's things in the kitchen? I'd say a lot easier now the cooker and fridge are up and running again."

Sylvia knew that the counsellor cared nothing about what went on in the kitchen. He was just trying to weasel his way into her good books, the way his type did.

"If only you had a microwave, eh?" he joked.

"We're grand with what we have," she replied, curtly. She poured herself a fresh cup of tea without offering Gibson any. It was as explicit a gesture in Ireland to show you didn't want someone around as a two-fingered salute would be everywhere else.

"I was wondering, Sylvia," Gibson began, still smiling, despite the frosty reception she was giving him, "would there be anything left I could eat? I was… er… busy, you see, and didn't get down…"

Sylvia looked sternly at the counsellor, her normally kind eyes hard and cold. "Sorry, Alan," she said, firmly. "There's nothing left, I'm afraid." She tried to force a smile, failing.

She watched Gibson hold his gaze, eyes fixed on hers. If it were true that the eyes were a window to the soul, then hers were frosted glass. There was no mellowing. She had locked him out and thrown away the keys. And good riddance, too.

Your days are numbered here, Mr. Gibson.

Sylvia was the provider for the group. The hunter-gatherer. Everyone trusted her, and she nurtured them in return for their trust. Such an arrangement wasn't likely to work in the favour of Gibson or Marshall. No one would be willing to break away from the security of the group in a world just riddled with insecurity. No one would be prepared to bite the hand that fed them. Sylvia knew all that. In fact, she had planned for all that.

She watched Gibson stand up from the table, smiling. "I'm sure I can make do with some chocolate and crisps," he said, nodding amicably before turning to walk away. Her frosty glance followed him.

Once he exited the canteen, Aida Hussein and Peter Stokenbergs gingerly approached. They had been hovering around, listening to the uneasy exchange as they wiped tables down and collected dirty dishes. Neither of them wanted to get involved, yet still they listened in on every word that had been said. It was as close to a soap opera as the survivors would get in the post-television world.

"Are you okay?" Aida asked, speaking first.

"Yes, pet," Sylvia replied, smiling warmly again. "Nothing to worry about."

"Did he mention the crazy man?" Peter asked. He stood awkwardly, his apron seeming far too small for him. His hands were full of dishes that he had been reluctant to carry into the kitchen, worried he might miss the gossip.

"No, sweetheart, he didn't," Sylvia said, looking into space. Even a reference to that Marshall man seemed to upset her.

She went to walk away, moving back into the kitchen, but then paused, turning again to the other two. Her face was rigid, her smile forced as if from an old photograph or painting.

"In the future..." she began, eyeing them both up poignantly, "I'll look after any food that's to be prepared for Steve Marshall."

"What do you mean?" Aida asked.

"Oh nothing, love," Sylvia replied, her smile still holding. "Just may be best that I take care of his food, though. You don't mind, do you?"

It was a threat in disguise, and they both knew it. They knew too that were anyone to object to this rather ominous plan, it wouldn't be long until they, too, were ignored and shunned the way Gibson so very obviously was.

Aida wasn't ready for that kind of treatment. Not again. Being a Muslim in Northern Ireland had been challenging. She had put up with racial insults and graffiti being sprayed on her house. Stones being thrown at her children. Strange looks and sniggers whenever she walked down the street in traditional dress. Although young and beautiful, Aida knew what it was like to be isolated, and she sure as hell didn't want to feel that way again. Not now. Not when she had so many other feelings to get used to. Like grief. Fear. Loss. (*Guilt?*) Rejection. Being made to feel so welcome, now, was a refreshing novelty that Aida wasn't ready to give up, regardless of the price to others. In this new, dangerous age, she had no problem justifying that to herself. But she didn't have to like it.

"Okay." She smiled back at Sylvia, sighing. "I'll make sure to give Mr Gibson the food you prepare for Mr. Marshall."

"Great!" Sylvia beamed, as if they'd just decided to organise a party rather than conspired to poison a man to death. "That's it settled, then."

They both turned, eyes finding the clock on the canteen wall. There wasn't much time left until they had to get things started for dinner. There were things needing doing.

...

"Fucking A, man!" Barry laughed, his eyes bloodshot. "Where the fuck did you score this from?"

Star smiled, carefully cutting the mass of white powder into lines on the elaborate grand piano in The Europa Hotel's main bar. Nearby, ex-DJ, Sean Magee, was getting the rounds in, pillaging a well-stocked bar to complete his order.

"Geez, girl," he mumbled upon catching sight of almost a grand's worth of cocaine being spread out on the piano. "You kept that little find a secret, didn't you?"

"Just waiting for the right time," Star murmured, her hand continuing to draw out perfectly straight lines of snort with a credit card maxed-out to its limit in the old-world, but still nifty for cutting lines in the new.

Since the two guys had shown up, debauchery had become the norm, the three revellers sticking their drug-addled and booze-fuelled fingers up to the stoical, dead world. As the days turned into weeks, conversation moved through grief at what was lost, finally reaching the coke-spiked nonchalance of what the three *wouldn't* miss about the old world.

"That *Raining Men* song," Star said, first to address the question. "You know that one that every girl jumps up to when it's played at weddings?" She ran a little coke under her lips, spoiling one of her perfectly cut lines. "I'll not miss that shit."

"I hear you, girl."

It was Barry Rogan speaking. Sliding by her, he filled his nostril with a line of white. Star watched his eyelids quiver as he took a moment to enjoy the hit.

"And if ever I tried pulling any of those bitches, they would look at me as if I was a piece of shit."

"You *are* a piece of shit, Barry," Star sneered, smiling wryly, pushing him away from the coke.

"Fuck you, Ellen," Barry retorted.

"I used to play that song," Sean muttered, pulling his seat closer. "Hen parties and divorce parties. I kid you not. They lapped it up in equal measure."

"What about you, Sean? What will you not miss?" Star asked.

Moonlight spilled through the windows near the grand piano, casting the DJ a fairly pleasant profile in the shadows. He may have been old enough to be her dad, but he still had that twinkle in his eye that veterans like him seemed reluctant to give up.

"Elvis."

"What? Elvis is dead!" Barry laughed. He made his way back over to the coke.

"Go easy on the snort, tiger," Star reprimanded. She was starting to regret sharing this with him..

"He may be dead," Sean pondered, "but fuck me, he roams free in the hearts of many music listeners. Me? I always hated him. Sounds like a fucking warthog on speed." He guzzled almost half a pint of beer then burped loudly. "And those fucking jumpsuits… What were they all about?! Did he think he was some kind of fucking super hero or something?!"

That one really tickled Star. She almost choked with laughter, stumbling back into one of the bar's chairs. Her nose was raw from snorting, and she could feel a nose bleed coming on. She dabbed it with a napkin that she retrieved from a nearby table, noting the red spots on the soft white paper. Yet the familiar confidence that the coke afforded her was welcome. She lounged back in her chair before scrunching up then discarding the bloody napkin, lobbing it behind her back. They were having a good time tonight. She felt happy. Content.

From where she sat by the window, the city of Belfast could be seen sprawling across the horizon, splashes of moonlight teasing with shadowy glimpses of its dirty secret of death. The Rain continued its nightly assault.

Her mood darkened, suddenly.

She recalled the dealer's bedroom she'd broken into in order to get the coke. The stench of the corpse was almost unbearable. Star tried in vain not to breathe as she stepped into the apartment, unable to blot out the first glimpse of the greasy son of a bitch, half in bed, half out of it, calloused hands no doubt reaching for the burnt-out spliff, lingering precariously on a large mosaic ashtray by his bedside. Flies had flocked around his body, seeking out new patches of rancid flesh to pick at. Shit had slipped out of the man's bowels, seeping through his boxer shorts onto his jaundiced bed sheets, creating a collage of colour and texture so foul that Star was forced to take a moment to puke over his carpet. She pushed back a thought that hundreds of residents, equally decrepit, remained within the city. Some on the streets, most in their beds, rotting obnoxiously like some kind of fucking hors d'oeuvre for the cold, deathly main course of Autumn.

But then there were the bodies that didn't seem to be rotting. The bodies that seemed as fresh as the day they had fallen. Perhaps fresher. Those ones really freaked Star out. She hadn't mentioned them to any of the others, but she knew she hadn't been the only one to notice them. Truth be told, Star reckoned that the things that didn't click, the bizarre subtleties that came with the territory of watching everyone around you suddenly drop dead, were ignored. It was as if some great hypnotism had been performed on the few remaining survivors, wiping out any ounce of shock or awe. Nothing could top what they had gone through. No loss could better the loss they had already suffered. Everything else, whether the fiery preaching at the Victoria Centre or the fresh, perfumed dead lying on the streets, was mere detail to their desolation. Perhaps forming a queue in their post-traumatic brains, behind the very real despair of the current situation. It was the only way to survive now.

"The thing I definitely won't miss," Sean said, "is trying so damn hard to make up for all the fuck-ups in my life."

Barry said nothing. Star, now back at the piano, paused in the middle of squaring up more lines of coke. She looked at the forlorn DJ as if surprised. They had both, no doubt, been expecting Sean's usual meandering grief about his ex-wife. They hadn't expected a soundbite like that, one which touched them both in different ways, yet on an equally profound level.

For Star, the effort of trying to define herself all the time, a constant struggle in days gone by, was pointless in the new world. She'd been freed of it. It was as if this realisation formed one small needle of hope within this new, chaotic haystack of hopelessness.

For Barry, the sins of the past seemed very far away now. Irrelevant. It was as if he had been given a clean slate. He was in the company of people he could trust and didn't want to take advantage of. People he could talk to, without being judged. And, hell, good Mother Nature had fucked over more women in the last weeks than he had even seen in his life, never mind—

Raped?

No. that was all behind him now.

For a few long, quiet minutes, no one spoke. In the sparse hotel bar, the three revellers' slurping of booze and exhaling of smoke was the most that could be heard, the odd cough and wheeze suggesting more decadence than was healthy. Through the perfectly pale silence of the summer night, another sound could be heard, that of drug-curdled daydreaming echoing around the forever-buzzing ears of the stoned threesome. The wind howled angrily before quietening. And in the bliss of that shared feeling, they sat comfortably together, each of them reflecting on days gone by. Days no longer relevant.

Within those pure moments, each of the three, together, remembered the world for all it was. A bittersweet cocktail of making do and making out. A paddling pool of piss and bliss, for all of mankind to dip their fingers into. And for that short time, none of them wanted to be back in there, kicking and splashing amongst the good and the bad, carving out an existence that made a lot less sense, somehow, than drinking and snorting coke in an empty hotel bar.

Star quietly flicked open the grand piano's lid. She had played well since she was a child, music being the only thing other than art that she ever excelled at. In the gentle chill of the evening, she ran her nimble fingers up and down the keys of the piano. She played elegantly for a girl so severe-looking, smiling in an almost lady-like manner as she poured her narcotic-enhanced emotion into a few gentle jazz numbers.

For another few minutes, she played, Sean sipping on yet another drink, whistling along with the sweet piano notes, Barry tapping his foot peacefully.

Outside, The Rain sang along.

SIX

As the rain beat upon his window, Herb sat back in his chair, listening to what the English voice from his Amateur Radio was saying to him. A tear formed in his eye, leading him to remove his spectacles, wipe his eye with his handkerchief (ironed to perfection by Muriel) then place them back on the end of his nose. The voice was telling him that the world had changed on that fateful Sunday morning, some weeks ago. It spoke so clearly and matter-of-factly, and Herb thought, for a moment, that it was all some sick joke. Finally, it stopped and the fuzz of the radio returned.

Herb sat motionless, considering everything that had been said to him. He knew it made sense. The streetlights outside his rural, Ballyclare home hadn't been working. No television broadcasts. No postman calling or any noise of activity outside. The world was dead, and to any other man, apart from Herb, it would have been very obvious.

He picked up the mic. "I asked you what your name was, sir. I don't believe you gave it to me."

Pzzt. "Terry. My name is Terry, and you, Professor Matthews, are the first Irishman I've made contact with through the radio." *Pzzt.*

"And where are you based, Terry?"

Pzzt. "We're at a small airfield just outside of Manchester." *Pzzt.*

"You said 'we', Terry. How many of you are there?"

Pzzt. "Ten in total. We have a couple of pilots, a few doctors and some others. Is there anyone with you, Professor?" *Pzzzt.*

Herb turned slowly to the armchair behind him. Muriel remained there, still wearing her best shoes—the ones that Herb put on her feet all those weeks ago. Perhaps it was because he was now talking to the living, but Herb was looking at her, now, in a different light. He didn't know why it hadn't been obvious to a man of his intelligence that she was, in some way, different than your average dead body. But then again, Herb wasn't accustomed to seeing any bodies, in recent years, dead or alive. The shock of finding Muriel like that was extensive. Herb could only surmise that his mind wasn't up to the feat of dwelling on much of anything since he'd climbed out of bed that Sunday.

Pzzt. "Professor?" *Pzzt.*

Herb didn't answer. Instead he stood up, steadying himself by leaning on his desk chair, before making his way to the armchair near where Muriel still sat. Her eyes remained fixed, as usual, on the television across the room, oblivious to the fact that it hadn't broadcast anything in weeks. Herb sat on the edge of the armchair, removing his spectacles as if about to kiss her. He ran a finger across her face, noticing how soft the skin remained. His other hand ruffled her hair a little, his ailing eyes straining to work out what colour it was. It seemed darker than he remembered, and so Herb wondered, for a moment, if she had started dyeing it in recent years without his noticing. He got up, standing back to study Muriel's face against the light beaming in through the front room window. He noticed a framed picture on the mantelpiece, taken many years ago. It was a picture of Muriel at Blackpool pier, taken on their honeymoon. Herb retrieved the picture, looking at it, and then Muriel, in comparison. She always seemed beautiful to him, but in those days she had been a knock-out. Her long, dark hair framed a heart-shaped face. Her eyes were so pale Herb almost felt himself swimming in their gaze. Her lips were full of colour and life, and he remembered, again, the first time he had kissed them.

Herb looked at her now, lying on the armchair, slowly realising how much the Muriel there seemed to resemble the Muriel in the picture taken thirty years ago.

Pzzt. "Professor? You still there? I was asking if there was anyone else with you." *Pzzt.*

Herb returned slowly to his desk, picking up the radio mic with one shaking hand, his other still holding the picture.

"My wife, Muriel, is with me," he began, bafflement and shock creeping slowly into his voice. "She… she was one of the ones who had fallen, yet I wasn't… er… in a position to bury her."

Herb paused for a moment as he choked back the tears. He could hear the rain scraping against the windows and it sounded grotesque to him all of a sudden.

"Terry, I think something's not quite right about her…"

…

The rain beat upon the windows of the canteen, blurring Aida's view of outside. She was glad of that. She wasn't quite sure why no one else in the canteen found what she was watching shocking, but they didn't. A few stragglers for dinner quietly worked away at their food. Sylvia Patterson and Peter Stokenbergs, washing the dishes in the kitchen next door, were laughing together, sharing jokes. Flirting, even. But Aida couldn't ignore what was going on. It seemed all too familiar to her, all too tangible.

Roy Beggs and his two cohorts, Trevor Steele and John McElroy surrounded another man on the football field, the fourth man on his knees, visibly upset and frightened. The three lawmakers each held guns, Roy's slung around his shoulder as he read from a piece of paper, fighting against the rain to be heard. Aida couldn't make out his words, but it seemed he was reading some kind of declaration, a prelude to whatever justice had been decided upon. She recognised the man on his knees. He was particularly known to the others in the canteen, having been caught stealing food by Sylvia herself, earlier on in the day.

As Aida watched, the man tried to climb to his feet and get away. But McElroy was quicker, tripping him up and then bringing the butt of his rifle down on the man's head.

Roy Beggs responded by pocketing the piece of paper, then closing in to sink his boot into the felled man as he lay on the ground, trying to cover his face. All three of the armed men did likewise, Aida terrified as she watched the brutal display escalate, the eyes of the three men wide and angry as they continued to deal out their justice.

She had seen this kind of thing before. Only then, it had been her husband she was watching through the window, caught doing nothing more than coming home from work by a gang of youths. They had berated him with racist slurs, spitting at him as he walked past in the street, trying to ignore them. One of them grabbed his coat, dragging him into their company, circling then tearing into him like a vicious pack of dogs.

All she had been able to do then, as now, was to watch on, terrified.

Finally, they stopped, Roy Beggs pulling McElroy away as he went in for one final boot. They left the man, wounded and perhaps unconscious, lying in the wet grass, and returned through the rain towards the school. Aida watched John McElroy as he sought shelter from his cupped hands to light up a cigarette. She could hear Sylvia's laugh from the kitchen, loud and bellowing as Peter continued with some humorous story.

This isn't right, she thought to herself.

...

Tim sat in the corner, gazing out through the hotel bedroom window. It was raining. The curtain was mostly closed, save for a slim gap between the corner of the window and wall. Tim shivered as a breeze blew in some random raindrops, his naked skin perhaps creeping against both the chill of the night air and the shame of his flat, useless cock cradled, like a baby, in his clammy hands.

"It's okay, Tim," Caz said from the bed in the middle of the room.

It was a clichéd thing to say, and she knew it. Truth was, this was meant to be her first time too, and she was every bit as nervous as Tim seemed to be. She knew that what she'd seen in the movies and on TV was not what it would be like in real life. She knew it from magazines, graduating from the teeny-bop 'position of the fortnight' features to Cosmo's frank and open discussion of the many, many things that could go wrong when a man and woman got down to it. But none of that made it easier to hide her disappointment.

Tim said nothing. From where Caz was sitting, the poor evening light gave him an almost ethereal look. His long, slender back was topped with a curled neck as his head bowed in the corner of the room. He looked like someone had told him off and put him in the corner for being naughty. He seemed almost dead, the only sign of life being his gentle yet constant shivering. Raindrops continued to blow in on him, sprinkling his pure, white skin like a handful of diamonds. In a way, Tim looked more beautiful to Caz than ever.

She wanted to tell him that, but couldn't think of any words that sounded right.

"Tim," she called.

He didn't even hear her. Inside his head were shadows, similar shadows to the ones cast over him whenever his dad would have come in to visit him at night, towering over his bed like a dark cliff. Tim smelt that same stench of whiskey from all those years ago, drifting gently in from the rain-swept night. The curtain caressed his back, swaying with the wind, its touch reminding him of that first experience of sex, the first of too many nights, when he tried to feign sleep to escape those bittersweet touches. He could hear his father's whisper, whimpering apologies for something he couldn't understand. He heard it whistling in the dark-stained wind of night. Tim pulled his legs closer to his chest, suddenly aware of how naked and exposed he was.

Caz watched as the candle they'd lit earlier, a feeble attempt at creating the serenity they both needed to make the evening of Caz's seventeenth birthday (she had lied—she was still just sixteen) special, fought bravely against the cold, damp night air before snuffing out. The darkness, The Silence, was suddenly unbearable. Quietly, she got up from the bed, the room having been chosen specially, due to its particularly ornate-looking bedposts, and tip-toed over to where Tim was. She covered him with the bed sheets, drawing in close beside him as she wrapped him up.

It was a good touch.

"I want to know what you're thinking, Tim."

"I know… but it's... like… difficult."

"Everything's difficult now, Tim… Difficult for all of us."

She knew it was the wrong thing to say even as she said it. In response, she could feel him withdraw, physically.

Yet she persisted, pulling him closer, hoping to bring Tim back from wherever he disappeared to whenever she seemed to reach for him. It was as if squeezing him tighter would stop him from spilling away from her, keep their connection watertight.

"Things happened… a long time ago… I don't want to talk about it."

She noticed him pause. It was as if he were worried that the tears pent up in his stinging eyes might suddenly gush out.

"But, I might need more time to get … you know… used to us being together, before… before we can do any more of what we were doing tonight."

She stroked his hair gently as he talked, ready to withdraw if she felt him tense. He didn't, instead slowly leaning his head into her hand.

This, too, was a good touch.

"I need… more of this, I think."

"I know. Me too," she whispered.

It was imagined peer pressure alone that had made her rush things. She felt, at sixteen, that she should make that transition from girl to woman, go down that clichéd road that every coming-of-age chick-flick told her she needed to take. She'd even lied to make it happen. She was suddenly very ashamed of herself. Bowing to peer pressure in a world without peers. Caz couldn't believe how ridiculous that was.

"We've all the time in the world," she comforted. "What else can we do now, apart from spend time together?"

Tim looked around, showing his face for the first time to her in over an hour. In the shadows, he looked even more angelic to her than ever. Light freckles were silhouetted against his pure skin. A faint peppering of stubble made him look a little more mature than his sixteen years. His shiny blue eyes shone like pearls. His innocence, his vulnerability hung like a wide open door. He was absolutely beautiful to her.

"I... love you, Caroline," he said suddenly. The words were both loud and soft, like the wind and rain outside.

Caz felt a sudden warmth flow through her body. It was what she expected an orgasm might feel like. A real orgasm, from sex, as opposed to her own hand. A sudden, euphoric, all consuming heat. A reassurance that everything, even for a moment, was completely and utterly perfect.

She felt for the small chain around her neck with the silver crucifix. Carefully, she took it off. Carefully she reached towards Tim, attaching the chain around his neck.

"My mum gave it to me," she said. "She wasn't religious or anything... it just reminded her to keep going, even when things weren't very good."

Tim looked at the figurine of Jesus clinging to the cross. He ran a single finger over the small silver torso, his mind seeming busy with the emotions conjured up by the imagery.

He looked at Caz, smiling weakly. "Faith, hope and love..." he whispered, as much to himself as to Caz.

There was a brief silence between them. Tim's eyes glimmered in the pale moonlight, damp with raindrops and bittersweet emotion. The breeze blew playfully through his hair, several strands catching on the newly-acquired chain around his neck. Silver Jesus remained suitably poised. He moved towards her. She thought, for a moment, that they might kiss.

But then they heard the explosion.

SEVEN

As time went by, each survivor at the school in Lisburn found themselves able to move away from the quiet comfort of the shared assembly hall dormitory and set up their own quarters in small classrooms. Some of the group still chose to share, shacking up with new partners, rushing passionately into fresh and desperate relationships that were more to do with insecurity than love or romance. For others, sharing was not sexual. It was simply because they were afraid to sleep without the presence of someone else. And then there was Alan Gibson. Although he would have preferred to sleep alone, the counsellor chose to bunk up with Steve Marshall, regardless of the man's mental health, lack of personal hygiene, and the ever-present stench that such encouraged within his 'cell.'

Gibson chose to bunk there for a variety of reasons. First of all, he figured that he could spend more time studying Marshall's habits. As a keen practitioner of cognitive behavioural therapy, Gibson hoped that being able to study the actions and words that Marshall seemed to repeat could help him get to the root of his problems, hopefully speeding up the man's mental recovery. Secondly, with Marshall's physical condition having improved a little (he was starting to eat again and seemed to sleep better at nights) Gibson thought that maybe this public gesture of sharing with the man might encourage others in the group to take an interest in him. In time, people might realise that he posed no threat to them, no danger to their stability. Maybe some of the leaders, even, like Roy and Sylvia, might become less insistent that he stayed locked up.

Out of sight, out of mind.

Thirdly, and a little more pessimistically than the other reasons, Gibson was beginning to fear for both his and Steve Marshall's safety. He had been sidelined almost as much as Marshall, of late, noticing how the whispers stopped as he walked by a group of people talking or wandered into the canteen for lunch. It was as if he too were possessed by the same demon they thought Steve Marshall to be possessed of. As if he too had nurtured a rotting corpse of a child in his arms, a cruel and visceral reminder to all whose loved ones remained somewhere else, unburied and unattended to. It was as if everything that had happened was Alan Gibson's fault as well as Steve Marshall's. Gibson valued the fact that he had the key to Marshall's classroom and took the time to lock up each night. He could deal with their victimisation when he was awake, and able to keep both eyes open. But he sure as hell wasn't going to sleep unsecured.

This was confirmed to him as more than simple paranoia whenever Aida Hussein approached him one evening before bedtime. There were fewer survivors around, most of them having retired to their classroom quarters for the night. A faint light still spilled out of the canteen, several doors down the corridor from Marshall's room, and it was to this light that Aida kept looking, as if fearful someone might open that door. She caught Gibson just as he was about to lock his classroom up for the evening.

"Mr. Gibson," she whispered, glancing towards the sleeping Marshall behind the ajar door.

"Yes?" Gibson replied, cautiously.

"You have to leave now. Take *him* with you. It's not safe."

Hearing a sound up the corridor, Aida turned quickly, her eyes searching, her ears listening.

"What do you—"

"Leave!" Aida barked. She turned again to see whether anyone was coming. "Leave now. And don't let *that man* eat any more food."

She said 'that man' with a mixture of revulsion and pity in her voice. It was as if she wanted to help Steve Marshall but either felt too scared of him, or too worried about the consequences of doing so. Maybe both.

"What's wrong with the food?!" Gibson called after her, somewhere between a raised whisper and a shout. But Aida continued down the corridor, back to the canteen, without looking back. Gibson cast an eye over towards the oblivious Steve Marshall. He looked to one of the desks, where Marshall's plate rested. He had meant to carry it up to the canteen after supper but forgot. Carefully, using a fork, he scraped in between the remnants of food left. It was some kind of cheese dish. Most of the cheese left was now hardened onto the plate, drying up like chalk. As he continued his investigation, Steve Marshall paying him absolutely no attention from the other side of the room, Gibson noticed what looked like a peculiar red powder faintly blended in with the food. It could have been chili pepper, maybe.

Putting Steve's plate down, Gibson picked up his own and compared the two. There was no powder on his. And, now that he thought about it, the cheese macaroni (or whatever the hell it had been) had been distinctly bland tasting. In fact, Gibson remembered splashing more than the usual amount of pepper to liven it up a little.

Gibson sat down on one of the small chairs in the classroom, taking his glasses off and setting them on the desk. He ran one hand through his thinning hair.

"Oh, Steve," he sighed, casting a glance over to his dazed patient.

From a corridor nearby, standing by the door to her own classroom which she shared with the groups' youngest, Clare McAfee, Mairead Burns listened intently. She watched Aida open the door to the canteen and slip quietly inside. Now she rubbed her eyes, allowing her hands to drop down her face and form a prayer-like shape over her lips. She had heard everything that had been said. And it worried her.

EIGHT

It wasn't as if explosions were something unheard of in Belfast. Quite the opposite. Almost all of the survivors could remember at least once, before the shit hit the fan, whenever a bomb blast near them rocked the foundations of their home, spilling neighbours onto the streets. Some had lost relatives, friends, or colleagues to the so-called Troubles; many had been innocent bystanders or even cases of mistaken identities. The Omagh bomb in the late nineties, a horrific and ruthless massacre of unbelievable proportion, was the most recent bomb blast any of them could remember. It was also the most senseless.

For those currently resident in the Europa, this latest blast, seeming to come from somewhere north of the city centre, was particularly poignant. Barry, Star, Sean and the two teenagers were staying in the most bombed hotel in Europe. Its four walls had enjoyed many a reworking over the years, shaken by more than its fair share of explosions.

For The Preacher Man and his sombre band of followers, this most recent blast was but a war-cry of the promised return of the Heavenly Host that they prayed for so fervently. Their almost hallucinogenic state, massaged daily by prayer/song/preaching, could see little other than signs and talismans, miracles and curses within the empty, soulless streets of Belfast. Even an explosion, brutal and devastating, with all the trademark, telltale signs of the gritty struggle of days gone by, now took on a more priestly countenance.

Yet, for those cowering in the shadows, the monosyllabic majority, the explosion was but another reason to remain quiet, hidden and alone.

It was just shy of 4.00am when the red-yellow light burst through the navy, pre-dawn skyline, and Barry Rogan was the first of the Europa survivors to wake. He had fallen asleep where he sat, still at the bar table, the smell of cigarettes and booze heavy in the air like mist. Sean stirred next, his messy shambles of a head jolting upright. He had fallen asleep as he did most nights, in the same chair, at the same table, by the same window, glass or bottle toppled nearby, fierce hangover pending. His eyes popped open, a short, nervous gasp escaping from his mouth.

"*Shhhhh*," Barry motioned to him, one finger over his lips. "I'm trying to work out where it came from."

Sean took a while to gather his senses. His heart was going like the hammers. His whole body ached. These seats weren't for sleeping in.

"What the hell was it?" he asked.

Barry shushed him again then whispered, "An explosion of some sort..."

"Where do you reckon it came from?" Star asked, pulling herself up from behind the grand piano. Eyeliner smeared down her gaunt cheeks like tears of ink.

"North, I reckon," Barry said.

His head was bent slightly to one side, ears listening intently to the slight reverberations.

The two teenagers entered the bar, joining the others, all of them suddenly brought together.

"Looks like a bomb went off out there," Caz said, stating the obvious.

She spoke in a low voice, as if worried that someone might find out where they were, too, and bomb them. Her glasses were clouded up. She took them off to clean the lenses, revealing her beautiful, China doll eyes. She was getting on like a kid at a firework display, excited by noise, dazzled by light. In sharp contrast, her boyfriend looked shaken, constantly running the finger and thumb of one hand over a silver crucifix around his neck. His eyes glazed over, as if he were drugged. He moved towards the front window, looking out onto Great Victoria Street. There he stood, fiddling with the cross, seemingly mesmerised by whatever caught his eye.

"Did you see where it came from?" Barry asked Caz.

"That direction," she replied, pointing north. "You can still see the smoke. It's so black."

Star was now at the window, standing next to Tim.

Sean joined them, following their gaze. On the street, he could make out a lone figure, tall and formidable-looking, one of the shadow people, maybe, or one of those religious nuts from the Victoria Centre.

"Are you alright?" It was Star speaking. She placed one hand on Tim's shoulder.

The two of them seemed to have bonded, of late, over a mutual interest in tattooing. Star the teacher, Tim her student. But Caz didn't seem so happy about this. Sean felt a bad vibe from her. The tattoo sessions. The things she had no interest in and couldn't even feign an interest in. It was like Tim and Star had formed their own little exclusive club, and Sean could see how that might cause problems.

He thought, again, of his Sharon. How he felt on seeing new family pictures dotted around the house he used to share with her. Pictures without him. The decor she had chosen changing so dramatically. There was a different dynamic between Sharon and her new partner, just like the dynamic between Star and Tim.

To see that had to hurt.

It didn't matter that Star's motives were far from romantic. This would be alien to Caz. Even if she did notice Tim's unnerving look, a look so pungent that it almost felt as if he might pop off, like a cork from a bottle, it would still hurt to see him sharing it with Star.

Barry joined them by the hotel bar's window, straining to look as far left as the glass would allow.

"Fuck me," he muttered. "That's gotta be something big that's just went up."

...

The Preacher Man stepped out onto Great Victoria Street. From his pocket, he took out a small brown bottle, bringing its contents to his lips, slowly and awkwardly, like a first kiss. He sniffed it first, reassuring himself that whiskey still smelled just how he remembered, just like it did all those years before he had found The Lord. Then he drained it half dry in one swift and fluid motion. A warm rush of relief washed through his tense, sober body, giving sweet release from the pressures of leading his flock, the pressures of preparing for the coming of his Saviour. He looked up, catching sight of the candles burning from the nearby hotel bar. Inside, no doubt, he would find more souls. More people to lead to The Lord. More converts to his congregation.

(And more temptations of the flesh.)

"Forgive me, Lord," he muttered, violently ashamed of himself.

He smashed the whiskey bottle in his hand against the side of a wall, bringing the jagged edges of the broken bottleneck against his face as if to slice the evil out of himself. He stood poised, staring at the lethal, sliced glass, eyes fiercely wide, hand shaking with frozen momentum. He moved the bottle to his hand, slicing a clean line across his palm, grimacing with the pain, sharply drawing in air as the glass dragged across his skin. When the line reached his wrist, he stopped, pulling the glass away, breathing out in relief as the blood was released from the wound. His heart was racing, but a familiar swell of relief filled his chest. He dropped the bottle.

"Be merciful to me, Lord," he muttered. "Be merciful to me, a sinner."

...

The world seemed even quieter after the explosion. The sudden and dramatic sound was a reminder of how loud and obnoxious the world used to be before The Great Silence. For Star, it had been a sudden jolt to her heart—a call out from the wild saying '*remember what it was like to be alive?*' It injected her with inspiration, and she felt a desperate need to tattoo.

The others had drifted off to sleep, finding themselves their own rooms within the hollow-bellied husk that used to be Belfast's busiest hotel. Caz and Tim had shrunk from sight first, followed by a hungover Sean Magee. Finally Barry Rogan, pausing long enough to steady himself with a swift shot of whisky, disappeared off to bed, his furrowed brow still, no doubt, pondering the mysteries of where the fuck that bomb/plane/nuclear meltdown had occurred.

Star waited a while, drinking up the inspiration that The Silence and The Rain had to offer her before pulling herself out of the empty bar and making her way down to her makeshift studio in the bus station next door.

She switched on the generator. The old thing whirred into action, its flickering light struggling to illuminate the otherwise black mass of tiled floor and sterile-looking seating. A gentle hum assured Star that the generator might just hang in there in order for her to grab another stodgy coffee from the machine, but she sure as hell wasn't going to rely on it to power up her needle.

Pulling up the old stool she had recently nabbed from her shop downtown, along with all of her other stuff, Star began the arduous process of unpacking her gear and connecting the powerpack to the car battery with a couple of leads. Once happy that the power was humming through, Star linked the whole lot up to her foot pedal and clip cord, clicking on/off to make sure everything was working okay. Only then did she click her beautiful girl into place—the old custom-made machine that had been passed down to her by the old-school tattooist who'd taught her everything she knew. Her mind drifted back to those days, a time when she knew where she was going. Just before the drugs and the booze took over, and her art was relegated to third place. She'd done some less-than-great tattoos when she was learning the ropes, yet nothing she would say she was ashamed of. As an artist, she'd grown over the years, honing a particular fondness for tribal tattoos, then black and grey, before revisiting the boldness of old school and graffiti-style tattooing. As a businesswoman, Star moved with the times and trends, with what people were asking her for. That suited her just fine. She always loved a challenge.

Star was just finishing up her preparations when she heard movement by the door nearest to her. A quick look around revealed Tim Adamson, his head hung low as if he were late for school.

"Hey," Star muttered, half-heartedly.

"Hey," came a similarly lack-lustre reply. "What's going on?"

Star looked up at the lad, a smirk spreading across her face. "I'm having a bath," she mocked. "What does it look like?"

He managed a smile, but Star could see almost immediately that Tim was less than on form for her quips.

"Can I help?" he asked, looking more bashful than she'd ever seen him.

He was a moody lad; that much Star had noticed. Until tonight, she would have put that down to his teenage years. And, hell, what human being was going to be all sweetness and light after the whole fucking world fell apart? But as he spoke, she saw something more sinister going on in his head. The vibes coming off him could have roasted heaven. He was here for a reason, Star realised. Here to cull the demons from within.

Star could relate to that.

"Tell you what, go and grab me some of that fake skin we were working on earlier. I'm guessing your arms need a break after all the action they've seen."

Tim looked down at his arms. Where there had once been untouched flesh, a chaotic ensemble of ink now resided. His lily-white skin developed into altogether more eclectic sleeves, featuring contemporary old school blending into graffiti-style colouring. Star was quite proud of what she'd achieved, albeit outrageously unique for a lad's first ink.

Tim moved as if to make for the two travel cases where Star kept all of her gear from the shop. Then he stopped, dead, as if he were some kind of puppet sent in another direction by an invisible string. As Star watched, he made his way back outside the station. In the poor, pre-dawn light, he moved through The Rain towards the boneyard, where all of the bodies had been dumped that very first day. He unwrapped the pile of bodies, perusing the makeshift grave like a kid in a candy store, before reaching in. His tall, lean frame strained against the weight of his chosen prey as he began the laborious and shocking process of dragging the body of a young girl out of the pile and across the tarmac, back into the station.

He presented the body to Star, like a cat with a bird. The Rain, although paling, had spat all over both him and the body dumped on the floor.

"This one looks good," he said, fighting to regain his breath after the exertion. "I want to work on this one."

NINE

At precisely 4.30am, Alan Gibson found himself on the school football field looking down the barrel of Roy Beggs' assault rifle.

It was John McElroy who had stopped Gibson at the school's gate as he tried to bundle a doped-up Steve Marshall into Roy's Land Rover. Gibson had stolen the keys from the soldier's bag when he wasn't looking. He might have been in with a chance of slipping past the dozing sentry, were it not for Marshall's boisterous behaviour. Rudely awakened, McElroy wasted no time in calling Roy Beggs on his two-way radio.

All kinds of thoughts raced through Gibson's head as he stood there, poised like a deer in headlights. He thought of escape. Simply running for it, leaving Marshall behind to whatever fate was in store for him. But that was cowardly, and he knew it. He then looked to the Land Rover, wondering if he could simply overpower his opponent and make a dash for freedom, but with Marshall in tow, things were a little more complicated. Even if he himself made it to the Land Rover, somehow able to push aside the wiry but apparently trigger-happy McElroy, he knew that Steve Marshall, in his present doped-up state, would get easily—and mercilessly—gunned down.

Roy Beggs appeared, flanked by another two of his militia, the devoutly religious and equally bigoted Trevor Steele and a small, nervous-looking man named Pat Black. All three carried rifles, trained on Gibson and Marshall, as they walked towards them.

"I *told* you, Gibson," Roy said. "I warned you what would happen if you went against my orders and messed about with this freak."

"Orders?" Gibson replied, indignantly. "For Christ's sake, Roy! We're not *all* soldiers. This man's sick, and whatever you are putting in his food isn't helping matters any."

Roy looked baffled.

"Careful what you accuse me of, you self-righteous fuck."

Gibson flinched. He needed to choose his words more carefully. He was starting to see the cracks forming in Roy's psyche..

"I just think that if we leave, Roy, it'll be best for everyone. We'll leave on foot. We'll take Steve's car. What kind of threat are we to you then?"

But Roy didn't look convinced.

"You'll be shot of us," Gibson continued, trying desperately to sound convincing. "Out of sight and out of mind before dawn. You can get on with building this community, something that you're clearly very capable of doing."

"Don't patronise me," Roy said. He was no fool, and Gibson knew it..

Gibson noticed the other three watching Marshall closely. Reading them, he couldn't be sure if their nervousness would work for him or against him.

"We'll leave here. Go to Belfast," the counsellor appealed, looking to each of the men in turn.

But Roy was having none of it. "And what example will that set, eh? What happens if *everyone* decides to just do what they want?"

He pulled a piece of paper out of the pocket of his combats. He pointed at it, enthusiastically. As if it were holy, as if the crudely scribbled words were from God Himself.

"The law protects people, keeps them safe. If you reject it, you reject me. You reject this community," he said as if preaching. "I've a duty here, Gibson, a *legal* duty."

"We're not doing anything wrong, for Christ's sake!"

Gibson was losing his patience. He'd met a lot of unbalanced people through his line of work, but none of them had had a gun trained on him. .

"Stealing?! What do you call that, eh?" Roy was angry now. "If I let you away with that, how long before everyone's at it? And then comes the rape—the murder. When law breaks down, so too does society. Look at what happened when those fuckers from before decided they wanted to take our base. I've a responsibility to—"

But Roy was cut off when Marshall suddenly made a dash for the graves of his son and wife, lunging forward like a man suddenly possessed. He had been relatively still up until this point, standing with his nose high in the air and his eyes closed, like someone smelling freshly cut hay for the first time. The militia raised their rifles. They watched Marshall bolt past, scurrying like an excited animal, finally falling to his knees by the makeshift cross.

"Wake up!" he ranted, maniacally. "It's time to get up! Nicky! Time to get up!"

Gibson watched on in horror, open mouthed, as Marshall scratched and pulled at the earth, clawing to reach the body of his son. His eyes were wide and desperate, drool falling from his crooked smile, tears and snot running out of his eyes and nose. His hands and mouth attacked the black plastic wrapped crudely around the dead child, ripping and shredding until the boy's decrepit flesh became visible. He lifted the tiny corpse up like some kind of trophy. It looked for a moment like he was going to eat it.

From where he stood, Gibson could see what happened next very clearly. As Steve Marshall cradled the putrid bundle of flesh that used to be his son, that used to be his reason to get up in the morning, go to work during the day and come back home to at night, another hand, a hand with flesh still pale, lush and angelic, reached slowly towards him from the grave. It was the body of Marshall's wife, Kirsty. Gibson was sure of it.

Roy Beggs fired. The young man, once an easy-going accounting technician, shook briefly, then fell, a shower of blood escaping from his head. Still clutching the small, rotting body close to his face, his body slumped awkwardly against the wooden cross. The cross buckled from his weight, tangling up with the sorry mess that had become the Marshall family grave.

Gibson looked to Roy's eyes, finding guilt there. He noticed the soldier's hands shaking, making his rifle shake too. Roy turned to find everyone looking at him.

The small fists of the normally reserved counsellor clenched. "You bastard!" he spat, pent up rage turning his face purple."Damn you to hell!"

"You s-see?!" Roy said. Sweat was running down his forehead, meeting his moustache. Like a sponge, the small clump of greying hair became soaked, its moistness glistening in the emerging light.

"How can I trust you now, eh? You'll want revenge. You'll want to kill me now. Didn't I tell you!? That's how it all starts. One person goes doo-lally, and the whole fuckin' unit falls apart!"

Roy shook his head. Seemingly reluctant to do any more killing himself tonight, he gestured wordlessly to John McElroy to finish Gibson. McElroy's weapon rose, taking aim. His hands, too, were shaking, suggesting that whilst gung-ho when it came to talk, the son of a bitch was less forthcoming when it came to action. He kept looking at the grave as if he expected something to crawl from it—to come for him, like some old-school zombie flick. McElroy's eyes fixed on Gibson. Beads of sweat were breaking across his forehead like glitter.

Gibson closed his eyes.

A shot rang out...

...

Roy slowly looked up at Gibson, waiting for his body to fall, dead, to the ground. With horror, he realised that instead of Gibson's body crumpling, McElroy had dropped. He flinched as two more shots broke the quiet, Steele and Black crumpling to the ground in a similar fashion.

"You're next, Roy."

As Roy turned, his gaze was met by the familiar, cold stare of Mairead Burns. Her hand remained steady, measured, and undeniably straight as she pointed her handgun squarely at Roy's chest. She was a natural killer. Roy had seen it in her before. Now she stood in defiance against him, having killed three of his men in cold blood with the very weapon he had entrusted her with only weeks ago. Fuck knows why he'd let her keep the gun so long. He knew she would use it against him eventually. He knew that, especially in a lawless world, Mairead Burns, would turn against him.

Roy let his rifle drop slowly to the ground.

The bettered soldier stood obediently, his eyes moist, his body hunched over. Mairead had wasted no time in executing his men, and Roy failed to see any reason why she would hesitate when it came to putting a bullet in his head too—and he didn't want to die.

Gibson looked to Mairead for permission, before moving, slowly, to take Roy's rifle from him. The counsellor paused, briefly and vehemently, to spit in his face before turning his attention to the mess that was the Marshall grave.

It shocked Roy. He didn't think the soft bastard had it in him..

He watched Gibson walk across the patchy grass of the school grounds towards Steve Marshall's body. The counsellor shook his head regrettably on confirming his patient dead. He could see Marshall's body lying entangled with the rotting and worm-ridden corpse of his baby boy and the simple broken cross that marked the grave. The scene looked almost sacrilegious, a brutal and unholy desecration of a simple family grave.

Guilt rose up within Roy Beggs again.

He watched as Gibson did the best he could to tidy the grave before removing his coat and covering Steve's body..

"You going to kill me?" Roy asked, turning to look at Mairead.

Mairead smiled. Her gun was trained for a clean shot to his head.

She spat, "I'll not even try and pretend that I haven't wanted to do this since I met you."

Roy waited for the shot. His eyes were squeezed shut, and his heart was pumping.

Other survivors were starting to gather at the front entrance of the school, having no doubt heard the commotion. There were gasps and sudden cries as they saw the bodies, the graveside, the gun trained on Roy Beggs. The full horror of what was happening was dawning on them. It threatened their security. It tore at the thin web of deceit they had spun for themselves, reminding them that all was most certainly not well with the world. Mairead wouldn't care. She would shoot a man like Roy Beggs in full view of anyone.

But not in front of the child.

"Mummy!" Clare cried, still in her pyjamas, eyes red and puffed.

Roy watched as Mairead's face fell. She hadn't expected this, hadn't factored it into her plans.

"Clare, g-go to Mr. Gibson!" she shouted, as if angry with the child.

But Roy knew she was angry with herself.

Clare obeyed, running to Gibson.

Gibson, still trying to regain his own composure, threw one arm around her, consoling her as she wept. He dried his own eyes, removing his glasses with his free hand before soothing the distraught child.

"Keys to the Land Rover," Mairead growled to Roy.

"Gibson has them."

Mairead looked to Gibson, who confirmed this with a nervous nod.

"Okay, let's go," she said simply, backing towards the Land Rover whilst still keeping her pistol trained on the soldier.

His look said it all. Through the fear, anger was starting to rise within Roy Beggs' eyes. He knew Mairead sensed it. He would hunt them down. He wouldn't let the others see him bettered by her. It would upset his standing amongst the survivors at the school, challenging his authority, and that wouldn't sit well with the soldier.

Roy watched as the rebels climbed up into his Land Rover, the very vehicle with which he had rescued them some weeks back.

Too bloody soft, he thought to himself. *That's your problem, Beggs, too bloody soft.*

As the military vehicle pulled out, Mairead at its wheel, Roy turned back to the survivors gathered at the door. There they all were. Sylvia Patterson, the cook. Sarah Jenkins, the young student. Seamus Moran, the retired bank clerk from Lurgan. Aida Hussein, the Egyptian woman. All of them looking at him with fear and trepidation in their eyes.

And something else...

Pity.

TEN

It was still early, and most of the others, currently living between the Europa Hotel and the bus station, were still in bed. But not Barry. He was dragging the body of a young woman from a red Porsche that had stalled awkwardly on Great Victoria Street. Chris O'Hagan, a stunningly beautiful estate agent in life, looked almost as radiant in death, but Barry didn't pause to consider why that should be, mesmerised by the sheer divinity of not her body, but the ever-so-smooth body of her car. Its red, polished metal sparkled in the sun. Bold alloy wheels seemed to boast of its power, zero to sixty in mere seconds. A pull-down roof offered that oh-so-sweet feeling of wind through hair that a summer day demanded.

He noticed Caz watching him from the steps leading up to the station, nestling a glass of fruit juice in her hands.

"Fancy a spin, sweetheart?" he asked, straining to pull the corpse out of the vehicle's open door.

"You can't be serious," Caz replied, running an eye along the road where other cars lay sprinkled like breadcrumbs. "You'll get yourself killed if you speed up there."

"I know how to handle a car," Barry boasted, flashing Caz a flirtatious grin.

He noticed her blushing.

"Oh *pleeeeazzze*," she groaned. "Don't come crying to me if you get yourself mangled."

"Oh, come on," Barry egged. "If you can't live dangerously when the world's ended, when can you?!"

He searched inside the dashboard for the ignition. Grabbing the keys with a celebratory rattle, he smiled up at her.

"I'll go slow. I'm not a fast driver, anyway."

There was something within Barry Rogan that drew the mischief out of anyone he met. And he knew it, too. He also knew that it wouldn't take much of his well-stocked charm to convince little-miss-pious to walk on the wild side. Behind those glasses, he could see her baby blue eyes just begging to be convinced.

"Get the wind in your hair, girl. What do you say?"

He was about ten years older than her, rough around the edges, but definitely good looking. Or so he thought, anyway. He also thought that Caz would feel guilty for noticing. He had known girls like her. They loved their boyfriends, sure, but another part of them, a part they didn't particularly like, would long for a bad boy like him. Someone to put an edge on their boring, humdrum, safe relationships.

"Come on," he said. "Someone has to check out that explosion from last night. Aren't you even the tiniest bit curious?"

Caz was definitely curious. That was pretty much why she was up so early. She had been staring towards the northern part of the city for the best part of an hour, lapping up the early morning sun and trying to bolster up enough confidence to take a walkup north. The smoke had cleared, giving way to another humid morning. But there still had to be clues as to what had happened and what it could mean. Yet, curious though she was, Caz didn't want to do anything without first checking in with

Tim for the day. Of course, that would be easy if he were about.

"Sure, you can bring your boyfriend too, if you like," Barry said, as if reading her mind.

But Tim had withdrawn from her again. Caz blamed herself. She knew it was something to do with what had happened the previous night. And she wasn't thinking of the explosion.

(Hadn't he said he loved her?)

Caroline Donaldson may have come across as a well-rounded sixteen year old. Wise beyond her years. A conscientious and intelligent girl who almost always did the right thing—whatever that was. But the real truth of the matter was that she was desperately insecure. A part of her needed this attention from Barry, no matter how much she resented it.

"I would have to be back by lunchtime."

It wasn't as if she were being disloyal to Tim. Anyway, he spent a lot of time with Star, talking about tattoo designs, learning how to use the machine. Doing all those things that didn't interest a girl like her. A girl who did her homework on time and cycled to school.

"Sure. We'll be back by noon," Barry replied.

He ran one hand over the smooth leather of the steering wheel of Chris O'Hagan's demonic-looking automobile.

"What about your wee man?" Barry persisted, almost to test her.

"I think he's still in bed," Caz lied, hurrying down the steps, setting her glass of juice on the pavement.

She knew he had gone into town earlier. She'd watched him go from the window of the room where they slept, longing to follow him but knowing that to do so would set her back about ten squares in the constant game of snakes and ladders they seemed to be playing.

"We'll probably be back before he wakes."

"Well, let's go then."

Barry opened the passenger door to the Porsche, mock-bowing to Caz as she climbed into the car's low seat. Shutting the door with a swing, Barry wasted no time in climbing in beside her and kicking the engine into action. With a couple of revs, the two were soon tearing up the street, Barry dodging the first stalled car with an ease and proficiency that sent a few butterflies rushing through Caz's belly.

On the pavement, at the bottom of the station's steps, the discarded glass and beautiful blonde hair of Chris O'Hagan shimmered together in the sunlight, a gentle breeze lapping playfully at her pretty dead eyelashes. Perhaps a trick of the light, one eyelid seemed to flutter briefly before all was still again in the quiet, lifeless city.

...

Tim Adamson sat eyeing the bandstand from the shadows of the shopping centre. Nestled in one hand was a lukewarm Pepsi. In the other, he fumbled obsessively with his small silver Jesus, given to him only hours ago by Caz. Two yellowed and bloated corpses sprawled across the ground nearby. Another girl, head covered by hair, lay face down in a nearby shop window, halfway through the arduous task of changing the window display.

None of these pungent, sickly sweet smells bothered him anymore.

Tim followed every word the desperate choir sang, quietly and reverently. He was waiting for something to happen. They all were. But nothing did. Neither the music nor the fervour with which it was sung stirred anything or anyone, the sparsely talented crowd's racket only seeming to amplify the vast emptiness around them. No trumpet sound blasted through the clouds. No bodies arose, longingly, to dance with angels or cherubs.

(Nothing was the new something.)

Yet still the small band persisted, as they had done all day, every day for weeks now. Their voices were hoarse and parched. Their throats were strained and sore. Still they sang, probably because they knew of nothing better to do. Nothing better to say. They prayed and sang and listened to The Preacher Man simply because it seemed to be the right thing to do. It saved them having to think for themselves. Tim knew that feeling well.

ELEVEN

Caz was dreaming again. Eyes closed, hair massaged by the wind as the open-roofed Porsche raced along the M5 motorway with all the grace afforded by such a luxurious set of wheels. She hadn't daydreamed so indulgently since being on the train the day the world went to hell. Bizarrely, until now, Caz felt too closed in, too preoccupied with life in an empty world to give any quality time to dreaming. As Barry shifted into 5th gear, tearing the dial up a notch, she felt a sense of freedom kick in along with the speed.

Barry's driving, although fast, was good enough to allow her to concentrate only on the warm summer breeze as it whistled by her face. Despite her guilt about leaving Tim, Caz was really enjoying the drive. Being in a car was one of those things she hadn't realised she would miss until it was gone. Well down the list from showering, but slightly above flying, Caz found the simple pleasure of being in a car to be a forgotten luxury.

The open road was gloriously empty, save from the occasional Sunday morning spinner who had found themselves and their car slap into one of the motorway's barriers. Carnage was minimal, therefore, as were obstacles. Apart from that, the M5 looked no different from how it always looked. Industry buildings, no longer industrious, provided much of the scenery, along with railway track and the occasional flash of green. A stalled train, its few dead passengers still seated randomly throughout, as if sleeping, posed uselessly in the warm, summer glow. Then, within a brief moment, it was gone, lost behind them as Barry's demon-like Porsche tore up the silent motorway.

Caz wondered if some of the survivors' depression stemmed from the fact that the world had ended on a Sunday morning. Notoriously the most hungover day of the week, and not just in terms of alcohol consumption, Sunday was a nationwide come down, shoved in after Saturday's revelry to allow a little adjustment time before the horror of another week of school or work slowly sank in. Now, most of the world was dead, leaving the clock stopped forever at Sunday morning, 11.48am. What could be more depressing?

"Holy fuck!" Barry suddenly yelled, slamming on the brakes.

Caz had forgotten why they were taking their drive. The explosion was almost irrelevant now. Yet as the car skidded to a halt, swinging in various circles, ripping Caz roughly out of her serene daydream, an incredible sight burst into her line of vision. Dead in front of the two survivors, just as the car came through the roundabout where the M5 met the Shore Road into Whiteabbey, lay the broken body of what clearly was a helicopter. Pieces of the crashed aircraft spewed across their path like a huge string of metal vomit. Wreckage and charred corpses dotted the blackened tarmac of the motorway. Glass sprinkled across the landscape like fake snow, some of its crystalline, sunlit sparkles tainted by blood-red stains. Spat out pieces of baggage and fly-infested body limbs jutted out horrifically from under mangled pieces of propeller and door. The crash site spread across the entire width of Shore Road, spilling into a nearby grassy area, where its trail of destruction had slaughtered several sheep that had wandered down the empty roads from nearby rural Doagh. A single small lamb grazed casually close to the corpse of its mother, pinned helplessly to a nearby signpost by a random piece of the aircraft's engine.

Caz couldn't take in all that she saw, choking back her tears with one hand raised to her mouth.

"*Christ*," Barry whispered.

This was as explicit as it could get. All the world's death seemed to be summarised here. The quietly polite dying that had gone on across the world was nothing compared to this mess. For long moments, Caz sat very still in the halted sports car, its open top and luxurious interiors now meaning absolutely nothing. It was like a ringside seat to the misery in front of her.

Minutes passed where nothing was said. Finally, voice suddenly lost, Caz croaked, "Think anyone survived?"

Barry laughed nervously. "A-are you bullshitting me, girl?" .

"No, but..."

She couldn't even finish her sentence. She didn't remember what she was trying to say. She clambered out of the car as if suddenly aware of herself, holding one hand over her mouth again, half in disbelief and half to try and blot out the sudden whiff of cooked flesh and burned-out oil that swept over her like a polluted sea.

Barry followed her. "Careful," he warned, noticing huge, brittle chunks of glass and debris scattered throughout the ground.

Her eyes were drawn to a single arm, constantly harassed by flies, clad in one sleeve of a dress she had lusted over in Topshop just weeks ago. Caz still recognised the design of the fabric, even though some of the material was torn, leaving patches of blotchy, sun-raped flesh on display.

“I think I want to go home now,” she said, hardly able to take her eyes off the frightful image. “This is all… *wrong*.”

“I hear you...” Barry said.

He wasted no time in returning to the car.

Caz climbed back in beside him quietly, as if frightened of waking the crudely mutilated dead.

Barry ignited the engine. Carefully, and almost reverently, as if part of some funeral procession, he steered the boastful car away from the crash site.

Caz kept her eyes open, staring as the brutality of the sight was lost in the scenery once more, as they made their way back along the motorway into Belfast.

For a long time, neither of them spoke.

TWELVE

The Land Rover pulled into the back of Great Victoria Street Station earlier that morning, but Star was still in bed. Having vaguely recalled something from Barry about stealing a car and the almost dreamlike sequence of the explosion amidst the revelry of the previous night, Star chose not to worry much about any further drama until she'd had enough sleep. It was close to lunchtime, therefore, by the time she dragged her ass, once again hungover, out of the hotel bed and into a pair of distressed jeans. Her gut was crying out for something other than booze to digest, and the cafe at the bus station was probably the closest source of all things healthy.

Staring at her shoes on the way over to the bus station, trying to avoid sunlight as best she could, Star didn't notice the military Land Rover vaguely concealed behind one of the parked buses. The usual smell of the pile of bodies, still festering where she, Tim and Caz had stacked them under the canvas covers, greeted her nostrils, bizarrely reminding her to grab a box of ciggies from one of the shops in the station's small mall. It wasn't till she swung open the doors by the rear entrance that she noticed that they had company.

Although it didn't surprise Star much to see three strangers at her usual spot, by one of the huge, glass-fronted walls, she would have to admit that it did piss her off. She had come to call the station home, especially since Sean and Barry had arrived, rigging the place up with enough electricity to get the coffee machine working and a delightfully spacious party venue made-to-go. Dealing with the sight of a small child and what seemed like her middle-aged parents was not part of the drill for Star's morning routine. She just wasn't that excited about rolling out the welcome mat, especially when feeling so fucking tender.

The male amongst them, a small, mousy-looking bloke with glasses and a beard, was the first to notice the tattooist make her shuffling entrance. His face lit up with well-honed affability.

"Hallo!" he shouted, or so it seemed to Hangover Girl, "We… er… just arrived in Belfast today. There's only the three of us, and we're looking for somewhere to stay that's, you know, *clean*?" He uttered the word 'clean' with a smile that said, *Do you know what I mean by that?*, glancing over to the small child as if it were an adults-only secret that bodies were suddenly everywhere, rotting in beds throughout the city.

Star smiled weakly. "You'll find a room in the hotel that's pretty much *clean*," she replied, over-emphasising the word somewhat sarcastically, "and with our bone yard out back," she thumbed in the general direction of where the bodies from the hotel were dumped, "further 'spring cleaning' is made that little bit more convenient."

Star flicked on the coffee machine, grabbing a cup from the counter of the station's café.

"How many of you are there?"

This time it was the woman who spoke, a forty-something bint with a world-weary complexion and heavy eyes that suggested balls of steel. It didn't take Star long to realise that she wouldn't accept bullshit from anyone, especially jumped-up little punks like her. Not that any of that bothered Star. Especially when hungover.

The healing steam of coffee caressing her nostrils, Star simply leaned back into one of the station's seats, eyeing her up suspiciously.

"A few," she answered, finally.

"Seen any others in the city?"

"A few happy-clappy god-types seem to congregate in the city centre. You hear them singing their Shine-Jesus-Shine bullshit from time to time. Fuck knows what they have to be shining about, like."

The little girl, who had been glaring at Star since clocking eyes on her, suddenly mouthed shock.

"*Awww...*" she whispered dramatically to the woman. "She said a bad word!"

"Oh, dry your eyes," Star whispered under her breath.

The woman pretended not to hear her.

"No military presence? " she quizzed in a way that put Star a little on edge. "You know," she elaborated, "trying to mobilise the survivors, hand out rations, that sort of thing."

Setting her coffee down, striking up her first ciggie of the day, Star fixed the woman a look that said it all.

"It's everyone for themselves now, doll. Grab a coffee, get yourselves a room, but don't expect any cuddly rescue mission shit happening. This is your lot. Fuck knows, you could do worse than a hotel with a free bar."

Again the horrified look on the child's face.

"Do you mind?!" snapped the woman.

"Oh, fuck off," Star retorted, rolling her eyes. "What are you? Some kind of Christian?"

"No. I'm some kind of *parent*."

Star looked up, silent for a second.

"Well, lighten up, eh? World's ended, honey. Swearing's legal now. Along with thieving, drinking in public and getting absolutely wasted on coke." She exhaled another lung-full of tobacco. "That's kind of our bag here. Eat, drink and be fucking merry. Or miserable. Or both. If you don't like it, then feel free to check into some other hotel. Belfast has a few, I hear. Rates are pretty low, what with it being off-peak apocalypse season."

The woman said nothing, simply staring at her.

The child giggled, nervously, before putting her hand over her mouth on seeing both the woman and Star suddenly glare at her sharply.

"Well," smiled the man, after an awkward silence was shared, "if you really don't mind, we'll see if we can sort ourselves out with a hotel room, then."

Star eyed up the three, wondering how the hell an entire family had managed to remain alive when everyone else died so haphazardly. She watched them disappear out the back of the station, making their way towards the hotel. She hadn't even got their names, nor offered hers. Names seemed to mean fuck all these days, anyway. Hell, she might even change hers now. Perhaps use a different name every day, just to wind up fuckers like that.

Star drained her coffee then stubbed out her cigarette. She was getting sick of feeling hungover all the time.

....

The red Porsche pulled off the M5, onto the slip road leading back into Belfast. Neither Barry nor Caz had spoken a single word since returning from the crash site, their minds still digesting everything they had seen.

The tank was precariously close to empty, and Barry couldn't be sure there was enough to get them back to Great Victoria Street. He knew there was a petrol station near Carlisle Circus, so he made his way back towards North Belfast instead of following the road into the city centre. He thought that even if the pumps at the petrol station weren't working, there might be some cans of fuel lying about. Worst case scenario, he could siphon some using a piece of tubing. The petrol station would be well stocked for both options.

"Where are we going?" Caz asked.

"Need some fuel. Don't think we have enough to make it back."

Caz turned back towards the road without saying another word.

As they neared Carlisle Circus, the familiar scent of rotting death got a lot more pungent. It hadn't been as strong on the open road, or as visible. Here, though, near the housing estates, bodies littered the streets. The hum of flies as they gnawed continually at sun-parched flesh competed admirably with the engine of the car to fill the potent silence that remained overwhelming, constantly reminding the few survivors that the living were now very much in the minority.

Barry steered the car carefully into the petrol station, no longer little-boy-racer with his driving.

The fuel pumps stood pretty much as they had since its owner, a man by the name of Dorean Lappen, had fallen behind the counter of the station's small shop while lost in a random daydream about fucking the pretty blonde (Patricia, also now deceased) who usually worked weekends. His fallen body, like that of sweet Patricia, meant nothing to those left alive. Earlier looters barely noticed him sprawled out awkwardly behind the cash register as they raided his shop of tinned food, chocolates and cigarettes. To Barry, sniffing around the place for cans of fuel, tobacco, rubber tubing and a couple of bottles of water, Dorean Lappen was simply another putrid stench amongst a multitude of others. Once nauseating, now simply the norm.

Caz waited outside, her mind still clogged full of nightmarish images from earlier. She thought back to the first body she had seen all those weeks ago. The old lady on the train, looking so peaceful, was very much far removed from the burnt-out, bloody mess she'd come across earlier. It would have given Caz some comfort to imagine that all of those passengers on the helicopter, torn limb from limb, had fallen as peacefully as the old lady. Blissfully oblivious to their brutal fate. But she knew that hadn't been the case. Somehow, like her, Barry, Tim and the others, they had survived.

But how?

"Nice car, love."

Caz looked around, startled. A small group of survivors hovered close by, shuffling around each other, the car, and Caz. Their legs moved to and fro, seeming too spindly to hold their skinny bodies upright. Their faces were hidden under tipped baseball caps. They were like clones, barely discriminate from each other, hands buried in the pockets of their almost identical joggers. Their ages were somewhere between sixteen and eighteen. Hungry looks etched into their hollowed-out eyes, fluff straining to grow just above their top lips. These pale-skinned youths had been known as chavs before the disaster struck. Caz didn't take much solace from the fact that whilst most of the world died, these little bastards had somehow managed to survive.

"My boyfriend's in there," she said, pointing to the petrol station's shop. "He'll be out in a minute."

She tried to hide her nervousness, desperately trying to mask it with feigned nonchalance.

"We're not doin' nothing!" one of the pack protested, his whiny voice irritatingly high-pitched and melodramatic. "We're just looking, that's all."

It was a well-versed couple of sentences.

"Go get your own car," Caz snapped, still trying to appear unaffected.

She looked quickly over to the shop to see where Barry was.

"We're not just looking at the car," another one of the pack said.

He seemed to be their leader. There was something about his face that immediately terrified Caz. A coldness, maybe. Or callousness that suggested that none of this END-OF-THE-WORLD shit had affected him the way it should affect a normal human being. Both his eyes stared right through her like glass, as if he were looking at something inside her, something that he very much wanted to rip out.

Caz lunged towards the Porsche's ignition, banging on the car's horn as she realised Barry was carrying the keys. The noise screamed out like a hoarse banshee, causing Barry to turn quickly from whatever he was doing inside the shop.

Barry's eyes widened as he noticed three of the pack alight viciously on Caz. She was screaming, kicking and scratching as the pack struggled to hold her down. He felt for his keys, breathing a brief sigh of relief as he found them, his heart then sinking as he noticed the leader of the pack flicking open his knife in order to hotwire the ignition. He knew he could waste no time in getting out to Caz. Within seconds they would be off with her to God-knows-where to do God-knows-what.

Quickly grabbing a brush shaft from the shop's storeroom, the only thing vaguely resembling a weapon at short notice, Barry rushed them. As he tore across the petrol station's forecourt, Caz's wide eyes met his, begging for help. She was shrieking, scratching and biting whilst two of the pack held her down, laughing maniacally, one of them even spitting in her face as he goaded her.

Whilst the leader continued to hotwire the Porsche, the third minion came at Barry, aggressively brandishing a flick knife.

"Aye! Would ye?! Would ye?!" he slobbered in his barely legible whine, noticing Barry raise the brush handle with intent.

A keen golfer in days gone by, Barry swung hard and fast, clocking the knife-wielding youth squarely in the jaw, slapping his scrawny frame to the ground with ease.

"Ah! Fuck!" he screamed, writhing on the ground.

Barry sprinted to the car, pausing briefly to lay his toe into his fallen attacker, but by the time he was within range, the engine suddenly was revving up.

The car skidded noisily out of the petrol station and onto the main road, Caz's captors still holding onto her, goading Barry. Although Caz's mouth was held firmly by one of the captors, preventing her from saying anything, her terrified eyes told Barry all he needed to know. Helplessly, he watched the car fly towards the motorway.

"Fuck!" he shouted, kicking a nearby pump.

...

"Sean Magee."

"I'm Alan. Alan Gibson. Great to meet you, Sean."

Gibson extended his hand amicably. Sean shook it, smiling. It wasn't even teatime, but already the smell of alcohol was heavy on his breath. He was slurring his words, too, suggesting more than a couple of beers were already down the hatch.

"And this here's Mairead." Gibson gestured across the spacious hotel bar towards the woman and child getting some drinks. "The little one's called Clare. We just arrived in Belfast this morning. A very pleasant young... er... *lady* told us about the hotel."

"Oh, Caz, you mean?" Sean asked. "Pretty wee thing, probably hanging around a lad about the same age."

"Em, she had tattoos."

Sean laughed. "That's our Star, then. Face like an angel and the tongue of a sailor."

Gibson laughed sheepishly. "Yeah. Well, she seems a unique lady, that's for sure."

Sean opened the cap on his hip flask. He cleared his throat.

"Want a drink?" he asked.

"No thanks," Gibson replied.

Sean took a swig, reclining back in his chair by the window. He looked out at the first floor view across Belfast's centre. Nothing had changed. Same old lack of activity that there always was and always would be.

Alan Gibson was sitting opposite him. He smiled constantly, as if Sean was interviewing him for a new job.

"Where did you come from, Alan?" the DJ asked.

"Lisburn. We thought there might be more survivors up here, you know. Maybe some help."

Sean laughed. "I guess you're not religious then?"

"Sorry?"

"No, it's just that the only thing organised up here seems to be a crowd of Holy-Joes at the shopping centre. You know Victoria Square, over in the city centre?"

"Oh, right," Gibson replied. "No military, then? Or police taking control?"

Sean laughed again in response. They were not joyous laughs. They were too hollow to be anything more than sombre resignation.

"Think you been watching too many zombie flicks, mate."

Gibson's English accent was quite obvious, and Sean felt it lent him a certain naïve quality. He realised that, with the exception of the occasional Stones disc he'd spun recently, it had been weeks since he'd heard an English accent. Before the shit had hit the fan, every day was swamped with English accents. Television. Radio. Soaps. They were part of daily life in Ireland. Now, it seemed, no one talked very much at all, in any accent.

Mairead and Clare came over to join them, setting a couple of drinks in the centre of the table. "Sorry, did you want anything… er…?"

"Sean. Sean Magee," he said, offering his hand.

Mairead shook it weakly, which annoyed him. He never trusted anyone with a weak handshake. It reminded him of the executive types at the radio station.

"And, no thanks. Got myself a drink earlier."

Clare sat close to Mairead, glaring up at Sean. He hadn't seen any children alive, apart from the two teenagers. They were as rare as English people, it seemed.

Suddenly the door to the hotel bar opened. Barry, looking dishevelled, ushered a scared looking teenager in.

"Sean!" he exclaimed, ignoring the others.

"Where's your wee man, Tim?"

"Barry!" Sean called out, smiling. "Who's your new friend?"

Barry's new 'friend' was dragged by the neck over to the table where Sean sat. His hands had been tied, and it seemed from the messed up face that he'd suffered a crack around the head.

"This is Joe. Say hallo, Joe!"

But Joe said nothing, instead sniffling back tears..

"His little chavvy mates took off with my wheels, and Caz in tow. We need to get her—"

One look at Sean's gormless grin said it all.

"Christ, Sean. You're pissed. Fuck, mate, what help can you be?"

Sean's grin turned sour. "What are you on about? Who's took Caz?"

"Never mind," Barry sighed. "Just tell me, is Tim around?"

"Haven't seen the lad all day."

"Good. Don't tell him what's happened. He'd freak."

"Anything I can do?" Gibson asked.

Sean watched Barry eye up the five-foot-nothing counsellor.

"Probably not," he replied, curtly.

"Wait a minute. Did you say there was a bomb last night?" It was Mairead speaking.

"Well… no, not really."

Barry looked impatient.

"Well, was there a bomb or not? There either was or wasn't."

"Listen, love…" Barry started, voice raised.

Sean could see the child recoil at the sound of shouting, her short gasp seeming to steady Barry somewhat. He took a deep breath and started again.

"Look, it wasn't a bomb blast. Seems to have been a helicopter that has gone down."

"What?" Mairead couldn't contain her excitement. "Don't you know what this means? Where did it go down? Where did it come from?"

Barry sighed, seemingly resigned to a conversation that wouldn't help him.

"On the M5. The explosion happened last night, but—"

Suddenly he stopped. Sean watched a sense of realisation slowly descend upon him. Neither of them had given consideration to what the crash could mean. Until now, the very shock of seeing it had been stifling the cogs in their brains. But the fact that someone had put an aircraft in the sky weeks after everything had gone to hell was now dawning on both of them.

Where did it come from? Yeah, the fucking penny drops.

"I'll go with you," Mairead said. "Help you find your friend if you show me that helicopter crash."

Barry smiled, patronisingly. "I don't know about that," he said. "We're talking about—"

Mairead slid a handgun over to Barry, stopping his sentence dead.

"Know how to use this?"

He looked up at Mairead, clearly impressed. "Might do," he said, slowly, lifting the handgun, sliding out its magazine and checking it was loaded.

"We have more guns in our Land Rover," Mairead added. "Now where were these guys headed, did you say?"

"I don't know where they're headed," Barry said, grabbing 'new friend' Joe by the throat and menacingly shoving his newly-acquired handgun in the boy's face. "But you do, don't you, Joe?"

PART THREE

"Heav'n has no rage, like love to hatred turn'd, nor hell a fury, like a woman scorn'd."

(from *The Mourning Bride*
by William Congreve)

ONE

The skies darkened momentarily, as if threatening to rain. It was an idle threat, though. Everyone knew that the rain only came at night now. Heralded in by a descending cloak of thick, dark cloud, the rain washed away the silence of the day with its sweet pitter-patter. But never before its time. High above the city centre skyline, a single white bird darted to and fro as if part of a flock, before making a beeline towards the north of the city. Its solitary cry was almost lost on the dwindled population of Belfast, but not to Roy Beggs.

Across the road from the bus station, seated in a large People Carrier, Roy Beggs watched intently as the bird hovered then fell before swooping north. It was almost as if it felt a little tension in the air, prepping itself for a shower before realising it was a false alarm.

Roy turned his gaze back to the tall glass building he was parked opposite. He had been watching the comings and goings from the bus station for the better part of two hours, having noticed some activity from it earlier. Roy didn't expect to strike gold so soon, but a silhouette wandering through the glass-fronted bus station made him suspicious. It walked the way Alan Gibson did. A worried walk. More of a scuttle.

When the Land Rover—his Land Rover—pulled out from behind the large bus depot behind the station's shopping and café area, Roy was sure he was on the money.

Pulling a rifle scope out of his bag, Roy scanned the station. He noticed a young, dreadlocked man (or was it a woman?) smoking in the shopping area of the station, downstairs. This person was alone. They were of no real interest to the scorned soldier. Swinging over to the hotel next door, Roy continued his search. On the first floor he found Gibson, the child, Clare, and an unknown third person sitting by the window.

"Gotcha," Roy whispered, smiling.

He reached into the back of the car towards a bag of assorted weaponry.

...

Every meal was now communion at the Kitchen Bar, one of Belfast's oldest pubs, rebuilt brick-by-brick some years back right beside the bandstand just on the edge of Victoria Square shopping centre. Breaking of bread (or oatcakes, now that fresh bread was a thing of the past) preceded every meal, followed by a communal glass of wine.

For Robert McBride, a man who in the old world had never ventured too far left of pie and chips, oatcakes tasted like soil. But he ate them anyway, regularly and reverently. He drank the wine too, his stomach turning each time The Preacher Man launched into his monologue, dramatically camped up to max the effect, of how communion was to re-enact how Christ died on the cross, spilling his blood and shredding his flesh for the salvation of all mankind. To McBride, a man not given to religious hoo-haa before WHATEVER-IT-WAS-THAT-HAD-HAPPENED had happened, The Preacher Man's graphic retelling of the crucifixion process was harrowing. It hardly surprised him to hear of how some Christians were so mesmerised and consumed by the horrific torture endured by their Lord and Saviour that their own hands and feet would bleed. McBride suddenly recalled how his mum and sister's periods had regulated whenever they lived together, wondering if blood had a life and soul of its own—a sense of identity and awareness of itself. Was it something that lived and breathed through us, or despite us? Was it possessing us? This was the kind of fucked-up line of thought Robert McBride was finding himself travelling along, of late.

McBride was himself a man very far from the sort of conviction that would have blood seeping from his wrists; that much was true. If he were to be completely honest, McBride wasn't sure what to believe anymore. The Preacher Man simply took his mind off of what was really going on—a drug, if you like, to distract him from the real challenge of dealing with the true horrors of this Brave New World.

Not so for the majority gathered at the table, however. They were hanging on The Preacher Man's every word, fascinated, almost hypnotised by his personality. His unfaltering faith. His yearning for their salvation—all their salvations. The Preacher Man spoke like a man who was truly in tune with God, truly in love with angels. His passion for his mission was so strong, so wrought with emotion, that he cried almost hourly. Thick, salty tears. Loaded with the holiest of ghosts…

(And rage… And guilt…)

The Kitchen Bar was the base of the mission by night. They sought solace there once their voices had become hoarse and their backs sore from standing singing all day by the ornate bandstand, nearby. Their numbers were growing, yet the bar still provided ample room for them all. There was plenty of floor space to sleep on. Food could be kept in the spacious kitchen, mostly tins, as the power had long died for the fridge freezer to work. The Preacher Man retired to the manager's office to pray and read scripture during the night, sporadically sleeping whenever his fervour allowed him.

His dramatic use of Olde English added flair to his message of woe, warning of a final calling for all who were saved. The Preacher Man begged and pleaded for his followers to dig deep within their souls for assurance of their undying and unquestioning faith. Like that of a child for its father. That, and that alone, would save them. That, and that alone, would decide whether they were to be among the Sheep (those gathered at the throne of their Heavenly Father) or the Goats (those whose faith waned, leaving them shunned by a demanding God).

Some of them would never measure up. The Preacher Man demanded unfaltering faith, the kind that many proved incapable of. He spoke of lesser men, characters in the Bible like Lot, who had lost their bottle at the last moment, ending in their doom. He watched Gavin Cummings, as he strummed that guitar daily, often to the point of his own hands bleeding, his heart struggling with the words being sung. Cummings was weak, a dead weight that threatened the mission. He would never have the faith that was needed. Things were heating up now, and The Preacher Man needed strong men like Moses and John The Baptist, primal men, whose sheer, unbridled love for God would drive them to do the most incredible things. Yet all Gavin Cummings could do was strum a guitar, and with all the chords he was missing of late, even that was questionable.

As The Preacher Man started onto another rant-like sermon, like some great monarch dishing out death sentences, he watched Gavin's hand begin to shake suddenly and violently. The sin was upon him, just as it had been upon the devil child from before, polluting his veins, racing through his flesh, its raw danger threatening to completely consume all around him.

Every breath, every thought, every idea was riddled with temptation. Curdled with sordid intention. It was as if The Preacher Man could actually smell the failings within him, sniffing out his fear and insecurity like some great, divinely inspired bloodhound. He could see right through his skin as if it were invisible and read his every hellish thought.

It was a sign. The devil's grip was tightening, a last ditch attempt to destroy the mission. But The Preacher Man wouldn't be deterred. His faith, his resolve was like the prophets of old, anchored into the very throne of heaven. Nothing could stop him now. Judgement Day was finally upon them...

TWO

The Land Rover pulled up by the edge of the run-down North Belfast housing estate. It was the most animated place any of the survivors had seen since the disaster struck. Pavements and lampposts screamed out with red-white-and-blue glory. Wall murals, one reading "TAIGS OUT" clearly stated who was and who wasn't welcome in the area. Rows and rows of identical houses, some with mahogany windows and doors, others run-down to the point of squalor, stood facing each other. Like the residents who had once lived here, hard-faced and paranoid, the houses had a weather-beaten look of pride about them, as if primed to march through the streets of Belfast, defiantly waving their colours and murals and roughly pruned gardens.

This was inner-city Belfast at its most grim. A place caught in a political time-warp since the seventies. It stood for everything Mairead stood against, and yet, bizarrely, her own house would have stood in a very similar fashion to these, only with a different colour scheme. As Mairead slipped a fresh clip into her SA80 rifle, her bottom lip curled. Even in the Brave New World, where none of this could matter a fuck, it still antagonised her.

"You sure this is the place?" Mairead asked Barry.

They were looking straight at one of the many terraced

council houses sprawling through the estate like cells.

Barry stuck his handgun in Joe's ear.

"Aye! Fuck ye," Joe replied, sweating profusely.

"Okay, remember the plan then, Joey. Up to the door. Call out to your mates. Wait for them to open the door, then walk in." Barry emphasised the next bit clearly, as if Joe were a child. "*Leave.The door. Open.*"

Joe nodded, looking from Barry and then to Mairead, clearly terrified. There was a stain in his joggers where he'd obviously soiled himself, the smell thankfully masked by the stifling stench of death ever rampant throughout the dead city.

"Any messing about, and I'll put you down like a manky dog," Barry warned, poking Joe in the back with his gun.

Mairead said nothing. But one look in her eyes was enough to see what she would do to Joe were he to step left of centre.

Joe's eyes darted about like a startled animal, staring back fearfully as he climbed out of the vehicle. They had parked some distance from the house where Joe and his mates had been holed up for the last few weeks. It was Joe's own home. He had lived with his mother there, and his sister Tracey, since coming out of foster care last year. Now the lads all stayed there together.

Beer cans and broken bottles littered the lawn. Whilst Joe's mother had been very house proud, the lads' standards of hygiene were more than lacking.

Joe banged on the door, calling out a couple of names. There was no reply. Looking behind him, worriedly, Joe once again called to his friends. Still no answer. He looked across to where Barry and Mairead were standing, having slowly climbed out of the Land Rover.

Barry motioned for him to go on inside.

Joe tried the door, surprisingly finding it unlocked.

That meant the others had to be inside. Although there hardly seemed much need to be security conscious, the lads usually locked up before going out. There were too many spoils in the house, (beer and narcotics, mainly) and being thieving little shits themselves, they were wary of making it easy for other looters to raid their gaff.

Stepping inside the small hallway of the two-up-two-down terraced house, Joe called out again. "Sammy! Billy! I'm back! Your man cleared off and left me! Where are ye's?!"

Silence. Well, almost.

From the upstairs room, Joe could hear an odd sound of commotion. Kind of like someone eating noisily. Occasional sniffing. He figured it must have been one of the lads.

"That you, Sammy?"

There was no reply. The house, usually full of chatter and banter when the lads were in, seemed uncharacteristically sombre. Just that sound of chewing again. And then a slight whimper. For his own sake, Joe hoped that the sounds he was hearing weren't what he thought they were.

"Mackers? You in, mate?"

They had taken other girls back. Random, frightened loners who were wandering around aimlessly when the shit had hit the fan. People from the shadows. Sammy liked them young, so they aimed for girls who were in their early teens. Promised them all sorts to come back with them. Food. Shelter. Booze. Drugs. Anything at all to make it easier. Anything to keep them quiet for as long as they needed to dope them out, usually adding pills to their drinks or food. That made them very drowsy. Drowsy enough to fuck them without any complaints.

Sometimes they held competitions—seeing which

one of them could finish the job the quickest, the slowest to shoot off being the one left to dispose of the girl when they'd all had enough of her. Usually that person was Joe. And that pissed him off to no end. It was his house, right? Sure, it was really his ma's house, but he lived there too. When his ma and Tracey had fallen (along with millions of others), he threw their bodies in the shed out the back and opened the place up to the others. Surely that should have counted for something, no?

A shuffling... from the main upstairs bedroom. Gingerly, Joe climbed the stairs.

"Quit muckin' about, lads," he said nervously, aware of Mairead and Barry stealthily coming through the door behind him.

The sounds continued.

(Shuffling, sniffing, eating?)

As Joe neared the door, an awful thought came into his mind. What if the girl was in the room, dead or attacked and abused. What if the sounds he could hear were her, tied up and fucked up, struggling. There was no way her friends, those two behind him with their guns pointed up his arse, were going to let him live then.

His mind began working overtime.

Maybe if he got inside the room quickly, he could clean up the worst of the mess. Maybe he could even escape, himself, out of the bedroom window, sprint up the Antrim Road into another estate. They'd never find him if they didn't know the area.

He was at the door now. From behind it, the sounds were louder. He could hear breathing, broken and strained.

Joe pushed the door open.

His eyes widened at the grim view that spread before him. The main bedroom looked every bit the typical forty-something woman's haven. Gaudy wallpaper clung to each wall, seamlessly applied. A few framed pictures dotted the walls, one of Joe, his mother and sister, side-by-side, serious-faced as they stood by a passing loyalist band parade. A large, messy double bed stood centre place in the room, tall, golden bedposts sparkling in the afternoon sun's invasion through partially open Venetian blinds. There was blood everywhere.

A young girl lay shaking severely on the bed. Another girl sat huddled in the corner, hair hanging over her face as she worked busily at something in her hands.

The sniffing had been Sammy, his mutilated torso, half alive, shivering deliriously in the corner. Blood spilled from where his leg used to be attached to his body, now just a gnawed bone, hanging from a bloody, bile-soaked stump. His eyes darted about, closing then opening again as he slid in and out of consciousness. The contents of Sammy's stomach—and what seemed to be the stomach and gut itself—spread out from his belly like a crushed slug. Occasionally Sammy would gag, clotting blood gargling out of his throat, his left hand shivering as it reached forth to nowhere. It seemed to be the only limb actually capable of moving now.

Joe puked all over Sammy, adding to the various bodily fluids and parts already seeping out of him. He started to cry, sobbing like a terrified child on his first day at school. Wiping his mouth with the sleeve of his sports top, he went to move away from the mess that was still, somehow, alive. Still, somehow, his friend Sammy.

That was when Joe tripped over Mackers. Or what was left of Mackers. Sammy's right-hand man was in three parts, savagely torn apart like a victim at the centre of a bomb blast. He barely looked human, anymore, one sordid mess of him indeterminable from another, only now recognisable from his ever-present (now stained red) gold marijuana leaf necklace.

Joe cried harder. He could hear the sound of his

heart racing in his chest, that and his own whimpering drowning out the weak, dying rasp as Sammy, in the farthest corner of the room, drew a final breath before choking on his own bloody mucus.

But Joey-boy hadn't seen the worst of it yet.

The girl stooped in the corner, now visibly chewing on the mangled corpse of the youngest of the lads, Billy, seemed to be his sister, Tracey. Her eyes were pure black, her lips and body scarlet-red with blood. Her long, dark hair shone in the sun that sprinkled through the half-closed blinds. She wore pyjamas, the ones she was wearing when Joe had dragged her corpse out of bed. Although Joe didn't want to believe what he was seeing, it was most certainly his sister, beautiful and intelligent in life, now seemingly feral in death. She was like some kind of fucking zombie or vampire from a one of those movies.

What the?!

Only still looking every bit his beautiful sister.

He screamed.

She looked up at him, keenly attentive to the noise. As Joe watched on, she stopped eating, her head tilting to one side. She drank his appearance in, and unknown to Joe, began the process of checking his face against the many dark memories in her primal brain, searching for any link to the awful things that the mangled boys on the bedroom floor had put her through. Her eyes, wide and jet black, seemed to suddenly flick between various different colours. It was like a slot machine spinning, flipping from black to red, to white, then back to black again. As they changed, a rough papery sound could be heard, as if someone was flicking through a book. Then they stopped, Tracey returning to her meal. She hadn't found him guilty of anything. He wasn't even aware of any of the atrocities his so-called mates had put her through behind his back.

...

Barry was next through the door, eyes and gun at the ready.

Hearing all the commotion whilst climbing the stairs, Mairead wasn't far behind him, her rifle raised to eye level like a trained marine.

The whole scene opened out before their eyes, a rampant mess of carnage.

Barry ignored the other bodies, his eyes clapping on the badly-beaten girl on the bed. He winced at the sight of her abused body.

It was Caz. Her virginity was obviously in tatters. Save for a grubby t-shirt, she was naked, blood having trickled down her legs, hardening on the bedclothes. The only signs of life from her were sporadic whimpering and constant shivering. For Barry Rogan, in a room full of explicit and violent death, the small, curled-up child on the bed was the most horrific part of a very fucked up scene. Yet, in some ways, it was a very familiar sight to him.

Reluctantly, his eyes moved to the bedside table nearby. There he saw the all-too-familiar bottle of pills he knew only to be Rohypnol, his drug of choice once. Barry swallowed hard as the familiar wave of dark guilt and shame washed through him. He knew deep inside that these little fuckers, now somehow mutilated, had done no worse to Caz than he had done to those three women, their faces still etched clearly in his own mind. For Barry, the new world provided a fresh chance for him to be a new person. A better person. Free of the sins of the past, the sins of another life before everything changed. But nothing changed as long as people were still around. Humanity had acted predictably throughout its long history. Breeding, killing, invading each other...

Raping.

There was no escape from human nature. From feral urges. The animal within only roared louder, unchecked in this new, unruly world. It roared within Barry even now. Fearfully and tearfully, he fought dark inner demons as he felt, amongst the more forgivable emotions of shame, guilt and shock, a powerful and all-consuming feeling of arousal.

"Jesus," Mairead whispered, lowering her weapon.

She noticed Caz on the bed and immediately ran to her.

"You're okay, pet," she soothed. "No one's going to hurt you."

The young, broken girl shook violently and let loose a scream as if possessed. Mairead held on tight, rocking her to and fro. She couldn't begin to imagine what she would have done were this to be Clare lying on the blood-stained bed. She couldn't begin to imagine what kind of sick fuck would even do this kind of thing. She looked over at Barry Rogan, hoping for some kind of support, but he seemed to have zoned out.

Suddenly Mairead stopped, still holding the teen tight but attention now fixed on the other girl backed into a corner nearby. The one chewing on a torn-off limb.

"Fuck," Mairead breathed. "B-Barry… What the fuck?!"

One look at Barry was all Mairead needed to realise he wasn't operating on all cylinders. His eyes were locked in a thousand-yard stare, almost lending the normally cocky young man an ethereal look. His whole body was shaking, and his breathing was audibly speeding up, as if he were about to explode.

Behind him, their prisoner Joe lay slumped against the wall, his head buried in his hands.

Mairead watched, frozen, as the young, blood-thirsty

girl in the corner looked up at her, smiling, then turned her gaze towards Barry, her head cocked slightly to the side. Her eyes, jet-black against her pale face, flicking to a shade of red, then back to black, narrowed menacingly as they lingered on the man.

Dropping the chewed body part from her stained hands, the young girl lunged at him suddenly, with all the speed of a wild cat, long-nailed fingers outstretched, snarling with feral rage. On impact, she was ripping and shredding at Barry's chest and throat, then his arms as they automatically raised to defend himself.

Mairead acted quickly. Dropping Caz back onto the bed, she picked up her rifle, aiming and firing in quick succession. The first burst of firepower, due to her shaking hands, went slightly left of her target, tearing a clean hole through the chest of the cowering Joe in the corner.

"Shit!"

Quickly firing again, the next burst of firepower tore through the head of the feral young woman on top of Barry. She shook violently and briefly, stepping back as if shocked, before finally falling.

THREE

The swish piano bar in the Europa Hotel sprawled decadently across the first floor. High walls met beautifully carved coving, framing the blank ceiling, emphasising the roominess of the bar. The dark, wooden piano stood elegantly by the main window, looking across Great Victoria Street. Perhaps in reaction to the pungent loneliness, spreading like a tattoo throughout the hotel's pristine, empty corridors and golden staircases, the survivors at the hotel had always chosen to sit by the window. They probably felt less alone there. Even though the city usually stank of silence, its occasional voice, random car or droll chorus of Shine-Jesus-Shine would offer at least some comfort.

Alan Gibson was glad of the simple luxury of company. Sean Magee was a man of a similar age to himself, a man with something to say, even if it were mainly about his ex-wife. It was something, and after weeks of nothing, the counsellor having shared a room with the barely-alive Steve Marshall, Gibson wasn't going to turn his nose up at anyone.

He started on orange juice, but Sean's continual tempting with the distinctively off-perfume scent of vodka finally became too much to resist. Gibson gave in, perhaps having buried his last ounce of hope and direction in the Marshall family's crude grave. Alan

Gibson no longer saw any reason to deny himself, and he wasn't alone with that one.

In the days that had passed, many survivors who had once smoked, once drank, once jacked off to porn or shovelled junk food into their gobs, returned to their respective vices with devil-may-care resign. Gibson was no different. He no longer saw the point of abstinence. His last refusal of Sean's offer of vodka resulted in a 'why not?' look from the DJ, leading him to wonder why not, indeed?

Before long, the mild-mannered counsellor was diving into the vodka with admirable fervour, downing sizable shots with ease and comfort. Years away from alcohol hadn't done much to his ability to stomach it. Nor had it quelled his thirst for it. Like every recovering alcoholic, when Alan Gibson fell, he fell hard and fast. As the drink went down, the words poured out, Gibson relaying his own tales of woe to a partially alert Sean. The two men swayed and pointed at each other as they spoke like two pantomime pirates sharing a bottle of rum.

Gibson continued speaking, caring not that Clare, fixing herself a drink in the corner, unchecked, could hear every sordid and child-unfriendly detail of his days in counselling.

It seemed to impress his new friend.

"You're one in a million, Alan," Sean said, almost tearful with drunken sincerity. "Don't you let anyone tell you otherwise, eh?"

Now Gibson found himself in an awkward embrace with the man opposite him, meeting halfway between a messy table full of drinks and empties. In the drunken gesture, he found relief from the pent-up confusion and fear that was buried somewhere beyond realisation. It was survival instinct alone which prevented such fear from bubbling over, and continued to do so even when filthy drunk. But through the language known only to drunken men, Alan Gibson shared a universal truth with Sean Magee:

Everything's fucked up, and I'm afraid.

Clare looked on from the next table, rather confused. Although supposedly under the care of Mr Gibson, neither he nor the other adult had offered as much as a glance since the big bottle had come out from behind the hotel bar. Clare found her own drink, a blue bottle of something called WKD. She liked the colour and, although a little odd at first, its sugary taste seemed to hit the spot. She was beginning to feel a little dizzy, but it wasn't a bad dizzy.

She looked up, head spinning, as the door near her slowly opened. As her eyes steadied, hoping to find Mairead coming through, Clare discovered someone else she knew. Roy Beggs, gun raised, full combat regalia tucked in. He was like a cowboy coming into a saloon, like they did in those old movies her daddy used to watch. The kind of entrance that would have demanded a DANGER theme tune.

It seemed that only she noticed him. The two adults across the room were lost in their own world to the point where everyone else was invisible. Clare remembered seeing her mummy and daddy coming in after a night out, getting on in a similar way. Her granny used to babysit her when they went out to the pub. When they got back, she and Granny would seem invisible to them, in the same way Roy was invisible to the other two men. Sober people, it seemed, played minor roles in the drunken world. Ever-present, yet ever-ignored. Forgotten as soon as they were seen. Or maybe even before they were seen, as was the case with Roy Beggs.

Clare was confused. She was glad to see Roy, a familiar and sensible face. The man who gave her chocolate bars and told her not to tell anyone else. She knew that Mairead had fallen out with Roy, the two of them shouting at each other and pointing guns in a way which made Clare cry, but she still liked Roy. He had made her feel safe, secure—and that was important to her in a world without certainty. She loved Mairead the same way she loved her real Mummy, but she had felt safe knowing Roy was around as well.

Sneaking through the door, Roy smiled at her, quickly raising his finger to his mouth in a gesture that let her know to be quiet. Although unsure as to what she should do, Clare played along. She watched as he looked over at the other men, maybe deciding whether to say something to them. Then he looked down at her, and seemed to decide against it.

He quietly ushered Clare down the plush, carpeted staircase towards the front entrance to the hotel. Within moments, both Clare and Roy Beggs had left the building.

FOUR

Barry sat in the back seat of the military vehicle with Caz buried in his arms. He was still bleeding from where the crazed girl had bitten and scratched at him. Caz was catatonic with the shock of whatever the hell had been done to her, but Barry felt every bit as broken. Everything raced through his mind. The fucked-up girl's attack. The bodies—how could they have been so cut up like that?

The faces of three girls, in particular, started to form clearly in his delirious head. Colours and lights seemed to be swimming around his vision, swaying from side to side with almost mocking treachery. The picture of a nightclub was forming. A local spot he used to frequent some years back. Barry rubbed his eyes, trying to snap out of whatever trance he was slipping into. He continued to bleed, blood seeping out and collecting against his shirt.

A moment of clarity swept him back to reality. "W-what was wrong with that girl?" he asked, voice shaking.

His eyes were wide and manic looking. He was hardly even listening for an answer, simply having asked the question to try to distract himself from the strange vision that was threatening to consume him.

"Don't know," Mairead answered, curtly. "But you

need to pull yourself together. That girl needs you."

Barry looked down at Caz, suddenly aware of her again. Her eyes were shut tight, as if trying to keep the dam of tears welled up inside from gushing free. Her bare legs were covered with an old blanket they had found in the house. She shivered constantly, her shakes almost rhythmic, keeping time to some self-deluding distraction playing out in her mind, far away.

"F-fuck," he said, slamming a fist against the window.

Mairead turned to look at him, her face hard and devoid of sympathy.

"You've got to keep it together," she repeated, coldly.

"That girl!" Barry began, yelling at first. "That girl… she fucking bit me! She was trying to do to me what she did to those…"

His words trailed off, his throat hoarse. His face was beetroot red. Beads of sweat were beginning to glisten on his forehead. The colours returned, swirling in around him, like stars in a cartoon where someone had been hit on the head. He fought them, swaying in and out of the same vision as before.

"She pulled them apart! She was fucking eating them!"

Barry was losing it. A kind of dizziness was dragging him in and out of consciousness. The sweat was streaming down his face now, breaking out all over his body as if he were somehow evaporating. He felt as though he were slipping into some form of outer-body experience.

In the vision, he was talking to a girl. Pretty. Blonde. The type he liked. As she excused herself and left for the bathroom, Barry saw his own hand hover, briefly, over her drink. He watched a small pill drop from his hand into her glass. The same scene repeated itself, two other girls sitting across from him with each repeat.

He swayed back into reality with all the motion of an out-of-control pendulum.

Mairead turned to look at him, her eyes darting back and forth from the road.

“Barry, keep it together.”

But Barry was losing it.

FIVE

A small, petite hand pushed through the dirt and stones, pausing as the weight of her husband stalled her for a few seconds. However, before long, Kirsty Marshall clambered from her crudely constructed grave, her face pale and nonchalant as she threw her husband's body aside with ease and a distinct absence of emotion. Her hair shone in the afternoon sun, blonde highlights glistening in beautiful contrast to her almost coal-like eyes. Even though pieces of the black bin bag she had been wrapped in still stuck to her bare legs, glued uncouthly with semen from John McElroy's one-for-the-road ejaculation over her, Kirsty still looked absolutely gorgeous. Dead for several weeks now, she looked every bit the young bombshell she was in life. Perhaps even better.

She walked across the grass like a fucked-up angel, the black bin bag trailing in her wake like a bridal train. Her mind was a collage of undigested images, faces and names. Although emotionless, Kirsty still operated with purpose, as if fuelled by primal urges. Yet there was no passion. Kirsty wanted violence—specific violence—but she didn't know why.

She elegantly walked through the open door to the school, as if it were the front door to her palace. Her filthy, torn clothes and shreds of black bin bag did little to distract from her catwalk swagger. As if dressed head-to-toe in Prada, the twenty-something ex-teacher strolled up the main corridor of the school. Her black eyes searched for something.

For someone.

Aida Hussein had been cleaning up in the canteen, washing down the tables after the last few people had finished their lunches. When the door opened, she expected it simply to be some straggler wanting his or her dinner after everything had been eaten. That always pissed her off.

"I'm sorry, we're cleaning up now..." Aida began, only looking up to finish her sentence.

Her words hung uselessly in the still air. A beautiful mess stood in front of her, Kirsty's beauty stunning her as much as the cold terror in her black eyes. The young Egyptian dropped her cloth. Her lips moved to say something, yet stopped short of an actual word leaving her mouth.

Kirsty sidled up to her, her eyes seeming to look somewhere above her rather than at her. It was as if she were blind. Suddenly Aida could hear a sound not unlike flapping wings. To her horror, the dead Marshall woman's eyes were switching from one colour to another. Her lips were slightly parted, her body swaying. She was lost in some kind of daze, as if she were in the middle of one fucking good orgasm, only in slow motion. Suddenly she stopped dead, her eyes a very definite shade of white. They stared straight at Aida, her nostrils drawing close to the Egyptian woman's skin. She sniffed once, twice in succession. Then she smiled.

After but a moment, the woman—the creature—turned, no longer interested. She moved past Aida. She was after someone else. Someone who was close by. Someone who she would know when she found them, but not before.

Her trail of black bin bags caressed the smoothly polished canteen floor, swerving around the various tables and chairs, neatly laid out, with the grace and precision of a ballet dancer. Aida looked on, still frozen to the spot, her cloth still lying on the ground where it had been dropped. As she watched, Kirsty approached the kitchen. An electric light shone from behind the corrugated shutter, half drawn to discourage hungry survivors from disturbing the post-lunchtime cleanup. Kirsty Marshall halted in front of the shutter.

From inside, the sounds of hustle and bustle could be heard. Kirsty's head cocked to one side, her mind drinking in every detail of each image, making sense of it in order to plan her next move. One hand reached to pull up the shutter, revealing what she had been looking for all along: the large frame of Sylvia Patterson. Chief cook and provider for the group, Sylvia fed, watered and nurtured the survivors in a way which helped many of them deal with their respective losses. She held them as they cried, soothed them as they grieved, put food on their plates and tea in their mugs. She helped organise the survivors as they generated a little power to keep the kitchen running. She took control of things when Roy Beggs had left the school to reclaim the child that was taken away from them, slipping smoothly into a leadership role because, whilst Roy Beggs wouldn't have admitted it, she had been leading just as much as he had, all along. In fact, Sylvia Patterson achieved what Roy Beggs could never achieve. She gained the survivors' full and unquestionable respect and support. Whilst Roy could provide security and structure for the survivors, Sylvia provided comfort.

But she had poisoned Steve Marshall, adding progressively lethal quantities of rat poison to his every meal. A part of Kirsty Marshall knew that.

As Sylvia's eyes met Kirsty's, she could hear what

sounded to her like a kitchen fan. To her horror, Kirsty's eyes flicked from white to red, finally finding a very deep, dark black. The cook didn't recognise her, having only met her husband—the man she had poisoned—as opposed to the entire Marshall family. Sure, she'd watched as they were buried, but only Roy Beggs—and the John McElroy, tasked with preparing the Marshall family's bodies—had actually seen Kirsty's body.

Yet Sylvia knew that whoever this strange woman-like being was, this beautiful shadow of what was once human, but now beyond human—and the very constraints of humanity—had ill intentions towards her.

Of that she was sure.

The cook reached quickly and fearfully for a large kitchen knife on the table, but Kirsty got there first, lifting then turning the blade on Sylvia in one complete movement. It sliced through Sylvia's throat as if it were wet paper, spraying the clinically clean, white walls of the kitchen with bright red and separating her head from her neck. The cook's full-figured body fell heavily to the ground, leaving the cleanly decapitated head held, by the hair, in the left hand of her beautiful assailant. The pristine white kitchen floor, usually polished within an inch of its life, now ran red with its chief cook's life. The decapitated corpse continued to puke blood onto the tiles, the red liquid at first running along the grooves of each tile before finally pooling across the entire floor like a thick quilt of revenge.

Kirsty Marshall stood silently, as if unsure what to do next. She was operating on raw passion, yet still seemed uncertain how to express such. After a few seconds of lull, she suddenly leaned her face towards the severed head hanging from her hand, drinking greedily from the throat's many veins, shoving torn flesh into her small mouth as if it were a jam pastry.

Once sated, she tossed the head aside.

She moved back through the canteen. A number of survivors were gathered there, having heard the disturbance. She stood in the middle of the hall, drinking in all of their emotions. She found fear, mostly, her eyes flapping until they turned a pale blue colour. She watched as the people before her backed away, their own eyes white and wide with alarm.

Only Peter Stokenbergs stood to challenge her, his eyes catching sight of the twisted, torn corpse of Sylvia Patterson, sprawled out on the kitchen floor, blood and cartilage splashed across the floor like a broken jar of relish. Stokenbergs made his move, charging with his damp, red face and gritted teeth bared like a mad dog. His rampant anger tasted salty to Kirsty, her eyes shifting like greasy gears to red. She stalled him before he could even touch her, swinging one arm in a perfect arc to slice his thick, fleshy throat with perfectly manicured and brightly painted fingernails. His skin opened like ripe fruit, blood spilling almost immediately. Kirsty leapt upon his stumbling body, feasting, lapping up the seeping life thirstily. The heavy-set man fell to his knees, at first, arms flailing uselessly, skin draining of colour. Soon, his body fell to the ground, lifeless and empty. Kirsty went down with him, eager to suck up every last drop of blood. She continued to tear at his moist flesh, scooping it up into her mouth insatiably.

Once done, she stood up and turned, wild with the taste of his blood and flesh. She licked her lips and fingers, eyes flickering wildly between colours as she searched the room for more prey. Most of the survivors exited, their screams echoing throughout the school's corridors, blending with the feverish pitch of voices and movement as word began to spread of what was happening:

There was a monster in their midst.

And Kirsty wanted more. Her feet gathered speed, seeming to glide along the smooth floor as she moved out of the canteen and into the corridors, her arms swinging busily as she shifted through the herd of people, felling as many of them as she could reach. The more skin she tore, the more blood she shed, the faster and more brutal her rampage became. Each kill seemed to fire her up for the next, the blood-dampened walls of the school reflecting her scarlet eyes as she soaked up the life and fear and panic around her.

Finally, she stood at the school's entrance, the more fortunate survivors spreading out in front of her as they fled the school's grounds. She lifted her face up to the sky and allowed a roaring keen to escape her lips.

SIX

"Maybe I should wait for Mummy," Clare said, seeming a little anxious and confused.

Her parents had split before the disaster struck, meaning she was accustomed to a tug-of-war between adults concerning her welfare. Yet now both Mummy and Daddy were completely off the map of her life, leaving the child desperately alone. Mairead was her new mummy, and in the Brave New World, her father figure might as well be a man like Roy Beggs. Unlike the softer Gibson, Roy actually seemed to have an interest in her and seemed strong enough to protect her. When the reset button was hit, basic needs like protection meant a hell of a lot, especially to a child. Especially to Clare.

Roy looked at her and winked, gesturing for her to be quiet by drawing one finger over his mouth. It was as if their escape was like a big secret that only they knew about. She liked that feeling. A feeling of being included, playing a part in some game with the adults. She was happy to go with him. She didn't like this new place, nor the people who lived in it. She had never been to Belfast before, and even in post-apocalyptic emptiness, the Big Smoke still seemed overwhelming to her. Buildings seemed too tall, roads too wide. The starkness of the world seemed a lot more explicit here than in the school.

But she didn't want to leave Mairead.

"I want to wait for Mummy," she whispered, still playing the game even if unsure what the rules were.

"We'll meet her back at the school," Roy chanced, hurrying the child away from the hotel to where his car was parked.

"I don't think she likes the school." Clare looked up to Roy, saucer eyes blemished only by a redness that suggested a few nights sleep had been missed.

"Sure she does," Roy coaxed, flashing a cheesy grin that made him look a lot like a teddy bear.

Clare had giggled the first time she had seen that grin. Now it was comforting.

"Where is she, then?" Clare persisted. "If Mummy likes the school, she'll come back with us, won't she?"

"She'll follow us later," Roy snapped under his propped-up smile.

"No she won't. She doesn't like it there. She doesn't like you."

She had tested Roy and found him lacking. Everyone knew that Mairead didn't like the school. Clare may have been a child, but she knew as much as that and, like most children, she didn't take too well to being patronised.

Roy got down on his hunkers, stroking Clare's hair with paternal love he always thought non-existent.

"What's most important is making sure you're safe, isn't it?"

Clare nodded agreeably. Her face was approaching the kind of pout that might lead to a stubborn strop.

"Well, I'm here to bring you back to the school. You know, where you went when your mu—I mean when everything got scary, eh?"

Clare nodded. She did like the school. It was where she had spent a lot of her days over the last few years. She didn't feel too scared there. It even smelt right,

Auntie Sylvia's canteen cooking reminding her of that noon feeling when lunch was on its way, and home-time would follow swiftly. The timetable of it all, steadfast and sure, was comforting.

Perhaps that was the attraction of the school for all the survivors. Perhaps that was why none of them, apart from Gibson, Mairead and Clare, had made any moves to leave. The small school brought them back to a place where things were more predictable, less volatile. It reminded them of routine, of stability, of structure. It reminded them of authority, and how much they seemed to need that in their lives to feel safe. That was their programming, ripped from their existence, like wires, on that fateful day, some weeks ago.

Roy gestured for Clare to get inside the car. She did so obediently. He turned on the car's CD player, sliding in a disc he thought might appeal to the child—some pop shite that his niece used to listen to. Still smiling, his face almost hardened into that stupid grin he used especially for Clare, Roy closed the car door and allowed himself to frown. He took a moment to lean back on the side of the car and feel the calm breeze blow against his face. It seemed even quieter now than it had before.

Roy had some nasty business to take care of before they left. Never a man who took being scorned lightly in days gone by, the self-appointed lawmaker wasn't going to let someone like Gibson, the middle-class tosser that he was, get away with what he had done. He cringed when he thought of how humiliated he had felt, how much of a fool he had been made to look—especially in front of the others, the people he had sworn to himself he would remain strong for. Gibson had to be punished for what he had done. It was that simple.

Calmly, the soldier reached inside his bag for add-ons to the rifle he had slung across his shoulder. Whistling nonchalantly, he screwed a telescopic scope onto the top of his SA80. Once satisfied with that, taking a moment to aim through the lens, following the hotel wall until it reached the window where Gibson and the other man still sat, he looked again in his bag, feeling around for something else. In the thick, heavy silence it seemed even more important to muffle a noise as obnoxious as a rifle shot. Roy found what he was searching for, fixing the long, top-heavy length of metal onto his rifle's tip. It was a silencer.

Checking again to make sure everything was well aligned, Roy loaded the rifle's mag then slid it into place.

He winked at Clare, who was looking out at him through the car window.

"Won't be a moment, sweetie," he mouthed into the silence, flashing that grin again.

SEVEN

The late afternoon sun cut like a knife through the grey clouds. With the evening, The Rain would come, shunning the sunlight like a condemned man. Last night's rain had been particularly heavy, and the paving around the ornate bandstand still bore the fruits of its labour. The marble of the band stand, its gaudy pink colour even paler with the kiss of sunshine, shone. Drips of moisture ran down each of the legs of the structure, meeting the street in small pools, gradually paling as the paving gave way to the large shopping centre.

It would have lent the area something of a gothic feel even if The Preacher Man hadn't been there. His small congregation stood almost stalactite-still, their dark sincerity and bowed heads choking the already Victorian atmosphere. For the twenty-third night running, they prayed the same prayer, ad-libbed to various shades of melodrama by The Preacher Man. It started with a low moan and built to a shrill whimper before spiralling dramatically to peak in a roaring finale. Sometimes The Preacher Man's body would open up like a flower, arms outstretched and head raised, to bring proceedings to an explosive crescendo. Yet regardless of how it was done, The Preacher Man was always praying for the same thing: for angels to come and claim their souls.

Tonight their prayers were answered.

Like rats from woodwork, they seeped out of the city. They descended upon the holy throng from every direction, their gentle approach peeking open an occasional eye amongst the pensive crowd. They poured towards the worshippers in unison, as if choreographed, their luminous faces cocked slightly to the left as they approached. Like holy ghosts, they seemed to hover across the ground, each picking out their respective target calmly and elegantly.

Then they stopped.

From a distance of exactly five metres from the group, they slowly raised their faces. As if searching for TV channels, their eyes flicked back and forth between various colours. It was as if they were tuning into the feelings of the small crowd before them. As the eyes flicked back and forth, a sound not unlike the clicking of fingers broke against the reverent silence of prayer. Up to this point, almost every member of the group, even sceptical freeloader Robert McBride, really hoped them to be angels. Really hoped them to be the salvation they each had prayed fervently for. Another reality dawned upon them, however, as a different set of eyes, finally tuned into their respective colours, stared upon each face in the group. They had been praying for angels, yet what they saw before them was even better.

Gavin Cummings looked upon the freckled face of his wife, Kory. For Robert McBride, it was his mistress Patricia, and the tearful, wide eyes of Jackie McCrory met with the dark, tiny, narrow face of his stepdaughter, Barbara.

It was Gavin who cracked first. His hands, shaking like wings, reached forward to touch the face of Kory, fraught with disbelief. He just couldn't understand what was going on. Was it some kind of trick? A test, maybe, from God or The Preacher Man? Thoughts and emotions blended together like paint in a palette as his quivering fingers finally reached the face of his wife, each fingertip feverishly sending the same message to his brain. This was Kory. This felt like Kory. Only better.

Everyone followed suit, their hands feeling all over the bodies of their respective loved ones, some of the men snatching them close as if scared they might be taken from them again. It was a moment charged with raw, passionate energy. An electric orgy of love and loss, played out in front of the one man who stood alone: The tall, dark Preacher Man, alone in his pulpit. His birdcage.

And then it changed. Almost as if sick of the feverous affection heaped upon them by their respective men, as if the groping and grabbing and embracing suddenly became claustrophobic, something within the women assembled cracked. Within a split second, each of them lunged for their former lovers, greedily scooping clawfuls of flesh and sinewy vein from the throats of those who loved them, barely leaving their prey time to gasp a breath, never mind a tearful hallelujah for the miraculous resurrection of their fallen dearest. Soon the screams of each man were tearing through the dead weight of silence, shredding any kind of serenity they had struggled to achieve through prayer. In the middle of the onslaught, each man falling quickly and on the scarlet-stained ground, The Preacher Man remained unchallenged, his eyes drinking up the sight with fascination, his sandwich board hanging limp and ridiculous around his neck, spelling out 'JESUS SAVES'. Staring as every splash of blood and slice of body part slopped out around him, The Preacher Man showed little emotion, stepping out of the bandstand and through the carnage as if this were all part of some bigger, divine plan. A part of him believed it was. Another part of him feared it wasn't. Yet as he moved, the weight of his sandwich board bearing down upon each soft step forward he made, it seemed as if the violence parted before him, a red sea of death and carnage happening around him, beside him, (because of him?) yet not *to* him.

It was then that he spotted Tim Adamson.

The lad's definitive awkward frame sent a raw stab through The Preacher Man's heart, a mixture of joy and pain, love and disgust. The boy was shivering, yet sweating at the same time. Tears ran freely down his face, shimmering like precious stones.

Jaw to the floor, The Preacher Man stopped briefly, only long enough to drink in the sight of Tim standing in front of him. He wondered if the boy had been in the crowd all along, perhaps standing at the back of the crowd, shadows from the shopping centre seeming to cast themselves over the bandstand like cliffs. It was barely a second The Preacher Man had stopped, but it was long enough to allow one of the angels, a large, full-figured beauty with her husband's blood smeared over her lips like crudely-applied lipstick, to reach for him, catching a lock of his hair. The Preacher Man was dragged to a standstill, his eyes filled with terror. He froze, his large frame and imposing stature dragged to a standstill by his assailant. He was trapped. Scared. Yet the terror was not from the cold, clammy touch ebbing its way through his hair for a tighter grip, nor was it from the doom that such a grasp would truly spell for him. Instead his terror came from looking again upon this boy's face—*his* boy's face. A face not washed with the disdain and venom that should have been there, but with *love*. The Preacher Man—Samuel Adamson by name—felt his heart break in unison with the sharp pain of teeth sinking into his neck, tearing veins open like wrapping paper. His lifeblood spilled onto his dark grey suit and sandwich board, the back print ironically reading, 'THERE'S POWER IN THE BLOOD'.

Samuel reached one long, powerful arm out towards his boy, flailing wildly for a last touch. A last embrace. His eyes closed, stinging with pain as the creature's teeth tore again through his grey skin. Deeper. He felt himself slipping away, an all-consuming dizziness swamping his mind. Golden dreams swirled around his head, seeming to almost search for an opening. There was none. There was only this.

And then it happened.

Samuel heard what sounded like a gunshot ringing out. He felt his attacker falling dead, a single bullet tearing through her face. He looked up with disbelief, finding his son, gun outstretched, staring back. A sudden tear ran down Samuel Adamson's face.

His son had saved him!

Hallelujah?

The Preacher Man—Samuel—had prayed for the salvation of everyone, including himself, so many times that he'd lost count. He rinsed out the sinner's prayer more times than he cared to even fathom, his own guilt and self-loathing stocking up more sackcloth to don than he could keep up with. He had looked everywhere for an answer to his rampant inner demons—a cure to sate his dark, bile-stained lust for everything that he stood against—yet he never expected that very answer to come from the very person who had seen the absolute worst of him. A single, enlightened tear trickled down his cheek. This was what life was about. It wasn't about death or eternity. It was about grace. Real grace.

That very look sealed Samuel's doom. It was too much for Tim Adamson. His hate for his father quickly overwhelmed any trickles of love seeping from his heart. Tim aimed his weapon, the same gun he had taken off the policeman's body that very first day, squarely at Samuel, pulling the trigger with a surety that was rare for a sixteen year old firing his second-ever bullet. It tore a clean hole through his father's heart with almost marksman precision. Within seconds, Samuel Adamson's life was ended, his soul simply evaporating into the ether. Tim was quite sure that no pearly gates welcomed his monster of a father, no flames of hell licked at his feet. Instead, his daddy-dearest left the world as simply as he had, no doubt, entered it. Tearstained eyes closed. Flailing arms searching, wildly.

Tim's own eyes blurred with fraught and raw emotion. His gun dropped to the street, now a paddling pool of blood and torn flesh. His thousand-yard stare met with a bloody face, beautiful and dark-eyed. The face cocked to the left, drinking in Tim's turmoil, before it fine-tuned a heavenly shade of white. As the beautiful yet deadly angel moved towards Tim, stains of violence in every finger reaching, his eyes closed. He felt no fear. Relief's anaesthetic soothed him.

One cold hand clasped around his neck, snapping for his silver crucifix, but he gripped tight, his fingers bleeding as he strained to keep hold of his little shiny Messiah. The creature persisted, reaching next for his face. As sleek, perfectly-manicured fingers tore at his hair and eyes, gouging out each pupil as if scooping out ice cream, Tim was left only with memories to look upon. Memories of the most precious sight he could remember from his sixteen short years:

The face of Caroline Donaldson.

...

The first burst shattered the front window of the hotel bar, dragging the two middle-aged drinkers out of their alcoholic stupor, but failing to kick-start their brains to take cover before the second burst. It followed the first within seconds, cutting through the empty window frame to slice a lethal hole in Alan Gibson's head. The pissed-up counsellor, barely conscious before the bullets violated him, lost all signs of life immediately, his small, rotund body hitting the bar floor like a burst football.

Sean hit the deck, covering his ears. As he stumbled to the floor, an entire table of glasses and bottles fell on top of him, smashing. Sean closed his eyes as the booze and glass showered him.

"Fuck!"

He looked over to Alan Gibson. A thick, dark liquid now oozed slowly from the man's head, a man Sean had only seconds ago offered another drink to. Now his brains were seeping out of his head like lentil soup.

This was fucked up.

Sean could almost feel the sights of the rifle search for him. It had nailed Gibson. Now it would want him. Desperately, he scrambled under the nearest bar table. He listened, straining to hear some sign or clue as to what the sniper's next move was going to be, over his own heavy breathing and racing heart. Nothing. Just silence.

Who the fuck would do such a thing?

Sean had heard very little commotion over the weeks as he downed the drinks. An occasional shout or burst of a window, looting now being as common and inoffensive as shopping. The firing of an engine or rev of a car. Random music, the distant, sombre singing of the Cornmarket god-botherers. But little violence. He'd heard the others talk about the odd scuffle, burning out quickly, as if too embarrassed to continue to a logical conclusion. In the New World, it seemed The Silence would do most of the policing. Like the wagging finger of God burned within a penitent sinner, The Silence was ever present. Ever watching. Ever measuring. Until now. Something else burst through with lethal insolence, ripping a hole through the head of Alan Gibson, and Sean knew that whoever was responsible would most probably seek him out, too.

His eyes fell upon the only entrance to the bar. One door ajar, dead in front of him. The sniper's next move might be to search him out on foot.

Sean didn't know what to do.

He felt too drunk for sensible, reasonable action.

...

Roy Beggs was almost sure his second shot had struck gold. He thought he saw someone fall, and from the angle he was shooting from, and the shape of the silhouette that his bullet was aimed at, he was about ninety-nine percent sure it was Gibson. He was about ninety-eight percent sure that his bullet hit the right spot to make the pious wee fucker a dead man. But Roy needed to be one hundred percent sure.

Turning, he looked in at the small girl in his car. She hadn't heard any of the shooting, the silencer having muffled Roy's shot and whatever shite CD he'd given her doing a fine job of masking the sound of the window shattering. There was no reason that Clare wouldn't be safe for another few minutes, just until he checked things out in the hotel—made sure he had finished the job properly.

Roy sighed heavily. A part of him regretted that it had come to this. He wished there were others who could share the responsibility for keeping things under control, protecting the innocent and punishing those who could be a threat to his community. Removing the scope and checking his rifle, the heavy-set soldier moved towards the hotel's front entrance.

...

Star watched the series of events unfold from the relative safety of Great Victoria Street Station. The girl,

Clare, being led to the car by a stranger in camouflage. The sounds of splintering glass and distinctive flash of muzzle as said stranger, evidently a soldier, opened fire on the hotel bar, where she knew Sean would be. She knew this because, frankly, Sean did nothing else, of late, except drink.

The DJ's obsession with lost love had got too much for the tattooist, leading to her withdrawal from him. She found herself spending a lot more time with the quiet, introspective Tim Adamson, the two of them diving into all things tattoo. Tim didn't have a lot of talent in the area, but nevertheless Star encouraged him as he dreamed up weird and (frankly) creepy designs, then practised applying them on false skin. More recently, Tim had moved to real skin—the skin of the dead. It was a little distasteful, one might have thought—*might have*, that was, before thinking of such things (or thinking much of anything) had become less of an issue. The body they had been using seemed strangely well preserved, and whilst Star and her young apprentice both clocked that, neither said so to the other. They needed skin, and this skin was as good as you could get, for whatever reason. The dead had become inanimate, in a way. Almost invisible in this Godforsaken city.

Tim had fucked up his first few attempts, drawing too much blood from the corpse, digging too deep into the skin, inking lines so crooked they looked like zig-zags. But the boy was coming on—or had been, anyway.

As for Sean, he continued to drink, regardless of whether or not he had company. If anything, his intake had risen. At times Star would have joined him (last night for example), but the wild all-nighters were fast becoming a one-man show. Sean, and Sean alone, would be found sitting in the piano bar, spinning discs on his portable CD player until its batteries ran out, downing shots of vodka like a broken man.

Sometimes he could be heard crying, his drunken tears and rants almost part of the décor of the hotel now, as if it were haunted.

As Star watched the whole scene outside the hotel, she wondered what the DJ had done to piss off Green Beret dude. Was it something to do with that weird family she'd met earlier? Weren't they asking strange questions about military presence? Barry had disappeared somewhere with the woman earlier, but Star hadn't noticed the creepy guy with the beard leaving. Maybe he was with Sean? Maybe the military guy was after him instead? Fuck knew what kind of politics were at play here, but Star didn't like to see Sean getting drawn into it, and with the hairy bastard having not surfaced from the bar today, she was starting to worry about more than just his liver.

She lit up a cigarette. She needed to think about this. As she smoked, she watched the soldier make his way towards the hotel. Probably moving in to finish the job. Star didn't know what to do. She wondered about the child in the car. Why was the soldier interested in her? A shudder went through her as she imagined the worst. Grown women (as Barry often reminded her through his many drunken passes) were a little scarce these days. Would-be-predators now had a free hand to practise whatever sick games they played out in their minds, in full, Technicolor depravity.

Star had to do something. She didn't like children, but no part of her was going to sit back and watch something like this happen.

Stamping her cigarette out before lighting up another, she grabbed hold of a large kitchen knife (the only thing even resembling a weapon), pulled open the front doors of the station and made her way across the road to the parked car. The army guy had gone inside. She had a few moments' grace.

As the doors swung closed again behind her, something else stirred from behind the counter of the cafe.

Her crudely tattooed mannequin was moving.

...

The creature that, in life, had been Kirsty Marshall, and in afterlife/death/un-death was something *similar* to Kirsty Marshall, sat by her own self-desecrated grave. The body of her husband, Steve, lay entwined in the simple cross that had been thrown together by one of the survivors, a decent man named Phillip, who now lay face down in his own blood and spittle somewhere in the school. He had been the last one Kirsty had managed to kill, succumbing to her bloody hands just after the young student girl had been torn down. The others, terrified, defenceless and disorganised, spilled messily out into the streets of Lisburn, caring not for each other or the ones they left behind. Their bubble of security, a façade created by the uniform of Roy Beggs and the routine of Sylvia Patterson, had burst open like a fallen egg carton. Now they were just scared children again.

Kirsty didn't need to chase them. She was sated, with the blood hardening on her full-bodied lips, lips Steve Marshall had begged to have around his cock on many occasions. Some part of Kirsty remembered that and became aroused. Sitting cross-legged on the school's lawn, Kirsty ran her hand roughly through Steve's hair. It was filthy. Uncombed and greasy. The hair of a man who had given up caring about life well before any bullet reached him. Kirsty felt a draw towards him. His smell, masked a little by the sun-scorched decay that had already set in, seemed vaguely familiar. Attractive, in some way. It touched a very basic, primal part of Kirsty.

A cocktail of raw emotions raced through her head. Somewhere between hunger and passion, she found love, then loss, her head falling sharply to the side, her eyes flickering again as she searched, finding red—for passion—before they settled on the purest white they could be, a purity that equalled the love she had shared for her Steve.

For a moment Kirsty's arms flailed wildly at the body of her husband, tearing skin from bone like peel from an orange. Water gathered in her eye for a reason lost to her. Her tears twinkled like tiny stars in the sunlight. Her eyes turned from its pure white, to red, and finally to a deep blue. A low, heart-wrenching moan escaped from her lips, ripping through the stifling silence like a bird through sky.

Grief.

Dipping, Kirsty Marshall sank her teeth into the skinless chest of Steve Marshall, tearing chunks of flesh with raw passion, the crystal tears seeping from her red eyes and mingling with the broken heart spilling onto her lap.

From close by, the solitary figure of Aida Hussein watched on, terrified and broken-hearted in equal measure. She had been hiding in a cloakroom, all too aware of the painful screams echoing through the school. She left when the familiar silence returned, hoping to steal away from the monster that had invaded their solace, yet now reluctant. This wasn't a monster. This vicious, desperate woman was so badly scorned that Aida could only feel pity for her. A tear caressed the Egyptian woman's cheekbone, shed in regret for the very emotions that Kirsty Marshall's crude, violent brain was discovering.

Aida moved slowly towards the confused, ravenous creature. As she approached, Kirsty paid no attention to her, lost in the bittersweet ritual of feasting upon her husband's remains. Aida reached a shaking hand towards the creature's glistening mane of hair, running her long, slender fingers through. Kirsty stopped, for a moment. She looked up at the Egyptian woman, her eyes flicking slowly from one colour to another with the same steady rhythm as a paper fan on a bicycle wheel. She was searching for a suitable feeling. An appropriate emotion. Somewhere deep inside she remembered tenderness. She remembered what it was like to be stroked and pushed her head into the waiting caress of Aida Hussein's hands.

...

Professor Herbert Matthews sat in the armchair across the room from his wife, Muriel. He was holding a shotgun retrieved from his garden shed. His hands trembled as the woman he had spent over forty years with—now looking remarkably young—climbed out of the armchair she hadn't moved from for weeks.

She had been dead and in many ways still was. The larger part of Herb understood that. A small part of him, however, wanted to embrace this new Muriel, no matter how deadly such an embrace might be.

Instead he snapped open his shotgun.

As he loaded one of the barrels with a shell, Herb noticed the colour of Muriel's eyes. They were once a very pale blue, so ethereal that Herb often wondered if she had elfin blood in her veins. Now those same eyes raged red—a deep, passionate red that Herb could only translate as aggression. The fact that pure, condensed love fuelled their intensity was lost on him. Herb only saw the danger and their very definite feral intent towards him.

She rushed him, moving extremely fast for a woman who hadn't as much as scratched her head in the last month. But Herb was ready for her. Still in his armchair, he aimed the shotgun at head height and blasted from close range. The sound was deafening, ringing out obnoxiously through the quiet country air. The contents of Muriel's head were splattered over Herb in a violent wave of blood. The remainder of her body immediately hit the floor.

Herb took a moment to gather himself before removing, cleaning, and replacing his glasses. A moment was all he needed. He had mourned his wife many times since her death—her *real* death. He didn't need to mourn her again.

He slowly got to his feet, his dressing gown heavy with her blood. He sat the gun down and moved towards his desk, stepping over Muriel's desecrated body. He switched on the power of the amateur radio and lifted the mic.

"Terry? You there?"

Pzzt. "Professor? That you? Thank God you're still okay. We've had some… incredible developments—"

Herb squeezed his mic, blotting out what the Englishman was going to tell him. He didn't want to hear what was coming next. He had worked out for himself that nothing good could come from the dead returning to life. Herb had let the end of the world pass him by, but he wasn't going to be fooled anymore. Hence, he had waited for the inevitable to happen, sitting in vigil by his wife's side as she became the girl he fell in love with once more before becoming... *something else*.

Then he did what he had to do.

"It's okay, Terry. I'm safe. Muriel… she came back for me... but I attended to her in the proper manner. "

Pzzt. "Professor Matthews… I'm sorry. I really am. If there was anything I could have done… anything I can do now…" *Pzzt.*

"Thank you, Terry. I appreciate it. This is difficult for

all of us. I'm sure you have lost people too."

For a moment there was nothing but fuzz on the radio.

Pzzt. "Professor Matthews. I know it's a difficult time, but we're going to need you to do something for us. With these new developments, time is of the essence. I know it's a lot to ask someone as… er… mature in years as yourself, Professor, but we're going to need your help. You're the only hope for Northern Ireland." *Pzzt.*

"What do you need me to do?" Herb asked.

Pzzt. "We need you to go to Belfast." *Pzzt.*

Herb's ear pricked up on hearing the word 'Belfast'. He hadn't been to Belfast since retiring.

"Go on," he said to his radio friend.

As Terry explained his plans, Herb looked to the front door of his two-storey cottage, remembering what had happened before when he tried to leave. He thought back all those years ago to the last time he was in the outside world, a time when his condition wasn't quite as serious as it eventually got. He was listening to Terry's each and every word, yet he couldn't help being distracted by the things in his home, the things he had come to know and love and… fear?

Herb looked behind him at the bloody mess on the carpet. Muriel would have hated that mess. He would have to clean it up before he went anywhere.

Pzzt. "Professor? Are you still there? Professor Matthews?" *Pzzt.*

"I'm still here, Terry," Herb said, squeezing the mic. "And, yes, I'll go to Belfast. God help me, I'll go."

His hand was shaking terribly. Herb didn't know what was making it shake the most, the shock from blowing his undead wife's head off, the excitement from what Terry had told him, just then, on the radio, or the fear from knowing that, in order to execute their plan, he'd have to go out that bloody door again.

...

The Land Rover screeched to a halt by Carlisle Circus. It was a local name for the roundabout bringing together North Belfast's Crumlin Road and Antrim Road, creating a flashpoint of sorts, two communities meeting where the roads met. Flags could be seen within a stone's throw of the beginning of each road, proudly yelling out their paranoid tribalism as if to ward off the 'wrong kind'. This place was no stranger to riots and clashes with police involving both sides of the divide. But now, a steady stream of women were marching suddenly from the houses on each side of divide, meeting at the roundabout to file on into the city centre as peacefully as sand pouring through an hourglass.

Mairead wound down her window to get a clearer look. There was something not quite right with the scene. First of all, where the hell had so many survivors come from? Without actually counting, Mairead would have reckoned on there being two hundred of the women. This was the second thing that didn't quite add up – why were they all women?

Manic laughter came from behind her. It was Barry, delirious and flipping out. Shivering in the corner beside him, now a little more with it (*thankfully*, thought Mairead), was the girl they had rescued. Her eyes were darting, catching her bearings. Wondering, no doubt, why the hell she was in the back of a military Land Rover. Mairead reached a hand to the girl.

"You okay, pet?" she asked, her normally hardnosed face softening. "Can you remember anything?"

The girl startled at her touch, backing further into the back seat of the Land Rover.

"What's going on? Who are you?"

"It's okay, sweetie," Mairead fawned, her maternal instinct kicking in seamlessly.

The girl looked to Barry. His eyes were swimming around his head as if he were drugged. Some kind of fever was breaking on his brow.

"Barry? What's wrong with him?"

Mairead looked at the young man. He was mentally AWOL after being attacked by that... Then it hit her.

Turning slowly back to the crowd of women pouring into town, Mairead caught sight of three staring in through the windscreen. Their eyes were switching between red and black as if some form of fucked up traffic light. One of them was naked. The other two were partially dressed. They were clearly of the same messed-up ilk as the 'girl' they'd encountered at Joe's house. And with the middle one suddenly taking it upon herself to ram the palm of her hand wildly against the bulletproof windscreen of the Land Rover, Mairead figured they were likely to be as violent as the last creature. This was what Mairead decided these things were. Not girls, not women—not even humans. They were something otherworldly. Something primal and deadly. Something that could be attacking her little Clare, right about now.

Mairead sank her foot onto the accelerator, knocking the three girls in front of her across the bonnet of the military Land Rover. Dodging a stalled car, still in possession of its now rotting driver, Mairead aimed the Land Rover straight for the crowd of creatures in front of her, advancing towards the city centre. She wasn't going to let this bevy of bitches keep her from her little girl.

As the Land Rover connected with half a dozen creatures, struggling as they were caught under its rough terrain wheels, Barry suddenly sobered from his drugged-like daze, his eyes drawn towards the three girls picking themselves up behind him. Their faces were more than familiar. They were etched into his mind. Tattooed with guilt-ridden ink upon his conscience. The blonde one was called Nuala. She was barely out of her teens when Barry had met her at a club in the city centre, notorious as being a haunt for off-duty hairdressers. The brunette was a German student named Simone. The red-haired girl had been his first. He couldn't even remember her name, even though her face, drugged and innocent, was burned into his memory. He had raped them all. Now they were coming for him. Barry knew it was that simple, and he was scared.

The Land Rover fought on through the crowd, some of which were now clawing at the reinforced glass and heavy doors of the vehicle. Blood sprayed onto the Land Rover's windscreen. The wheels spun menacingly, the engine revving in anger as more and more of the beautiful monsters fell foul of the heavy-duty machine's progress.

Although seeming to be on the winning side in terms of safety, the three humans inside the vehicle were completely surrounded by the deadly females. The constant chaos of noise as each creature scraped and clawed, punched, kicked and even bit at the windows and doors of the vehicle was unnerving.

Barry's three girls were shrieking like banshees, staring in at him.

"Fuck! They're coming for me! They want me!" he cried.

His embarrassing whine was, perhaps, pissing Mairead off even more than the creatures outside. A dark part of her considered opening a window and feeding Barry to them, just to shut him the fuck up.

The young girl beside him, suddenly alert, climbed up beside Mairead.

"Don't worry!" Mairead yelled above the collage of noise and activity, as the Land Rover rocked and jolted against the deadly sea.

The girl looked incredulously at her.

"What the hell are they?!" she yelled back, over the noise.

Mairead didn't answer her question, instead pointing to the door on the passenger side of the vehicle where the young girl now sat.

"Make sure it's locked!"

The teenager checked the lock. Twice. Then again. Numerous black eyes stared in from the road, competing with one another as they clawed and scraped at the window. Their outstretched and bloody fingers, nails splitting and smearing against the window, were less than ten centimetres away from tearing her pretty young eyes out. Even their teeth scraped against the window, some cracking and bleeding as they dragged across the tough glass repeatedly.

A feeling of terror crept up Mairead's spine, a warm dampness that seemed to settle somewhere in between her skin and backbone.

"They can't get in, can they?!" the teenager cried.

Mairead didn't answer. She was ignoring the difficult questions now.

Suddenly Barry's voice rose to an even more manic level.

Mairead turned and that's when she saw it: a crack creeping across the rear window. The hand of the red-headed creature pounding upon it, blood seeping out of her broken fingers. Barry, now entirely beyond reason, raising his handgun and firing, blowing chunks out of the damaged window.

"Fuck."

Mairead said it more calmly than was demanded of the situation. They were entirely surrounded by them, now, stuck in a Land Rover that's only saving grace was reinforced glass and armoured doors. Those bitches had done enough to make an impression upon the rear window, but it was Barry's sheer stupidity, in the midst of all the panic, that had changed their situation from grim… to *very* grim.

It seemed like a hundred arms were reaching through the window as Barry scrambled backwards, still shooting, into the already occupied front seats of the Land Rover. Bullets tore through each arm of his assailants, shredding skin and splintering bone as they showered the window and rear seats with blood. Yet still they reached. Frantically feeling for something to tear, something to drag into their beautiful but lethal sea. Soon, one of them, a blonde-haired girl with eyes black as hell itself, had pushed her whole upper torso through the windscreen and was straining to grab hold of Barry, now sitting on top of Mairead.

"Fuck! Fuck! Fuck!" Mairead spat.

She pushed Barry over to the seat that Caz was curling up in, eyes welded to the dramatic danger inching towards them in the suddenly overcrowded vehicle. Grabbing Barry's gun away from him, Mairead turned herself towards the rear window. With one shot, aimed precisely at the creature's blonde locks, she had split the damned thing's head open, pieces of bloody brain and hair showering the three humans. Each shot at the advancing horde, scrambling and competing against each other for Barry Rogan, or anyone else who stood in their way, ended with more bile and blood soaking them. Mairead was spitting out pieces of flesh after each shot, then wiping her face before unleashing another. Some blood got into her eyes, and she struggled to maintain the vision she needed to shoot with precision.

Caz yelled directly into the terrified lad's face, "Barry, do something!"

But it was no good. Barry was crying, tears mixing messily with the gore splashing across his face with every shot fired. He reached shakily for the second rifle, feeling the flailing hands of the bitches, inching closer, scratching at his skin, grabbing for him. Screaming with effort and terror, Barry dragged his hands back, keeping hold of the weapon. He opened fire indiscriminately on the back seat, the semi-automatic fire shattering the remainder of the window along with half a dozen heads.

Caz reached her foot into Mairead's seat, pressing down hard on the accelerator. They could make more headway, many of the creatures having streamed towards the back of the vehicle and its broken window. Progress was still slow, but they were inching through the crowd a little more promisingly.

Barry continued firing wildly, his bullets tearing open skulls and breasts in equal measure, the fruits of his labour lapping back against him. A fever was building again on his forehead, his mind struggling to stay focused. He felt a mixture of dizziness and nausea sweep over him, disturbing his aim. Before he knew it, he was pumping a round of ammunition, at close range, through the side window next to Mairead.

"Fuck's sake, Barry!" she yelled, grabbing the barrel of his gun with her free hand, scalding herself in the process, moving it away.

The heavy din of weapons firing so close to her ears had deafened her, and with the constant shower of blood clogging her vision, Mairead neither heard nor saw the window beside her give against Barry's firepower and the incessant sea of deadly beauty before it was too late. Arms reached in, grabbing her hair, dragging her towards the street.

...

Roy confidently stepped through the doors of the hotel bar. His weapon was readied. His eyes carefully scaled the entire view of the bar, still lavish-looking despite the remnants of many a night's partying. Most of the tables looked disused, a thin coating of dust shimmering against the light now pouring in from the broken window at the front. The bar itself stood proud and dapper in the centre of the room, well stocked with all manner of spirits and fine wines, some drained more thirstily than others. Vodka, it seemed, was the drink of choice for those most recently resident here.

Roy stepped a little closer to the broken window. Gibson's body lay on the floor, shreds of glass coating it like diamonds. There was no sign of anyone else. He figured the other guy who had been drinking with Gibson must have bolted, running like a scared little girl when his friend had hit the floor. Roy caught a strong whiff of alcohol as he bent towards Gibson's body, just to make sure the job had been finished. The little cunt must have been drinking from early morning; the scent of the alcohol was almost overwhelming.

Then he noticed something a little odd; Gibson's body was soaking wet. That's why the smell was so strong. It was as if he'd not only been drinking booze, but swimming in it.

Like a glorious, drunken phoenix, the ginger mop of Sean Magee rose from behind the bar, a lighter in one hand, flaming bottle of Sambucca in the other. With one fluid motion and all the skill of a West Indian fast bowler, the flaming bottle left Sean's hand, hurtling towards Roy Beggs. The bottle smashed against the soldier, coating his uniform with its contents, immediately catching fire from the burning rag at its neck. The flames licked up the heavy coating of booze that soaked Alan Gibson, sending up a chorus of fire that almost drowned out the hoarse screech emitting from Roy Begg's mouth as his raw flesh fried like a slice of steak. His gun reacted against the sudden and immense heat, shooting off wildly against his own torso, lifting and hurling his whole body out through the broken window like a firecracker.

As Sean watched on, the human fireball jettisoned out of the first-floor window of the hotel bar, seeming to move in slow motion as it sailed through the air towards the street. The man was blazing, bullets slicing through the windows of shops and offices on the opposite side of the road from the hotel. Even from the first floor, he could hear the body hit the ground with a slap that seemed to echo throughout the city.

...

The beautifully suited-and-booted Chris O'Hagan had no recollection of her former glories as a businesswoman, making over twice her weekly target each day, affording her respect and Porsche alike. She had no memory of her endless quest down at the Gym each evening, after a gruelling ten hours in the office, sweating profusely against the lack of sleep, food, and constant popping of antidepressants to make even more targets. She cared even less for her family (long since broken down after the murder of her brother all those years ago) and longsuffering boyfriend (now dead, his corpse having decayed, textbook-style) as her dead eyes flickered open, and her mind slowly kicked into a most basic form of action. Chris' only target now was fuelled by dark, raw emotion.

Vengeance.

As she rose to her feet, rather awkwardly at first, finally standing tall, svelte and elegant, her senses kicked into overdrive. Her vision flickered between colours, white at first, then black as her hatred simmered to boil. Her sense of smell—this most primal of sense—sought out the blood of the man who had ruined her brother's life, making her the girl she was today, beautiful, successful, barely human.

Miserable.

The distinctive odour of Roy Beggs filled her delicate nostrils. His very smell was all around her. It filled the air, slightly more pungent due to the current state of his charred body. Her dark eyes fell upon his dying face, remembering him sitting so defiantly in the dock as the verdict of 'innocent' was read out and her life shifted into a new, cold, emotionless gear. Chris sauntered over to his burned-out husk of a body, the barbecued flesh reminding a deep, distant part of her of all-too-familiar hunger pangs from days gone by.

She fed.

Nearby, the over-inked naked form of Sonya Bailey, her body bearing the marks of Tim Adamson's crude, childlike attempts at tattooing, stumbled, then steadied herself. Her face pressed against the window of Great Victoria Street Station's front doors, staring down to meet with the disbelieving eyes of Tim's some-time sensei, Star.

From every corner, every nook and cranny, every street and alleyway throughout the quiet, dead city, more women emerged, swanlike in their almost musical approach. A sea of dark-eyed, ravenous vixens. Some came from Victoria Square, blood hungry with the taste of their loved ones still fresh on their lips.

"Fuck me," Star whispered, more to herself than anyone else.

She looked to the car where Clare remained, eyes glued to the approaching women, palms pressed upon the window. She moved towards it, quickly, dragging on her cigarette with one hand, grabbing the car door and shaking it violently with the other.

"Open the fuck up!" she cried.

Clare looked out, her distrust of the crude young woman hesitating her from opening. She wondered where Roy had got to, having missed his glorious exit from life while she was dancing in her seat to the loud music that blared out from the CD. Now the music was turned down, seeming an almost irreverent soundtrack for what she saw happening all around her.

They're all so pretty, Clare thought, having not seen or smelled anything less than gruesome since The Great Whatever some weeks ago. The women reminded her of fairies. Overgrown, wingless, but still graceful. They washed towards the car like a shoal of mermaids, a choir of angels, a toy store's worth of dolls, their pretty hair shimmering in the fairytale sunshine.

"Open the fucking door, you stupid wee bitch!"

...

Barry grabbed hold of Mairead's legs, wedging his foot against the side door as leverage. His lean, tall frame sprawled messily across the driver seat, obscuring Caz's view as she continued grinding the Land Rover against the thick, fearless crowd of women that swarmed thickly around them. She felt a little give, continuous bitch casualties seeming to bear the brunt of her sinking foot on the accelerator, blood squirting against the window as the Land Rover's large wheels churned against the fallen.

"Fuck… these… bitches!" Barry screamed, straining to keep hold of Mairead's legs, sweat continuing to pour down his forehead.

Mairead fought valiantly, trigger finger busy, her gunfire tearing through the masses. But it was useless. Like vultures, they pecked and tore at her abdomen, her freshly-spilled blood splashing in against Barry and Caz. Her legs kicked violently with the pain, catching Barry in the face with a heeled boot. He almost lost his grip, yet scrambled again to keep hold of her. He fought against the almost overwhelming urge to let go, to give into the fever, slipping back into his drugged state.

Finally Mairead's spine gave way, the creatures having gnawed at her like a dog would a bone. She snapped, upper body disappearing out the window, lower body falling against Barry as he tumbled against Caz. The two of them screamed blue hell, the legs, lower abdomen and fleshy spine of their friend shaking and jittering against them as if still alive.

Soon the doll-like creatures were scurrying up on the roof of the vehicle. Like bees around a hive, they closed in, pushing, stretching, snapping at each other in a passion-fuelled drive to reach the distinct cocktail of blood and sweat filling their nostrils. A horde of arms stretched into the vehicle, grabbing, pulling and ripping at anything they could grip. They tore the remainder of Mairead out into their mass, fighting over her flesh and bone like starving dogs. And then they came for Barry. The one they had wanted from the start. Led by the girls he had recognised—raped—they scrambled forward, pushing a screaming Caz aside to get hold of him.

They dragged him out, tearing him mercilessly across the jagged edges of the torn windscreen. Grouping together like hungry animals, they held him down in chaotic unison as the red-haired one whose name he couldn't remember—his first victim—strode across him like a lap dancer. Tearing the belt from his jeans with one fluid movement, she went down on him, her mouth wide open.

Barry screeched like a newborn puppy as her teeth sank into his cock.

...

From his vantage point by the devastated window in first floor bar of the Europa Hotel, Sean Magee looked down upon the fantastic sight of hundreds—maybe thousands—of young women swarming onto Great

Victoria Street. They came from everywhere, pouring out like marbles from a tin, their dense numbers and choreographed approach somehow lending both an erotic and sinister quality to their mass. A part of Sean thought he was dreaming, perhaps having fallen into his daily drunken coma earlier in the day than normal. But it didn't feel like he was asleep. He was still shaking from what had just happened with the soldier.

The ageing DJ ruffled his mop of unkempt grey hair in an expression that could only say 'what the fuck?!' This couldn't be real. And yet the women continued to come, their numbers and density swelling. At the centre of the mass, almost the very reason for the direction of its swarm, stood the dreadlocked and comparatively rough-looking Star, poised on top of a people carrier type car parked opposite the hotel. She was lying on the roof, beating the front windscreen passionately. This was beyond fucking odd.

"Star!" Sean called.

"What the fuck?! Sean! Jesus… Sean! You've got to help me here!"

"How?! What's going on?!"

"I... they... fuck! Sean! These… women… there's something not right about them!"

"How do you know?! Talk to them! See what they say!"

A large part of him couldn't believe that anything so collectively beautiful could be so dangerous. Another part of him was so pissed he couldn't see anything wrong with the world at all, and yet another part of him was still reeling in post-traumatic shock.

"Sean!" she yelled, understandably frustrated with him, "Their eyes are fucking black!"

He bent down a little to look closer, still unable to see clearly from his height. He watched as some of the women looked up at him, a few turning their direction from the main herd in order to move towards the hotel's front entrance.

Fuck. That wasn't good...

It wasn't long before Sean Magee was able to see first hand exactly why Star was so freaked out by the women suddenly swarming from everywhere. They breached the hotel, drawing towards him and the hotel bar like flies to meat.

Suddenly Sean felt very sober. Very alone. Very afraid. Since his whole world had turned itself inside-out, he'd been responsible for the deaths of two people (three if you were to count his ex-wife, Sharon – which Sean would, no doubt). He had always thought of himself as a lover-not-a-fighter, but something about this (brave, new) world changed him. Fucked him up. Maybe the same something that had created whatever insanity he was witnessing now.

The inhuman-looking women filled the room quickly and quietly. Their mouths remained incredibly expressionless. Their faces seemed almost radiant. Apart from their eyes, they were the picture of health and catwalk-quality beauty. Sean's eyes fell on one in the middle of the crowd as they approached. She was naked, and one of her breasts was so stained with blood that it looked as if someone had thrown a tin of paint around her. Sean couldn't take his eyes off her. She was beautiful and repulsive all at once, like some kind of fetish. She led the slow, calm charge towards him.

Sean backed away, inching closer towards the broken window. He weighed up his options. They were extremely limited. There were too many of them, and they were drawing closer. He thought of climbing out onto the window ledge and trying to find some escape from there. That was only going to delay the inevitable, as they were now literally everywhere.

It was useless. Sean lifted his glass, tipped it to the approaching horde and drank deeply. Dutch courage.

They say that a person's life flashes before their eyes just before death. Sean's eyes closed as he heard the familiar low-ebbed guitar sound and brash voices of the Sabbath gig he had attended back in '77. It was the most energetic night he could remember, with pogo dancing and head banging so extreme that he left with a bloody nose to go with the smile across his sweaty face. It was the first time Sean had stage dived into the crowd. He'd loved the experience, chasing the thrill of it several times during the night, higher each time until Ozzy himself pushed him into the waiting fans, hands raised to lift and carry him both gently and gruffly back to ground level.

Turning towards the window, Sean Magee hurled himself forward into the throng below.

...

"Sean!" Star cried, powerless to do anything but watch the DJ's swansong. "Fuck!"

She turned her attention towards the approaching hordes again. She looked in all directions, met only by hundreds of black eyes looking back at her. She could see some of them swarming towards the spot where Sean had landed.

"Jesus, Sean..."

She took his advice, mainly because she was flat out of any other options.

"H-h-hey…" she stuttered, heart racing. "Look… Can any of you, like, speak?"

There was a unanimous lack of reaction. Star looked all around, for anyone—anything—which could resemble communication from them. Only the eyes… Flickering. Blending colours. Narrowing. Star's heart sank, realising that whatever was happening all around her wasn't going to be talked down. Nervously, she lit up a cigarette. There was still no response from them. They collectively ignored her, turning their attention back towards the people carrier she stood upon. From inside the vehicle, palms still pressed against the windows of the car, Star could see the small, delicate eyes of the child, Clare McAfee, staring back at her and the doll-like creatures swarming towards them.

All of a sudden they were shaking and clawing at the people carrier with a fury that seemed demonic to her.

Star stood, balancing on the roof of the vehicle. They continued to swarm around her like a plague of locusts. Her weighty Doc Marten boots acted as the ideal weapon to land some of their mass on the ground, blood pouring from gashes in their pretty heads. Others felt the wrath of her cigarette, now a weapon to be thrust into their sadistic eyes, still flapping from one colour to another as they flocked in. Those assaulted fell back, embers, puss, and blood staining their porcelain cheekbones as others thrust forward in their place. Yet still they ignored her, her frantic violence against them hardly even acknowledged. Their faces, elegant and hungry, shone in the late afternoon sun as they fought forwards to the prize inside the car. That of the child.

The windows shattered, and what seemed like a million pairs of arms reached in.

From inside, Clare stared at one of the creatures, her bright, innocent eyes twinkling as tears began to build up. The broken glass had showered her like snowflakes, several shards slicing her soft cheeks and leaving a trail of bright red to blend painfully with her rich, salty tears. The hands kept reaching forward, then pulling back, some of them managing to tear at her long blonde locks, freshly washed and conditioned in the hotel earlier. Yet she ignored these creatures. She was interested in only one of them. Clare McAfee smiled, tearfully, as the face of her mummy—her real mummy—seemed to draw nearer to her. The crowd of fairies seemed to be parting, allowing Mummy to glide towards her as if on a cloud. Her face seemed more expressive than the other fairies, her eyes whiter than snow. Clare felt love beaming in at her, like sunlight. She reached towards her mummy, arms outstretched, blood and tears streaming down her cheeks.

"No! Get away from her!"

Star was in the middle of the crowd, screeching and clawing like a mad banshee. Her kitchen knife came out of her pocket, the blade flashing in the sun as she ripped skin from bone, digging into flesh with an animal thirst. She swung and sliced with a fervour beyond sanity, her voice cutting through the air like a siren.

"FUCKING WHORES!"

She was suddenly taken back to the horror of that first day, when she had seen the birds outside the church, the corpse in the pram. The stained innocence stung her deep, making her feel as if her heart had been pickled from the inside out. Star was a mess who cared little about her own life. But she couldn't let this fucked-up world steal another innocent soul.

Her boots were kicking out as several of the creatures attempted to grab her before meeting with leather sole. Half in the crowd, half on top, she fought like a wild cat, trying in vain to reach the little girl as the creatures passed her, some gently, others scraping and clawing at her tiny body as it moved through their ever-swelling numbers. It was useless. There were just too many of them. Before long, the child was lost within the sea of beauty, blood like raindrops from a petal dripping onto each of the creatures as she passed over them and through them. Some of the blood even fell upon Star. She was so close, yet so very far away.

Yet still Star screeched, arms still flailing, feet still swinging as the creatures turned their full attention towards her, their eyes flashing a colour so dark that it almost hurt to look upon. She grinned maniacally back at them. They were going to pay for what they'd done, all they'd stolen.

All of a sudden, these glamorous, shiny monsters represented everything fucked-up in life, everything that had ever stood in Star's way. They were the drugs that had messed up her mental health, spitting her from one fucked-up situation to another in the arsehole of London, years ago. They were the people she knew then, users like her. Abusers and veterans of self-destruct who knew no boundaries in their relentless thirst for hedonism. These callous bitches represented the very essence of 'wrong' to Star. Like ghosts from her past, they pressed against her again, their primal rage ignited.

Star licked her knife clean of the blood that she had already spilled. It trickled from the side of her mouth. She was ready for them. Ready to face her demons…

They turned to look at her, their eyes flicking back and forth between various colours, finally stopping at red.

"Come on, you bitches," she spat, smiling sinisterly.

They swarmed her like angry wasps.

Then came The Rain.

EIGHT

It rained hard and fast, the skies turning black with cloud. The water mingled with blood, streams soon flowing through the streets like watered-down wine. The rain came heavy, its monotonous patter breaking The Silence like glass. Soon it was joined by thick and deep moans of thunder. It was as if Great Mother Nature had finally decided to mourn Her loss, crying out in gut-wrenching, heavy tears. It was Her turn to grieve, and grieve heavily. A storm swept through the whole of Ireland, wiping clean every street and field. Its fury beat upon the flesh and bones of fallen animals, broken down cars and half-decayed corpses. Little escaped its touch as riverbanks gave way to rising tides, floods soon invading every hill and incline. Buildings were beat upon, billboards stripped clean. Corpses, some still untouched, others half eaten by beautiful ex-lovers and family, were sterilized. Where there had been Silence everywhere, now there was only Rain.

A solitary vehicle came into view, slowly crawling its way down Great Victoria Street. The van pulled up by the hotel, its worn rubber tires avoiding Sean Magee's henpecked body to roll over the charred remains of Roy Beggs. The front windscreen of the van remained intact, despite a large stain of blood, diluted somewhat by the recent fall of rain. The van ground to a clumsy halt, as if the driver were still learning how to drive.

The driver's door opened, and a rather scruffy-looking elderly man climbed slowly out. He carried a shotgun under his arm, wearing the bizarre ensemble of pyjamas, dressing gown, and work boots.

Shutting the door, the old man walked towards the bus station, head bowed low. He had endured the most horrendous journey and really needed a glass of bourbon.

...

The rain pounded hard and fast upon the scarlet-stained paving at the bandstand, cleaning the torn bodies of daily worshippers with an almost clinical precision. Pink water still pooled densely in pockets throughout Belfast's whole city centre, an indication perhaps that many of the shadow people had also fallen foul of the women's lethal and feral charms. Whatever number of survivors remained since The Great Whatever, that number had almost certainly become as diluted as the blood, leaving humanity in Belfast an incredibly endangered species.

Star's eyes opened, Cornmarket's whole brutal scene spreading out before her like modern art. Her hearing returned next, droplets of rain from the bandstand's ornate roof splashing delicately into the pink puddles below. She drifted almost blissfully back into consciousness, the gentle splish-splash noise whispering into her ear like a lullaby, a soundtrack for the blood and rain washed, landscape before her. But then it all came crashing back, the art before her suddenly morphing into the picture of carnage that it truly was, the young tattooist longing for unconsciousness to reclaim her again.

She couldn't remember much of what had happened since those bitches had decided, all of a sudden, to take an interest in her. She didn't know why she was by the bandstand, slightly east of Great Victoria Street. She saw no sign of the child she had tried in vain to protect. All she knew was that she was alive, albeit covered in blood, and the rain seemed to have washed more than just the sunshine away. The beautiful and deadly whores, all several hundred of them, were currently nowhere to be seen.

Star ran an eye over the sterilised chaos before her. The bodies of several men, (*the God-lovers*, she reckoned), lay spread-eagled before her. A sandwich board proclaiming 'THERE IS POWER IN THE BLOOD' was itself stained pink. Bones jutted out from the bodies, some of the men having enough of their faces left to allow Star a little glimpse of the pain and sheer terror they had experienced before death.

There was nothing but devastation. Cars, once just abandoned, were now ravished with the same ferocity afforded the bodies. Shop windows lay in glittering pieces. Even advertising billboards, their models seemingly too glamorous for chaos, couldn't escape the carnage. Strips of paper hung lifelessly from their corporate nests, ripped down by violence or the rain—or both.

But Star saw something else in the half-baked twilight, something twinkling differently to the shards of glass littering the damp streets like glitter. Something that stood out like a gem, its precious nature all too poignant. Her heart skipped a beat as she realised what it was that had caught her eye.

"Oh God..." she whispered, a tattooed hand rising to cover her mouth.

She walked, slowly and tearfully, towards the slender, half-devoured body of Tim Adamson. As she approached, her stomach turning with every footstep she took, she was able to see the full atrocity of the lad's final seconds. Both arms and legs had been torn greedily from his torso, leaving ragged stumps of bone and vein. His hair, having grown since she first met him, was ripped out in clumps. But worst of all was the expression on his face.

He was smiling.

Bending down, Star noticed the last tattoo she had worked on with Tim, still perfectly intact, despite the desecration of the boy's corpse. It was a small black and white star, wrapped in spirals of colour to form a circle. It was one that Tim had worked on for himself. He had told her that it represented hope.

Lying close to Tim's corpse was a small silver crucifix. Star picked it up, running one finger over its tiny, longsuffering Jesus. Looking back at Tim, she noticed how the position of his body's head (cocked slightly to the right) wasn't dissimilar to that of silver Jesus.

...

Professor Herbert Matthews was thoroughly enjoying his bourbon, its dark and bitter taste sliding down his dry throat like velvet. He sat in the cafe area of the Europa bus and railway station, admiring its architectural anomaly of glass and steel.

The door opened from behind him. As Herb turned around, a curious looking individual walked in. In her one hand was a cigarette, its embers shaken to the ground with the absolute minimum of respect. As she drew closer, he realised the other was holding a silver chain—a crucifix—if Herb's eyes could be trusted. Her appearance was almost tribal, blood having hardened in patches around her strange tattoos and piercings. Dark shadows of make-up swirled messily around her wide, hungry-looking eyes. Her boyish clothes were torn in a fashion almost unseemly to a man of Herb's mature years.

Herb felt intimidated by her. A cold sweat ran up his spine, reminding the professor of his age-old 'condition.' This was why he stayed indoors. This was why his doctor had prescribed the quiet, rural plains of Ballyclare to him instead of his old city haunts. The city could be quite unpredictable, bringing you into contact with all kinds of folk you wouldn't want to meet.

"Who the fuck are you!?" she said to him.

Herb couldn't abide ill manners, especially from young people, but he didn't pass the comment, instead standing up to introduce himself.

"My name is Professor Herbert Matthews," he politely began, despite his chronic nervousness, "and it's an absolute—"

"Where did you come from? Did you see any of those bitches on your travels?" she snapped back.

Herb tried desperately to maintain his composure as he spoke, "I came from Ballyclare, and 'those bitches', as you so very eloquently describe them, swarmed me briefly before the rain seemed to chase them away. We haven't quite worked out why that is the case."

"*We*? Who's we?" the impertinent woman snapped.

Herb explained to her his mission, of Terry from Manchester and how they'd been talking through the HAM radio. He informed her of how the team at Manchester had made contact with others across the world, people that were survivors like them.

But the young woman didn't seem very interested.

"Bullshit," she said, curtly. "Did you see any other vehicles? A military Land Rover?"

Herb ignored her. He hated it when people tried to knock him off track. He paused briefly before continuing, as if he needed to say everything now, lest it all be forgotten.

"Terry's people are trying to organise themselves

against the new threat… the threat of our own people returning from the dead. I can see by your appearance, young miss, that you've fallen prey to such, already."

"Wait a minute," she snapped back, "are you trying to tell me that those bitches are some kind of fucking zombies? Cause I, for one, am not going to buy any of that Hammer Horror bullshit, Grandpa."

Herb's voice suddenly rose.

"You'll watch your mouth, young lady," he said, sternly.

His heartbeat was speeding up, so he took a moment to calm down, sitting himself back in his chair and reaching for his glass of bourbon.

"I'll have you know that those creatures are much more than mindless zombies."

"What are they, then?" she snapped back. "Come on! You have all the answers, old man. What are they?!"

She was seething now, her rage, pent up to overflowing, pouring out like lava from a volcano. Her sudden aggression startled Herb, the old man retreating back into his seat. But she came after him, spitting and shouting.

"What the fuck are they?!"

Herb cowered. As his aggressor's face drew closer, wild with rage, Herb could see that tears were building in her eyes. Her voice was cracking with emotion. For a minute it looked like she might grab him, but then she turned away, perhaps becoming aware of how raw terror had twisted her.

Herb fought for breath, chasing away the pending panic attack.

The young woman was simply leaning against the station's glass wall, her appearance all too visible to the Professor. She was crying quite uncontrollably.

For a moment, neither of them spoke. Herb, too, was quiet, fighting against his condition, trying desperately to hold onto his own composure and calm. He needed to be strong not only for his own sake, but for Terry's sake and the sake of the damaged survivor he was trying to win over to his cause. A cause that was vital to the very survival of Northern Ireland's dwindled population.

"They used to be human, like you and me," Herb began again, once he had reclaimed his breath. He took a swig of bourbon, swallowing hard before continuing. "Now they're more than that."

"What do you mean?" the woman asked him, without turning around.

"What we're seeing here is a fundamental change. Not evolution, but something much more profound. I don't know much about the human body, but I'm led to believe that it's a machine quite like any other machine. And machines are something that I know quite a lot about."

Herb's voice suddenly morphed to that of his lecturer persona, his vocal cords exercising in ways which hadn't been heard in a long time. He was focusing on the young lady as he spoke.

"You see, my dear, in order to make any machine better, you have to turn it off, take it apart. Then you put it back together again, perhaps adding some new and innovative parts to make it work more efficiently. That is precisely what has happened with the human machine. Great Mother Nature has turned the majority of the human race off—unplugged us from the wall, if you like—before rebooting."

"Is there anything left of what they were before?" the young woman asked, still staring at her own reflection.

Herb paused, solemnly recalling that harrowing moment whenever his dear wife had reanimated. He remembered the photograph he had displayed on his mantelpiece, the picture of Muriel in her prime, all those years ago. He smiled.

“A little, perhaps,” he answered, quietly, “and in time, perhaps, they could show a lot more of the thoughts and feelings that they once had. But they are a deadly threat to our continued survival as a species now. We have to take the greatest of care when dealing with them. Research from Terry’s team suggests that they feed not only on flesh and blood, but on the very fabric of humanity itself. These creatures both thrive and feed on our emotions—the most raw and fundamental part of us. We must therefore take the greatest of—”

“They didn’t attack me.”

She turned back towards Herb. She was clinging to the small silver crucifix in her hand, and blood was beginning to seep through her fingers where she gripped it. Her hard exterior had been broken, her defence mechanism now short-circuited. Herb felt his feelings towards her change. She was as broken-hearted as he was. Deep beneath the hardened and violent front she had erected was a whole reservoir of grief that was only now becoming visible.

“They didn’t attack me because I feel *nothing*! I feel nothing for myself or anyone else.” She was sobbing hard. She banged her fist against the glass wall of the station, its dull thud doing no damage.

“I’m hardly fucking human. That’s why they left me, like some fucked-up and unwanted ragdoll.”

Herb looked at her as she shivered and cried before his eyes, opening up to him like some rare flower. It was as if this release of unspent emotion was her first real expression in a very long time. Herb could see that where the hard exterior had crumbled, a beautiful and fragile young woman appeared. She even looked pretty, an angelic and vulnerable face hidden underneath all of the blood and dreadlocks.

Herb walked over to her, pausing briefly before using

a sleeve of his dirty dressing gown to wipe away her tears. She didn't resist.

"Still waters run very deep, my dear child," he whispered softly to her, unclenching her fist. "Those bitches just aren't smart enough yet to see what a beautiful and wonderful young woman you are."

He smiled at her before continuing.

"They only sense raw emotion. The heart that we wear on our sleeves. They, themselves, seem fuelled by that very same primal energy, according to Terry, possibly leading to them seeking out those who they feel... *felt*... their deepest connection with in life. Those who would have drawn the most primal of emotions from them, for whatever reason.

"Of course, we can hide our feelings from them, protect ourselves. It would be possible, but in a broken down world like this, a world where the few of us who have survived are wild-eyed and raw, our cover is well and truly blown. They smell those feelings off us like blood."

Herb's face turned very serious. "And it draws them to us like wild dogs."

A sudden interruption led the two survivors to turn their gaze towards the huge glass walls of the station, looking out upon the bus depot. Straining his tired old eyes, Herb noticed upon looking out what seemed to be a small line of bodies, all decomposing, half-covered by a canvas sheet. Some of their number had, no doubt, already risen to join the unholy throng of women and Herb thought, for a moment, that another was rising to join their ranks.

But this most recent interruption hadn't come from there.

As Herb's eyes adjusted to the growing darkness outside, peering through the huge glass walls, he noticed a beat-up Land Rover stuttering to a standstill by the station's side entrance.

EPILOGUE

The rain continued to fall that night, its familiar patter welcomed by those at the bus station.

Caz remained in the bus station's waiting area, tending to the delirious Barry Rogan. His wounds were extensive, those callous bitches having mauled him in places that would really hurt… but Caz didn't feel any embarrassment. She felt very little of anything.

She nursed Barry with a clinical approach, wrapping what was left of his penis in sterile bandaging, tending to the bloody sockets that had been his eyes, brutally torn from his face. She did it all without any emotional attachment to the young man, a man who had lost his dignity, and just about everything else, in order to rescue her. She nursed him with apathy, more out of duty and loyalty than concern. All of her innocence had been torn mercilessly from her, and it had left her devoid of feelings now.

Professor Herbert Matthews remained vocal, expounding his theories and plans for setting up a new base at Belfast International Airport with surprising gusto. Neither Caz nor Star had a better plan, unable to articulate anything much. Just before dawn, therefore, while the rain still tumbled from the grey sky, the small group of survivors set off. The darkness was beginning to recede, and the Professor thought it best for them to get on the road sooner rather than later.

Barry was wrapped up in warm blankets, still shivering. He hadn't said a word. Nothing except the occasional guffaw of disturbed laughter came out of his mouth. They weren't sure how much he was aware of, or how bad his injuries were. Once at the airport, they intended to make contact with Terry's team in Manchester to get Barry some medical help. But it didn't look good for him.

Caz sat in the back seat of the bus, Barry's long, thin body draped across her. She felt like a shell, devoid of hope. Her eyes were bone dry. She couldn't shed as much as a single tear as Star handed her the small, blood-stained crucifix, her present to Tim Adamson, reclaimed from the boy's ravaged corpse. For a few moments, Caz simply ran her finger along its square edges, feeling the dry blood crumble against her fingertips, reading it like Braille, capturing the story of Tim's last moments: his courage, his war against the demons in his mind and the closure he finally received, his final smile on thinking about her.

She smiled, faintly, as the cross began to feel less rigid, metallic and cold to her.

Then she simply placed it in her pocket.